COURAGEOUS BOOKS

PLANET WALKERS
Book one of the Planet Walker series

A. V. Shackleton

Published by Courageous Books
1081 Wallaces Gap Rd
Ballalaba
NSW
Australia 2622

ISBN 978-0-9925814-7-3

Thank you to my family and friends for your tireless support and honest feedback, and to my intrepid fellow Planet Walkers - I'd be lost without you.

GLOSSARY

(Go to **www.avshackleton.com** for more detail)

Annangi: a dimorphic race consisting of angels and archangels.

Djan'rū: the point at which a planet can be joined by a navigator's song.

El: deity. Annangi believe that the Breath of El blows through all. **Asheru** is El's consort.

Great House: There are ten Great Houses, each with a home planet and a leader accepted by El.

Haze: easily visible aspects of an individual's aura.

Mark: the soul mark granted by El to those who become proficient in a particular psychic gift. The Mark appears as a symbol shining through the skin.

Qalān:

> **Personal Qalān** is a sub-dimensional space that surrounds every individual. Annangi access this space for storage of personal items.
>
> **Planetary Qalān** surrounds every planetary body in a web of interconnected wormholes. Skilled Annangi can create portals in this Qalān for instantaneous travel between locations on a given planet.
>
> **Galactic Qalān** connects the stars and planets of the galaxy. It merges with **planetary Qalān** at specific points known as Djan'rū. **Navigators** travel between Djan'rū.

Sajhar: both Mark and title of one who has mastered all powers entailed with the working of metal.

Screen: internally, a psychic construction that hides private information; or externally, a shield that hides one's presence.

Shamkar: the Mark of one who is a master of the power of voice.

Shamkarun: the title of one who bears the Shamkar.

Tiamät: the Imperial House; the God-Emperor and Empress are of House Tiamät. The three clans of Tiamät are Gok, Enna and Ashik.

Tsemkar: the Mark of a master of mind power. This ability is often strong in those of clan Ashik.

Tsemkarun: the title of one who bears the Tsemkar. Although the current God-Emperor is a Tsemkarun, not all God-Emperors are Marked.

Veil: a psychic construction that hides thoughts and feelings from the perception of others.

Ziquarra: the Mark of one who can leave their body at will and send their soul to far distant locations. Ziquarra is also the name of this skill.

Ziquarudjan: the title of one who bears the Ziquarra.

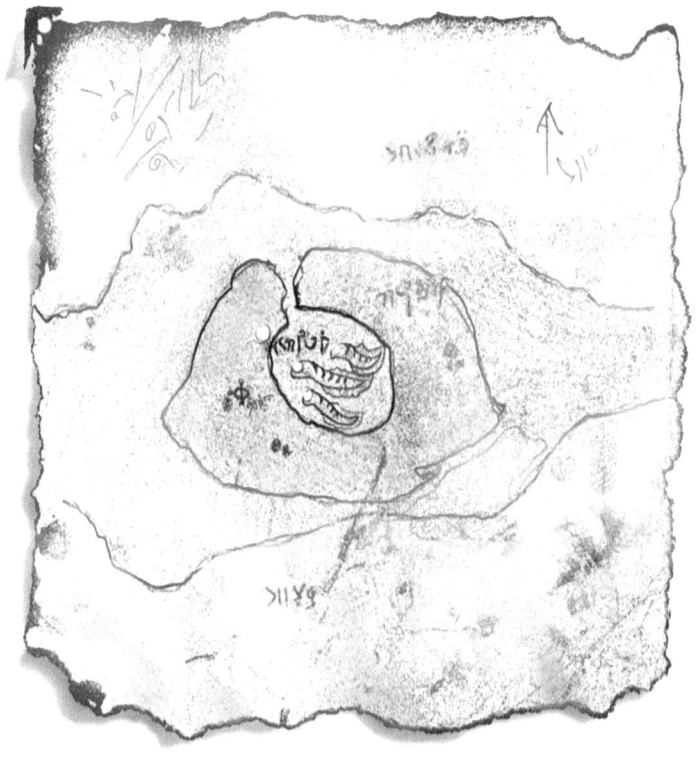

Duvät Gok's map.

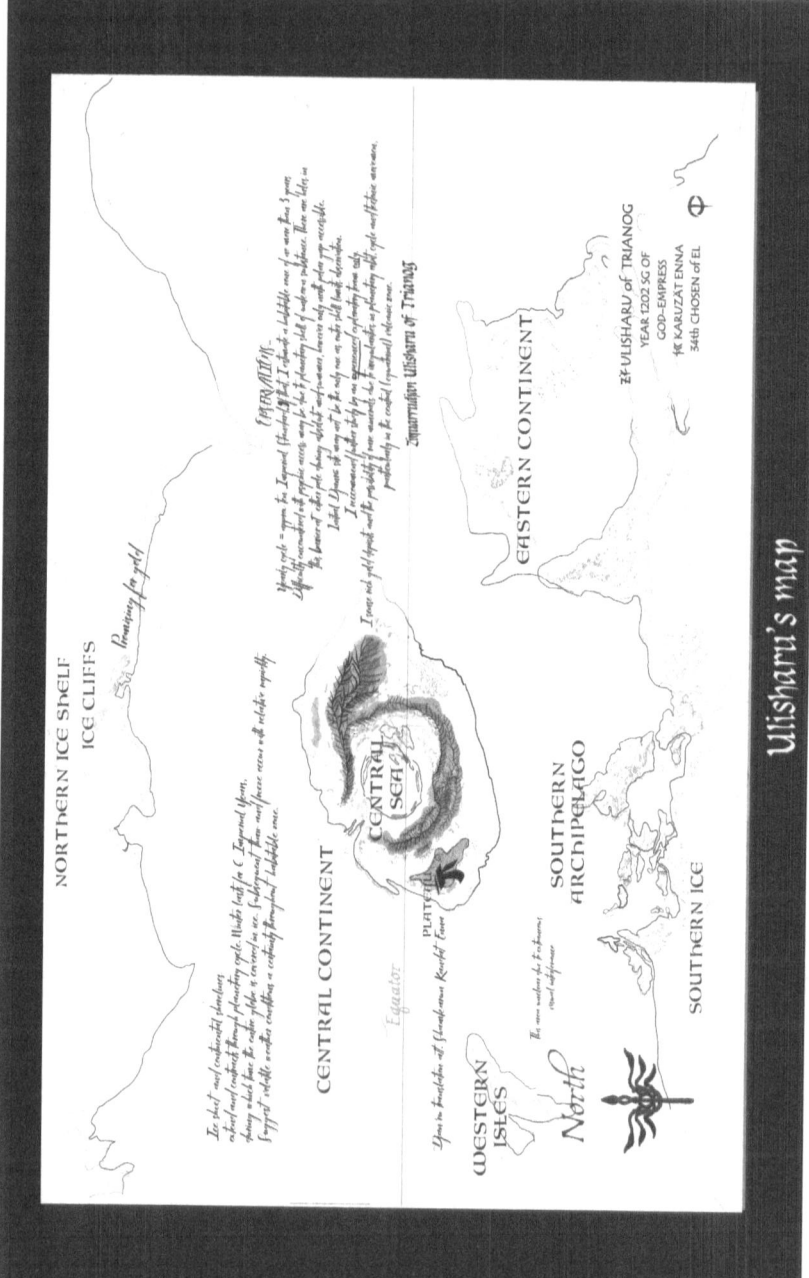

Ulisharu's map

A.V. Shackleton

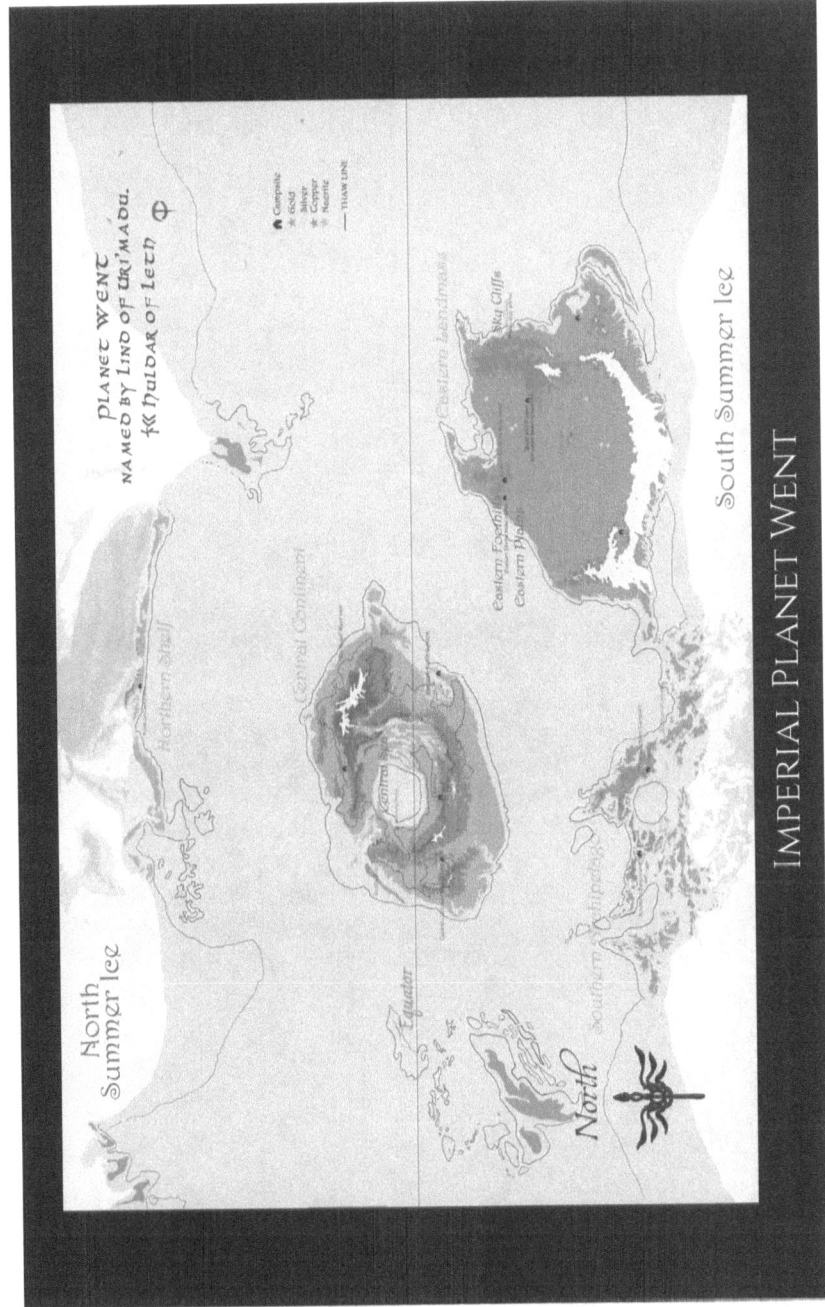

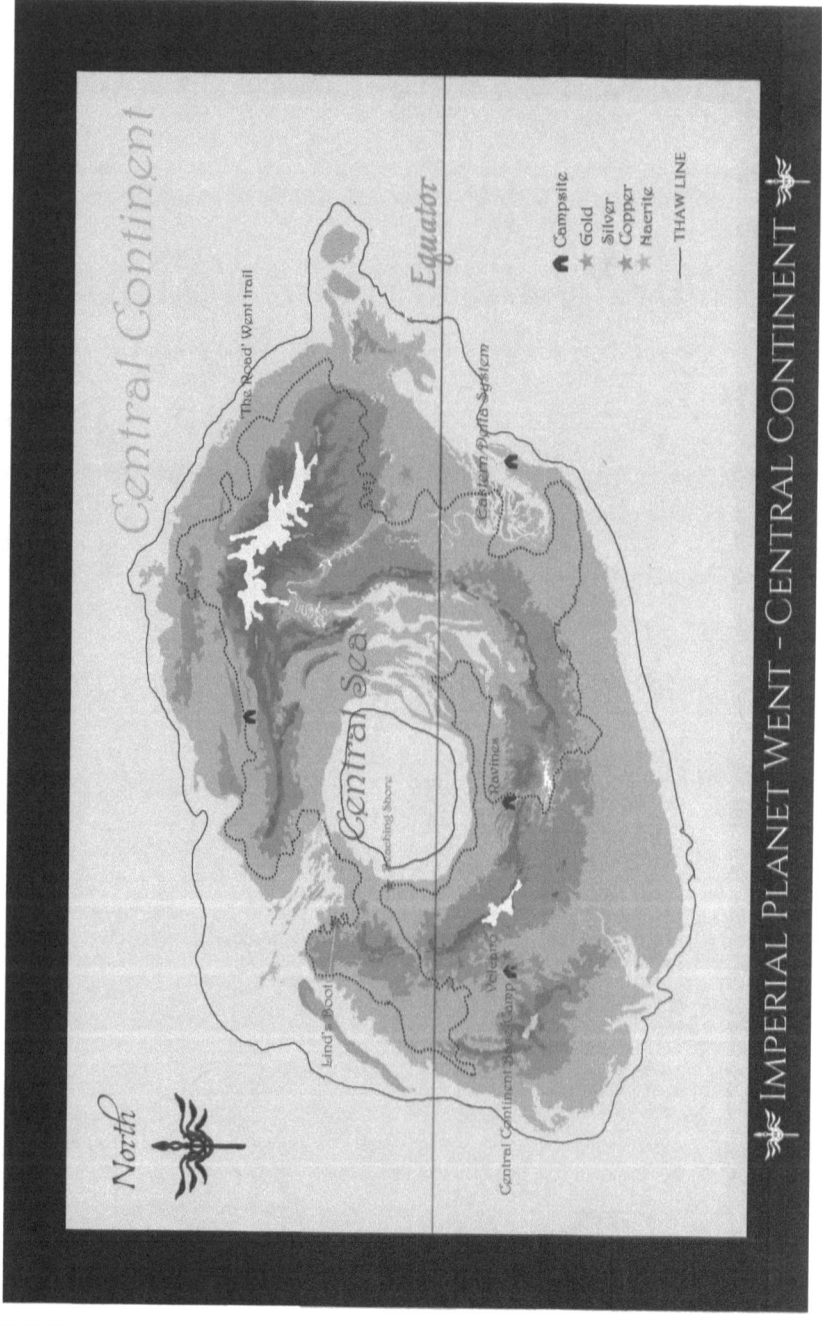

PALACE OF GATES

In a distant sector of the galaxy, far from the more heavily populated regions known as The Belt, spun a small planet with a string of small moons and three distinct continents. Few regions beyond The Belt held planets of interest; however, this one's transformation over several years from harsh, white wasteland to gem-like beauty of green life and blue waters then back again captured my attention. The Imperial navigator composed a song of translation, but for many long ages this song was unused.

Eventually, despite the climatic extremes posed by this planet's eccentric orbit, an exploratory expedition was proposed, and, in due course, the Thirty-sixth God-Emperor, Tsemkarun Ishät Ashik, dispatched a team of explorers to make the long journey. But this was long after my retirement to the blessed solitude of my own lonely planet, a gift to me from his father, the generous and kindly God-Emperor Tsemkarun Zohrät Ashik.

… Within the Palace of Gates, the Journal of *Ziquarudjan Ulisharu of Trianog,* Imperial Scryer to the Court of God-Empress Karuzät Enna, Thirty-fourth Chosen of El, and God-Emperor Zohrät Ashik, Thirty-fifth Chosen of El.

THE NEW DIVINER

She looked around and saw him running.

Rough terrain crunched underfoot. Small branches clung to his legs.

He couldn't move fast enough.

The bushes behind her rustled.

"NO!" he screamed, *NO!*

Ten prehensile fingers exploded outward. Red streamers wrapped the lean explorer in an unbreakable grasp. The giant plant's nest of teeth scythed downward and a bloody stump bloomed where Joumelät Enna's head should have been. Her body twitched and jerked as if it still fought. Viscous fountains sprayed the monster's leaves red. Joumelät's death-cry brushed his cheek with icy psychic fingers as it passed …

Huldar woke with a gasp. The sound of snapping bone echoed in his mind. He threw the covers aside and staggered to the washbowl to splash his face with cool, clean water, then wiped it off savagely as if blood and gore still stained him.

The image in the mirror was haggard. Helpless to stop himself he repeated the mantra: Why hadn't she sensed it? She ought to have known it was there. Why was she so reckless? If only she had scanned as he'd asked her to do – time and time again.

He leaned by the window and watched the dark streets below. The moons had long since set, and high above the Imperial City stars peppered the ageless skies in a web of silvery trails.

Had it been his fault? The healers said no, but they weren't there at the time.

Tomorrow he would meet Joumelät's replacement. He knew she was Trianogi, and quite accomplished, but what would she be like? How would she take to life in isolation from the Realm? Would she fall prey to monsters as yet unknown, or even the monsters within herself? Many of her people found the inner silence too much to bear, but on this assignment, once they'd arrived, it would be too late for a change of heart.

He suspected the new planet's unique and very harsh climatic pattern would test the hardiness and ingenuity of his team to the limit. Would the new explorer survive? And for that matter, would they?

The stars had no answer.

With a groan he padded back to bed, but sleep was slow to return.

His first choice for Joumelät's replacement had been a Nhadu, un-Marked, but very experienced, however, while the Overlord dithered, he had taken another position.

There had been another applicant from Clan Enna. Huldar had nothing against them, but so soon after losing Joumelät – the team would be constantly reminded of her loss. And if he was honest, the average Tiamäti came with an abrasive sense of entitlement and took direction poorly. Joumelät had been no exception, and now she was dead.

Andel of House Trianog was highly credentialed, but lacked experience in survival situations. They were to meet as she arrived in the Imperial Bays.

Everyone has to start somewhere. He sighed. *Let's hope she has better luck.*

Brown hair caught back in a fourth-level braid; gait … a little unsure.

"That's her there, Casco," said Huldar.

Tsemkarun Andel of Trianog recognized him and made her way through the travelers and piles of cargo that crowded the Imperial translation bays.

Huldar weighed up the immediate cues and added them to what he already knew.

His logistician, Casco, waited with him – no doubt summing her up as he was.

Casco leaned closer. "She seems a bit delicate."

Huldar tipped his head. Perhaps Casco was right, but on paper she'd made it to the top five on his list. "She's a Marked Tsemkarun with experience in the field, and she was keen to sign up."

"In the *fields*, maybe," Casco retorted. "A novice. Knew no better."

"Some Trianogi find the isolation a little overwhelming," he conceded, "but she looks determined, and she's been briefed on the conditions."

If the Guild has chosen wrong, it's you who'll take the blame.

"Casco!" Mind-speech in public was frowned upon by polite society, and especially between classes – all very well once they were away from the social strictures of the Imperium, but not there.

"Still true," Casco muttered.

Huldar glanced toward him. "So, what do you think?"

"Not what my kind are paid for," Casco grumbled. "And who'd listen anyway?"

The diviner hesitated as if steeling her nerves, then advanced the last few paces with her papers clutched tight between her fingers. Her mind leaked tinges of excitement. Huldar stifled a scowl. First Casco, now this one – was there something about him that invited people to take liberties? But when her buoyancy was suddenly contained, he regretted his moment of annoyance.

Casco gave a barely audible grunt.

She bowed and offered the credentials. As he took them, he noticed her hands were small but not soft. She was used to working outdoors then.

"Tsemkarun Andel of Trianog." He bowed in turn. "Welcome to the Uri'madu." He turned to his friend. "This is Casco, our logistician."

"A fellow Lethian, I see?"

Her eyes were a warm tawny-brown, like her hair. She waited and he blushed, realizing he'd forgotten to introduce himself.

"Yes … my apologies. I am Shamkarun Huldar of Leth." He made another small bow.

Her eyes danced. "I have heard of you," she said. "When I found I was accepted into the Imperial Explorers and to be part of your team, the Uri'madu, I – "

More excitement leaked from her mind's veil and Huldar didn't know whether to be shocked or embarrassed.

She smiled an apology. "I can hear my mother now – always one for decorum – but I hope you will excuse me, this once? It has long been my ambition to join the corps of the Explorers' Guild and today, despite her lack of faith, I have realized that dream."

"Dream?" Casco snorted. "Might not be so thrilling when we're alone in the wilds and shitting in the woods."

"Casco!" Huldar snapped. "You forget yourself! Tsemkarun Andel of Trianog is an archangel, and Marked."

Casco bowed deeply. "My apologies, Lady Andel. Our last diviner died horribly, and the shock has not yet left me."

The diviner accepted Casco's defense with a gracious nod, but when their eyes met again her excitement was withdrawn behind a veil of steely calm.

"I am new to your team, Shamkarun Huldar," she said evenly. "I have presumed on my acceptance and I am sorry if my exuberance offends. However, I have some experience of new planets and I am aware of the conditions we shall be working under. As I said, this is my dream appointment, and I have, I hope, trained for every contingency, even, as your friend so eloquently puts it, shitting in the woods."

Too late, Huldar realized that her show of emotion had been a gift – an early invitation to find out more about each other. Were her feelings hurt? Now that her psychic emissions were impeccably controlled, he couldn't tell, and he sensed it might be a long time before he would get the opportunity again.

"The Uri'madu leave from the Imperial Bays at daybreak in one week from today," he said. "Shamkarun Kandät Enna will be our navigator. The recommended kit list is included with your acceptance papers. Please try to keep personal belongings to a minimum. If you have any particular charms or substrates you need for your work, please ensure the list is discussed with Casco here." He paused. "Any questions?"

"If I may?"

He opened his palm. "Please."

"Why the limitation on personal effects? Not that it is a problem," she added. "But things stored in personal Qalān can have no effect on our manifest or a navigator's song."

"A few things are good, but too much can impede our acceptance of exploratory conditions …" He hesitated, not wishing to sound harsh, then explained, "It's something I've observed. Life in isolation from the Realm can take some adjustment."

"I see." She nodded. "Well, I will bear that in mind, and I need no special equipment that is not already listed, thank you."

"Very well. Please, contact me if you think of anything else. Otherwise, I'll see you here at daybreak, seven days from now."

A touch of frost had crept into her gaze. She bowed with almost mocking precision and inwardly he sighed. It was only as she was walking away that he noticed how small she was.

For the next three years, the Uri'madu would be beyond contact with the Realm and utterly dependent upon each other, and if the group were not compatible, those three years could become an eternity.

"What's next?" Casco asked.

He tipped his head vaguely toward the Explorers' Guild. "Meeting up at head office."

"Just to make your day complete." Casco sniggered. "What's it about?"

He gave a cynical snort. "Can't wait to find out." He pictured a group of shiny-pants officials who had never strayed from the Imperial City, telling him how best to run his assignment.

"The joys of leadership." Casco smiled. "Will Duvät Gok be there?"

"Most likely."

Casco nodded sagely. "The honey in the cake."

A broad grin spread over Huldar's face as he imagined their pompous Overlord as a spongy confection. He shared the image with Casco.

"There's one dessert I won't fight you for," Casco chuckled. "Did I tell you about that clunky old desk he's insisted we lug along? Had to ditch one of our kitchen trestles to make room."

"Only the spare, I hope?"

"Still ... what if one gets broken? Can we use his desk?"

"Might have a struggle on your hands! Still, we have to keep the esteemed Gok happy, I suppose. Perhaps I can bring it up at the meeting."

Casco shook his head. "See you later down at the Red Weyfal? You can tell us all about it over a jar of ale."

Huldar waved his friend goodbye and strode through the familiar streets of the Imperial City toward the Guild's offices. A persistent grin spread through his mind as despite the puzzle of the unwelcome desk and lingering disappointment over his interaction with the new diviner, the ridiculous image of Duvät Gok as a cake wouldn't leave him.

JOURNEY TO THE NEW WORLD

The navigator's voice rang on and on as it hurtled the Uri'madu through the vast emptiness of space toward an unnamed planet on the edge of the Known. The chord had surrounded them at every moment for over a month now, pervading their souls with the song of passage.

Although an Imperial Scryer had been to this planet in spirit, this was the first time anyone had made the physical journey, so this was an exploration as much for their navigator as it would be for the Uri'madu once they arrived.

Andel of Trianog sat on a crate and watched the crew operate. Of the seven spinners, three would be singing at any one time, four when the navigator himself rested. They were experts in their field, of course, but there was always a blanching of tone in Kandät Enna's absence, as if the heart had gone out of it.

During the early stages of their journey the jumps between rest-stops had been short – no more than a day or two between the inner planets of the Realm, but those times were well gone. Now they were traversing unknown territory, weeks had passed in eerie monotony and there was nowhere to rest.

After a while, the richness of the material world had come to seem dreamlike and barely relevant. Team members occupied themselves with games of ashut but she didn't know how to play and no one offered to teach her. She longed to feel something solid beneath her feet again, to reclaim her reason for life. Only the storytelling brightened the hours, and as the Uri'madu vied with props and charms to make their tales more entertaining, it became clear that Huldar was the best of them all.

The envelope juddered. Andel shuddered slightly as the chord wandered the edges of dissonance.

Kandät Enna waved a spinner forward and the thin Tiamäti entered the song with seamless precision. Andel watched as the navigator wandered toward his sleeping mat. His lean frame folded to the floor with a barely audible sigh. Most navigators were of House Maatu, but this one was of House Tiamät, the Imperial House. Shamkarun Kandät Enna, he was called, and woe betide anyone who did not address him by his full title.

He noticed Andel's attention and brushed her mind with reassurance. She smiled her thanks, but looked away when he winked, hoping he wouldn't sense her embarrassment.

It was said that navigators had a lover waiting for them on every planet, and recalling the amber flash in this one's eyes, she could see the allure – mystery and intelligence – the status of the extensive Shamkarun's mark on his cheek – but the instability of a navigator's lifestyle would be hard to deal with, and she knew they rarely married.

She looked up as their team leader, Huldar of Leth, laughed and continued his chat with Casco. He was also a Shamkarun, but his vocal talents lay in a quite different direction. He was taller than the navigator and perhaps not as handsome – but nowhere near as arrogant, and his clear blue eyes and a ready smile were hard to look away from.

Andel smoothed her thumb along the top of the crate and barely noticed its woody grain. She wished she'd been in on the joke, but he'd made it perfectly clear at their first introduction – if she were to be accepted into the tight-knit group she would have to prove herself.

She knew about the terrible death of the team's last diviner, killed by a moment of carelessness. She would have to be sharp if she wanted to survive, and never complacent. But that misfortune had been her gain, because there she was, a member of the Explorers' Guild at last, team Uri'madu, no less, and on her way to an adventure of her own.

She lifted her hand to the memento against her chest, a delicately patterned driftwood twig suspended on a leather thong. She'd carried it with her since childhood. Her brother had found it in a cave on the turbulent wilderness world of Germane, its rounded ends tumbled to smoothness in an ancient watercourse. She closed her eyes to envisage the complex trails of honey brown and ashen silver on the dark wood, and remembered the grace of his hand as he'd presented it to her. They had often played at being explorers. It had been his fondest dream. Would he be have been proud of her?

She wondered how the new atmosphere would taste. What strange life forms would she see? The world they were assigned to spent much of its cycle as a snowball … how would the cold have shaped it? She wished she could share it with him. Soon after their arrival her work would begin. As a diviner, it would be her job to search the bones of a planet for mineral ores and assess whether they could be mined. As planetary ecologist and team leader, it was for Shamkarun Huldar to decide if they should be.

———

Kandät Enna summoned Huldar to his side. The navigator leaned close and said something. A palpable sense of excitement rippled from their conversation.

Huldar raised his hand to gain the team's attention.

"Best get some sleep now," he said. "The navigator tells me it will be a big day tomorrow." His thick Lethian accent brought a covert smile to her lips.

The Uri'madu cheered.

"Daylight at last, and the wind on our faces!" said Casco.

"And silence," called Nachiel. "The chord, it never stops!" The gentle artist seemed out of place among the rest of the team; however his partner, Ronnin, looked more than rugged enough to make up the difference.

"We'd be in trouble if it did." Ronnin growled.

Andel turned to the angel by her side. "To be honest, Sari," she said, "I thought the journey might never end."

"Never end?" Sari replied. Her gentle manner and lilting speech always made Andel smile. "Yes, it has been a particularly lengthy translation. Is this the longest time you've been in the chime, Lady Andel?"

Andel nodded.

Around them, the discussion went on.

"At least I'll have something to do besides beating you at ashut."

"I let you win," Ronnin grumbled. "Otherwise you'd sulk."

Glass clinked as a box of ale was opened.

"Oh, yes please – and one for me brother!" ... A male voice, Andel thought it was either Topper or Bush. The brothers sounded so alike that if her back was turned she found it hard to tell them apart. Then she heard the confident voice of Lind: "Breath, that's good!"

The festivities continued but Andel slipped away and shuffled into her bedroll. Around her, the pseudo-liquid walls of the envelope resonated softly to the noise of the party. It was fortunate they were in a quiet part of the chime. When things got wild, silence was crucial.

"Big day tomorrow," she repeated to herself. "Tomorrow ..." She tried to imitate Huldar's accent, but Lethian vowel sounds were hard to reproduce and before long she had given up and drifted off to sleep.

She was woken by loud clapping, and saw the Imperial Overlord, Duvät Gok, stagger as he tried to find something to hold onto.

Bags and boxes jostled back and forth. Andel clung to a crate, ashamed of the startled squeak that had escaped her lips. How could she have slept through the onset of this?

"Why are the sides heaving? she cried. "Is it meant to do that?

A surge of song pounded through her mind as Kandät Enna and his full crew fought for control.

The Overlord clung to a sturdy wooden desk and shouted, "Stay calm! Have no fear!" but his face was white and his eyes were very wide.

Huldar swayed in place as if the wild motion was to be expected. Casco even seemed exhilarated by it. Andel strove for similar bravado but it was a difficult façade to maintain.

The envelope shuddered again. Its sides fluctuated like cloth in the wind.

"I saw stars!" she gasped. "There are stars out there!"

"This is the final approach," Huldar said quietly. "Bound to be a little rough with an un-tried entry. The navigator needs silence right now." He looked pointedly at Duvät Gok.

Andel pictured her mother's disparaging face and strove even harder to veil her fears. *I am tough*, she recited to herself, *I am resilient*. Of course she was up to the challenge. They were the Uri'madu, not tourists traveling in tameness.

Huldar's mind was calm and strong, his gaze steady, and suddenly Andel knew how much she wanted to be one of this team. Once they made landfall, the Uri'madu would be there for her, and she for them. If they died during the entry phase, they would taste the Breath of El together.

Then the navigator's chord chimed in resolution and the envelope shuddered to stillness. The spinners' voices softened at last and Andel released a breath she had barely known she held.

Kandät Enna strode to one end of the envelope and lifted his arms. Before him, the envelope dissolved into a doorway and the new planet was revealed at last.

"Theatrical." Casco sniggered.

Huldar shook his head. "Tiamäti," he said quietly.

The Overlord glared as if he'd heard their disrespect.

The landing site, or Djan'rū, was on a plateau surrounded by huge grey boulders. Fresh air caressed Andel's face with lively fingers. She took in sights and sounds unseen by another annangi. Poised on the threshold, she waited for the signal, for the first touch that would make this reality hers.

As she blinked in the sunlight, the Navigator pointed to the ground and sang a few phrases. Huldar echoed him as if committing the sounds to memory.

"Come on," said Sari. "Let's start unloading." She glanced across to a group of team members and called out, "Casco! Lind! Work to do!" then she leaned closer to Andel. "If we left it up to them they'd be lazing about till nightfall," she chuckled. "And he's no help!" she added, and tipped her head.

Andel followed her gesture and saw the Overlord standing as if transfixed by the view.

"Huh!" Sari pitched her voice so that only Andel could hear. "Clan Gok are famous for it! Three years we'll be here, Tsemkarun Andel, and I'm sure that stretch will do nothing to sweeten him."

The Overlord lurched into action as someone lifted his desk – "Mind out! Be careful, you oaf!"

Andel gave a dry grin. "Lord Duvät Gok *is* a real charmer, but I guess our navigator earned his moment."

"Earned his moment, that he did." Sari's eyes twinkled.

The cool air seemed clean and sweet, and in the absence of the constant ringing chord, Andel could hear the chirrup and clack of small creatures in the landscape with absolute clarity.

A light breeze moaned softly through the stones. "Brrr!" She shivered. "I thought the Djan'rū was supposed to be at a tropical latitude, but look, there's snow in the shadows, and the ranges are cloaked in white."

She looked up as Huldar came toward them.

"Don't worry, Tsemkarun Andel," he said. "The planet's in its warming phase, or so we've been told. Soon white will turn to green and the long summer will begin!"

Something about his smile jogged Andel's memories of her brother, and with a quiet nod she patted the twig in her pocket.

Here we go!

THE TENT

Andel shivered in the breeze. Although they must have been exhausted after the difficult entry, the navigator and his spinners stopped only long enough quick meal before departing again for the Realm. They were long gone now and would not return for three years. A short time afterwards, Huldar and the Overlord disappeared on a mission of their own.

She looked around the barren plateau and tried not to despair. All around her, tents were going up quickly and without fuss, sprouting like a ring of pointed mushrooms; but right now hers looked more like a sack of entrails than something she could sleep in. She poked the pile of rope and leather with her foot.

I've been camping before, she said to herself. *With my family ... many times.*

She started on one edge and began to pull the tent into shape. The leather felt slick in her hands.

So how did I do this then?

Every so often, her uncle, the navigator, had whisked them away to a surprise destination, often to planets where few had been before. But when she thought about it, if they'd camped, there had always been someone else who knew how to erect a tent, and later on, as a diviner on assignment, the facilities had been set up for her, but within Huldar's team here there were no such distinctions.

Well, if they could do it, so can I!

The charm to sing the rigging taut was a simple one, but of course it had to be performed with precision or it wouldn't work. She rehearsed the sequence of notes in her head as she dragged the sides into place. With great effort she tugged the center to where she thought it should be, but it was heavy and awkward and took several attempts.

Just a little more ... she puffed. *There! Now for the ropes. They ... should ... look ... like ... spokes.*

With the guy-ropes in place she pushed the central pole under the panels, then, after a quick glance to make sure no one was looking, clambered beneath to position it in its central notch.

She gripped the pole with her mind and hoisted it vertical, then took it in her hands and paused to catch her breath. The flaccid tent hung like a translucent flower bud, filling her nostrils with the smell of leather. Then came the tricky bit ... the charm to set the guy-ropes. With the tent pole gripped firmly, she took a deep breath, closed her eyes, and sang.

Ropes rustled, joining, she hoped, with the ground beneath them and tightening until the tent was fixed in place, but when she looked again the leather still hung like a shroud. She heard quiet laughter and it seemed to be directed at her.

She tried once more. This time she kept her eyes open and saw the ropes dance as if each had a different idea of what the charm meant.

She rubbed the Mark on her forehead. Surely a gifted Tsemkarun could manage this small chore!

Muffled footsteps drew nearer and she sensed Sari outside.

"Let me help," Sari offered, but Casco arrived right behind her. "Haven't you done that yet?" He spoke as if her ineptitude had scored him a point.

"I … I'm trying!" Andel said. She felt more than a little ridiculous beneath her leather caul. "I've never used this style of tent before, or the charm that tightens the rope … things."

"It's no trouble," Sari said. "Here, let me –"

"The Tsemkarun needs help to put up a tent?" said Casco.

"I can do it myself," Andel found herself replying. "Thanks all the same."

"Of course you can," Casco sniggered. "It's a three-year assignment. Take all the time you need."

Andel tried again, but although she sang the charm as precisely as she could, the ropes twisted like a nest of snakes and only stopped after they had knotted themselves into a macramé mess.

Casco laughed aloud and she could feel the rest of the team homing in on her dilemma. Her eyes burned as she fended off tears. It wasn't fair.

Outside there was heavy silence as the Uri'madu waited to see what would happen.

She keenly remembered her first meeting, when she'd assured Huldar and Casco that she had trained for every contingency. With a conscious effort, she groomed her veil to show nothing of her feelings. They would not get the pleasure of seeing her snap. What should she do? What would she advise someone else to do?

Be still and think it through, of course.

She had quite enough mastery of her Tsemkar powers to hold the tent pole up and lift the leathers into place at the same time: she just needed to focus.

Once she was calm, she pushed upward with her mind, keeping her influence light, just enough so the tent was hovering nicely above. Then she turned her mind to the ropes. This time, she noticed a faint aura around them and an almost imperceptible hum. Someone had charmed them! She almost laughed aloud. Although she was no charm-singer, this one seemed simple enough. She analyzed flow of the song until she had identified the loop, then with a single note sung at the right pitch the charm dissipated, taking its aura with it.

The next time she tried, the stays secured themselves as they should, and with a sigh she realized she'd been singing the charm correctly all along! When she released her mental grip the leathers they stayed up – a triumphant brown roof held taut by obedient guy-ropes.

"Yes!" she congratulated herself, but who had played the trick in the first place?

When Casco's reluctant approval came through, she understood. The whole thing had been a set-up. A joke. And she had played right into it! How silly she must have looked; the great Tsemkarun, the diviner, unable to erect a simple tent.

With a quiet laugh she straightened her hair and smoothed her jacket, then emerged from her shelter with as much aplomb as the Empress Ishiquel herself.

Her team-mates cheered.

She inclined her head in a regal manner. "Your accolades are acceptable."

Casco bowed. "Tsemkarun Andel, congratulations. The last newcomer took all day to solve that puzzle. You did well!"

"You did well," Sari echoed. "I wanted to help, I did, but it's a tradition!"

"An initiation prank?"

"Exactly," Casco said. "Shows us what you are made of."

"Here, have a drink!" Tam, the cook, thrust a brimming mug into her hand. "You're one of us now. Uri'madu!"

"Uri'madu!" they toasted, shouting it to the skies. A sense of belonging swept Andel's heart and she tossed her drink down like a champion, only to cough and nearly choke as the ferocious alcohol gripped her throat.

"Come on," Casco laughed, "we'll tackle the marquee next. Thank goodness it's not too windy."

Andel walked beside him as the group arranged themselves around another, even more intimidating pile of leather panels and poles.

"My uncle was a navigator," she ventured.

"Oh, yes?" Casco replied.

"Umm, Shamkarun Roshu of Trianog?" She visualized the sturdy planes of her uncle's face.

"Can't say I've heard of him," said Casco.

This was understandable, she thought, since there were few Trianogi navigators, and her uncle had rarely taken work from other Great Houses.

"Well, most Trianogi enjoy the unexpected," she continued, "so long as it isn't too far from home – but sometimes my uncle would take us somewhere truly remote. I suspect he enjoyed the surprise. Once, we even ended up on Manziat. Have you been there?"

Casco looked to the skies. "A world of endless muck and steamy swamps."

"True," Andel said, "but the sky-veils." She paused, remembering. "The most beautiful sight I have ever seen! All day, wild colors rippling across the sky like silken fabric hung out in the wind … shawls of liquid opal." She hesitated as a new thought came to her. It seemed so right! She hurried a little to catch up. "Like the veils of life and the veils of the mind, don't you think?"

"Hmm … I'm not sure." Casco scratched the side of his neck.

"It's the way they move," Andel said earnestly. She crossed her hands back and forth before her face. "Revealing then obscuring each moment with yet more life, do you see? Like the layering of psychic screens … interpretation and propriety."

Casco nodded uncertainly. They continued walking.

"But we didn't camp on Manziat – too dangerous," she said.

Casco nodded again. "Yes, it can be." They stopped near the pile of awnings, watching as the first of the poles went up.

"Will Huldar will be back soon?" Andel asked.

"And he'll be worn out," Casco answered. "Always is after contact with a fresh planet. He'll want all in order and dinner waiting!"

"And Duvät Gok is with him?"

"Yes." Casco shook his head. "Hopefully Huldar will've managed to lose him in wild Qalān, but failing that, I guess we'll have to feed him too."

A TOUCH OF ICE

Duvät Gok wrapped his warmest cloak tighter and kept watch for predators while Huldar knelt and buried his hands beneath the snow. The Qalān of a planet manifested itself in a network of wormholes, and with his palms pressed against the ground Huldar felt for these channels. When the Uri'madu arrived on a new assignment his first priority was to set up a transport grid. Without tuned portals, the team could not properly traverse the planet – they wouldn't get far on foot! – but the work was arduous and he was nearing exhaustion.

"I'm freezing!" said Duvät Gok. "What's taking so long?"

"I can't understand why you wanted to do this now," Huldar muttered. "We're still setting up camp, for Breath's sake!"

"Just hurry."

"We should head back – leave this till later in the thaw," Huldar said. "If we go further north, the cold will be far worse. We'll be risking our lives."

"Is that why you made me come?"

"Someone had to."

I wish I'd never left the comforts of Giahn, Duvät Gok moaned.

Then why did you? Huldar asked impatiently.

None of your business, the Overlord snapped.

Huldar laughed to himself. Word was that Duvät Gok had some serious marital issues. Perhaps this was the way he'd chosen to escape them.

Before them was just the sort of strong nexus he needed. With a determined breath, he pushed back his tiredness and honed his senses to feel the flow. Through psychic touch, he followed the streams and tributaries of the planet's network until he found a path that would take them directly to an island on the southern coast of the northern continent.

The Mark on his cheek tingled as he set his voice to resonate with the song of Qalān … soothing, smoothing, asking permission. At first the nexus was reluctant. It had many strong branches. And why should it obey this request to shut them off? Huldar refined his pitch to convey the benefits of harmony. Every time the gate was used the web would be strengthened, he explained, not reduced.

Abruptly, the pact was sealed and the portal was opened. The thrill of permission granted never paled. He stood and brushed the snow from his hands.

Duvät Gok grunted. "Don't you feel the cold?"

"Yes," Huldar said.

"You're not shivering."

"I accept it." He shrugged. "The cold is not my concern right now."

"You ignore it." Duvät nodded as if he understood.

"No, I accept it." Huldar knew the Tiamäti could never grasp it.

"Whatever." Duvät rolled his eyes. "Are we going north now?"

"Are you sure this is what you want? It will be dangerously cold."

"Just go."

A pulse of bloody-mindedness tightened Huldar's lips. Although a direct order from the Overlord could be ignored where the welfare of the crew was an issue, Duvät Gok should see what he meant when he said something was unsafe. "Stand closer would you? This is hard enough as it is."

With a sullen grunt, Duvät huddled nearer and together they stepped onto the side of a mountain deep in snow. Here, it was sunrise, and pale new light sparkled over creaking glaciers. Far away, the ocean bulged as an ice-river calved into its turgid, floe-bound waters. There was no sign of life. No ebb and flow of psychic conversation, no emotional under-stories, nothing to not-hear or shield his thoughts from; only peace. For a moment, Huldar stood and bathed in the stillness.

Duvät hugged himself tight, shocked by the raw power of the cold. "By the Breath, Huldar! Get me out of here before I freeze solid!"

Huldar wrapped his scarf around his face. His limbs were already starting ache.

"Get on with it!" Duvät snapped.

"Breathless moron," Huldar muttered to himself. "Maybe next time he'll understand." But his anger was as much for himself. For the sake of giving the Overlord a shake-up he might have killed them both.

He spotted a bright point in the local energy field and started toward it. He'd hoped the walk would warm them up, but the result was disappointing.

Once more, he immersed himself in planetary Qalān, seeking a quick exit to warmer climes. During previous negotiations he'd sensed the possibility of a gate that would return them directly to the Central Continent. Duvät's impatience beat against him, but the process could not be hurried. Engrossed in his work, Huldar could hardly feel the ferocious cold, but soon it was as if a thick blanket muffled his thinking, growing heavier by the second.

The branch was there. He forced himself to focus, each step thorough and sure. If the portal was not correctly negotiated they could end up lost in Qalān, unable to extricate themselves, and they would die there.

"Come on!" Duvät rasped, but Huldar barely heard. He was tired. He wanted to sleep so badly. Something slumped into the snow beside him. A voice was singing and he was almost surprised to find it was his.

Suddenly, the way was open. He grasped Duvät Gok's arm and dragged him, half falling through the gate and stumbled into darkness.

His teeth were beyond chattering.

Far ahead he could see the orange glow of a fire and his mind reached out, *Casco! Help!*

When Casco answered, Huldar was so relieved he could have wept. It didn't seem right to die on the very first day of their new assignment.

On our way! Casco answered. *Stay with me ... just trying to locate ... got you! We'll be there soon!*

He had an impression of Casco and the two healers running, but didn't have the strength to keep the contact open.

Duvät Gok lay unconscious in his arms. He looked down at his face; limp hair pale in the light of the moons, skin tinged blue with cold. High, flat cheekbones and fleshy hooked nose, heavy eyebrows and coarse lips … features typical of Clan Gok. He strained to find beauty there. The effort was too much.

He felt as if weights were pulling his eyes closed. He wanted to sleep but knew he mustn't. His mind wandered to their new diviner … had they played the tent-rope trick on her?

"Casco won't make her sleep outside," he murmured. "No, he wouldn't. When I get back I'll tell her the charm … but she's smarter than you think, my friend, she might have worked it out by herself."

He hugged the Overlord, trying to find warmth, but his strength was fading. "I should have turned back," he whispered. *No one should be this cold …*

MEETING SPACE

A freezing draft whistled through the marquee as the door was pushed aside. Andel wrapped her coat tighter as Lind strode toward the bright flames in the central fire-pit, hands held out to the warmth. Hot tea and honey-cakes waited on a wooden trestle toward the rear where Tam had set up the kitchen area. The stout cook leaned toward Lind as she reached for a cake. "Just three days since we got here," he muttered, "and already there's lives almost lost. Arko!" He pointed at the fire. "More wood, please. And I need more coals for the cookfire."

Arko looked at their skimpy pile of firewood. "Casco says we have to ration it until the snows lift and there's more to be found."

"I'll deal with Casco," Tam said. "You get wood. And hurry! Lord Huldar will be here soon."

"Just keep that Breathless Gok from my sight!" said Lind.

The brothers, Topper and Bush, looked up from their plate of cakes.

"I doubt he'll show his face for a while," said one.

"This'll be his excuse," said the other. "Mark my words, he'll not do another lick of work for the next three years."

Topper aimed another little cake at his mouth. "So, what's changed!" He laughed.

"Shush!" Sari frowned at them. "They're almost here."

She looked up as the tent flaps parted. Huldar entered with Casco close behind, observing his every movement. Andel winced as he lowered himself painfully onto the rugs around the fire. With a brusque gesture Casco signaled Sari to bring tea and cakes, and she obeyed with barely a blink.

The healer, Ubaid of Naghar, entered quietly and waited within easy call.

Huldar's hands were still swollen from their icy ordeal and fumbled painfully with the mug. His thanks rasped from lips cracked and raw. Part of Andel wanted to look away, but the blue of his eyes blazed from the redness of his face and she stared as if mesmerized. Flakes of dead skin clung to his cheeks. His long, shapely nose was raw like meat. When he seemed about to speak, the Uri'madu clustered closer. The specter of Joumelät Enna hovered in their thoughts.

Huldar pushed his face into a smile. "Ubaid of Naghar assures me that I ... that Duvät Gok and I ... will make a full recovery." He raised his hand to forestall comment. "In the meantime, there is work to do despite the shortage of available portals. We will have to walk overland until I am well enough to resume that task. As you know, Uri'madu means 'planet walker' in the ancient tongue of the navigators, so this will be a chance to live up to our name."

"Tam might lose some weight!" Arko muttered, but few responded to his attempt at humor.

"As the weather warms," Huldar continued, "we will travel to the Eastern Continent, then from there to the Southern Archipelago. As the thaw gains pace, many of the southern islands will be submerged beneath rising sea levels. Some will keep their heads above water, and it is those we will try our utmost to get to.

"The north will only be open for eight weeks either side of the summer solstice, but the Imperial scryer had high hopes of gold deposits in the sub-polar ranges, and Duvät Gok insists we explore there ... So, as you see, our itinerary will be dictated by the ebb and flow of extremes. But before we venture onto other continents, there is work to be done on this one."

Huldar bowed his head and breathed deeply. Ubaid of Naghar took a step closer. Casco looked at Ubaid, but the healer gave a small shake of his head.

When Huldar resumed his briefing, the Uri'madu leaned closer to hear his voice.

"This central continent has a circular inland sea. Are we camping on the edge of a caldera," he asked, "or is it an old impact crater? We need to know. Volcanism will be increasing as the ice lifts. Expect tremors. Beware of potential eruptions. Sea levels will rise rapidly. We have already seen the violence of the storms. Flash flooding ... tornadoes ... be aware of the signs. Never go far from camp on your own. All expeditions are to be undertaken with three of you, minimum. You know the drill, people. You know the dangers."

Andel found herself nodding with her team-mates.

"We know the dangers," Sari said to her quietly. "You can never be too cautious, Lady Andel."

Andel's breath caught as Huldar looked directly at her. "Tsemkarun Andel, the volcano on the ranges opposite – go with Casco, Lind and Cobar to assess the risks of eruption. You are in charge. Anything to do with the geology of this planet is your domain."

Her heart raced. "I'll be in charge?" she murmured.

"In charge?" Sari echoed. "Well, of course, Lady Andel. You're an archangel." She smiled. "Don't worry, Casco will look after you."

Huldar turned to the healer. "Ubaid of Naghar, you and Sari should stay nearby and search out edible plants. The sooner we can supplement our diet with fresh food, the better.

"Tam, basecamp, of course – you and Arko. You have the inventory. Water is rationed until a fresh source can be located.

"Bush and Topper, that's your department. Go do that thing you do with finding water. Priority to a well near here, but we'll relocate if we must." He eyed one of the two barrel-chested Rukh. "Take Gento with you for muscle – all right, big fella?"

Gento grinned and flexed his biceps. "I'll keep them safe, boss. Don't witter yourself!"

Huldar's brief smile cracked the scabs on his lips, but he continued speaking as if he felt no pain. "And you two! Nachiel and Ronnin, do the expedition day-packs and see that all kits are up to scratch. Ask Tam or Arko if you need something. Don't just take it."

The couple glanced at each other. Tam and Arko slowly nodded.

Huldar gazed at the Uri'madu, each in turn. "Any questions?"

Tam stepped forward. "What did this to you?" he asked, and others murmured with him.

"Was it just the cold," said Nachiel, "or are there monsters out there that we should know about?"

"The cold," Huldar replied. "Northern portal damn near froze us to death."

"Have you sensed any predators?"

"None so far, but the weather is a predator in its own right."

Andel nodded in agreement. "He's right about that, Sari," she murmured. "Those last two storms were ferocious ... One minute the sun was shining, the next, horizontal snow – and the wind!"

"The wind, yes. Didn't we run for cover!"

"But there's a wildness in it," Andel added. "Exhilarating, don't you think?"

Sari looked at her strangely. "Exhilarating? Maybe not the word I'd have used."

"That's not to say that there are no predators," Huldar continued. "They could be hibernating, or not viable until the ambient temperature rises."

"... Like Duvät Gok," Tam murmured.

"Oh," Huldar paused, "and the Overlord has asked that you keep your reports up to date."

"There's a surprise," Gento grunted.

"Speaking of predators ..."

Casco bent to help Huldar to his feet, but he shook his head. "Thanks, Casco, but I can manage on my own." He turned to them again. "With Ubaid to look after me, I'll be back to my best in a few days and ready to make more portals for us. Meantime, keep one eye on the weather and never let this fire go out."

Ubaid held the tent flap aside, admitting a shaft of golden light, and Huldar walked stiffly toward it. For a moment he was silhouetted against the outer world, then the door closed.

Casco watched the exit for several moments, then wandered over to Andel. In his measuring grey-blue gaze she glimpsed great intelligence, but she sensed a life of hardship and wondered if her suspicions about his mixed heritage were true. He was certainly tall enough, and the texture of his skin was surprisingly fine, but his eyes had round pupils like any other angel would have.

"You are not as tall as most archangels, Lady Andel." Casco held her gaze. "That does not mean that you are of mixed blood."

Andel's cheeks flamed. "I'm sorry, Casco. I didn't mean for you to hear my thoughts."

"I didn't."

"My apologies." She nodded a bow.

"No matter." He looked around as Lind and Cobar joined them, then returned to Andel. "What do you want us to do?" he asked.

Andel fought back feelings of awkwardness. "Oh, um, Casco, can we work together on this?"

Casco's eyebrows lifted slightly. "We are working together," he replied, and they waited, the three of them measuring her now.

"Umm ..." She thought of years spent divining in the field, always knowing beforehand where she should look. "Do we have maps to work from?"

"Rudimentary, but I have one here." With a whisper of song, Casco whisked the Imperial Scryer's drawing from his personal Qalān and handed it to her.

"Let me see," Andel murmured. Two major continents were outlined; the central one they were on, and a second, much larger one to the east. There was an island continent to the west – an elongated blob surrounded by endless oceans – and the top of a vast archipelago to the south. The rest was covered in ice. There were few details.

She put her finger where the Djan'rū was marked. "This is our Djan'rū?"

Casco nodded. "It's the only one."

The mountain range rough-sketched to the north-west of the rune must be the mountains they could see on the other side of the valley. Several of those peaks looked to be volcanic, but the prospect of walking through miles of virgin scrub to reach them was daunting.

"We should cross the plain here …" She traced her finger across the chart. "But it's a long walk."

"I have some farsight, Lady Andel," Casco said. "I can scout the path ahead. Lind, here," he placed his hand on the wiry angel's shoulder, "has a good eye for detail. Show her what to look for and she'll not miss it."

"And you, Cobar?" Andel addressed the burly Rukh standing with them.

Cobar studied her for a moment then rumbled, "I make sure we all survive."

"Oh."

Casco nodded. "All Rukh are warriors."

And Cobar is no exception, Andel thought to herself. *I've never seen such massive arms … or shoulders!* She looked to the tent flap. "Well, let's go to the bluff," she said. "From there, I can show you where I want to go first.

As they stood on the plateau's edge, Andel tried not to look down. A cold wind sighed among the boulders, tugging at their coats. "There!" She pointed across the basin to the string of snow-covered peaks that stretched from horizon to horizon. One in particular caught her eye. It was tall and conical, the classic shape of an active volcano.

"Casco, if we find somewhere comfortable for you to work, can you scout the way? Then, Lind and Cobar, once we know how long the walk will take, if you could organize supplies?"

Cobar squinted at the mountains. "Two days. No more," he said.

"Are you used to walking overland?"

He nodded, then looked her up and down as if questioning her ability to do the same.

Andel frowned. If they imagined her incapable of a long-distance trek, they'd be mistaken.

Lind bumped Cobar's ribs. "She's got nowhere to hide now. Stuck here for the duration like the rest of us."

The comment rang over-loud. Andel was dumfounded. "Excuse me?"

Casco and Cobar scowled at their team-mate.

Lind shrugged. "It's a joke, right? ... Sorry." She lowered her head in a brief bow but Andel was not convinced. She turned to Casco. "If you can you scope the best path for us, please? I'll leave you to it. We'll set off tomorrow at dawn. Pack supplies for the journey there and back, plus two days' surveying and one day spare."

"Breakfast first." Lind lifted her palms. "Can't walk on an empty gut."

"She's right, Lady Andel," Casco said. "It would be best to eat before we go."

Andel frowned, all too aware of her inexperience. "Well, of course! Please, tell Tam we will eat before first light. The sooner we get going, the sooner we'll find what we need to know."

Casco's eyebrows lifted. "Very well. I'll tell Tam. Daybreak it is."

"Thank you, everyone," said Andel. "We'll talk again after the evening meal. If there are any problems, come to me straight away."

They nodded and took their leave, but Andel remained, gazing out over the plain. A patchwork of foliage covered the ground: mostly green, but she noticed purples and ochers, and areas of deeper green that could denote swampy ground. What dangers would they find? Bogs and sinkholes … strange creatures hungry from hibernation and ready to eat anything in their path? The cacophony of shrieks and calls that issued from below told her anything was possible. She sat with her back to a boulder and wrapped her coat tight. Although she was no stranger to rough terrain, part of her quailed at the prospect of walking through uncharted wilderness – but even more unpleasant would be doing so in the company of an antagonistic team-mate. Lind's attitude was mystifying, but she was right about one thing; the navigator was gone. There was no backing out of this assignment now.

JOURNEY TO THE VOLCANO

In the pre-dawn gloom, Andel hurried toward the marquee where her team was waiting. Lind stood by the door. A steaming mug of tea sat beside her on top of a lumpy bag. Three more such packages waited in a haphazard line. Inside the sturdy leathers, Casco and Cobar stood with their backs to the fire and shoveled down breakfast from wide bowls clasped in their hands. From behind a bubbling cauldron, Tam greeted her with a welcome smile and dolloped a large portion of soft brown porridge into a bowl.

"Here you are," he said. "Hot hamarsi with krale-leaf, just in case there's blood-sucking critters down there."

"Krale?" Andel asked.

"It's worked before," Casco said. "There should be some in our supplies?"

"There is," Lind said. "And speaking of supplies, this one's yours, Tsemkarun Andel. All the packs are much the same, content list in a pocket on the side. Best to spread the essentials between us, just in case one goes astray."

As Andel hefted the heavy bundle and stowed it in Qalān, Casco said, "I didn't ask yesterday, but I seem to remember that you have some farsight, Lady Andel."

"Some," she admitted, "although I am no Ziquaran – more used to directing my vision downward through rock."

"Still, you're unlikely to lose your way." Casco nodded.

"Lose my way?" Andel's brow furrowed.

"Well," Lind sniggered, "if the tent was any indication …"

Andel knew she wouldn't lose her way. She was a diviner! But if she tried to justify herself to Lind she would seem weak. "Are we ready?" she asked, proud of the steel in her voice.

They left the warmth of the marquee and made their way to the bluff. As she descended the first few awkward paces down its side, Casco coughed. Three faces looked down at her, pale in the dawn twilight. He touched his forehead, almost as if by accident, and made a circular motion.

"Oh! Yes, of course!" She was glad the light was low enough to hide the pink flush on her cheeks. "Link with me please," she said, "… and with each other if you haven't already."

She opened her mind's veil enough to allow light contact from each of her team. It was important that they stayed in touch at all times. She had known that. Already she'd made a mistake. Casco's gaze was understanding and she sealed her inner mind more tightly, embarrassed to think he might have felt her pulse of self-recrimination, but before she could look away he surprised her with a wry wink and a fleeting touch of respect.

We'll maintain this light level of contact at all times during the expedition, she said. *Agreed?*

They responded in tight unison, and she realized the team were well used to being in each other's minds. Casco was their unspoken filter. They were linked more strongly with him than with her, but that was to be expected. She was still a stranger, and it was Casco, as Huldar's deputy, who would make their evening report back to base.

Step by step, they clambered and slid down the side of the steep plateau. As the first rays of dawn hit the icy plain below, they squinted against the stark white glare. By the end of the descent they were waist high in tough vegetation. All color had been subsumed in the shimmer of frost, and although bright, the sunlight seemed ineffective against the valley's deep chill.

Andel was delighted when Casco projected an image of their destination and his proposed trail directly into her mind. After months of solitude as they travelled with the navigator, she had come to enjoy the silence and sanctity of her own head-space, yet now she appreciated how much she missed the fluent banter only possible through the sharing of familiar minds, and she longed for that opportunity – an invitation to join in.

I've had a closer look at this ridge-line, Lady Andel, Casco said. *We should set out this way,* he pointed toward the sun, *more to the east.*

Right you are, Casco, she replied, but when she peered ahead at the impenetrable scrub, she was unable to perceive even the slightest of paths.

"I'll go first," Cobar said, and Andel laughed in surprise. *Oh! You've put an image in my mind! You are a … a giant boulder? So you're going to roll the path clear!*

"Don't break anything, big boy," Lind said. "You know the boss won't like it."

I know what I'm doing.

The party began to pick their way along Cobar's rough-cleared track. As the morning wore on, they passed through seemingly endless fields of tight, twiggy bush. Around them, the chirp and bleat of a million tiny creatures saturated their ears. If not for their mental connection, there would have been no way to make oneself heard – not that there was much conversation.

By noon, the temperature had climbed to almost warm.

Casco's mind showed them the sullen glint of dark water ahead, clogged with slightly greener shrubs and paper-thin reeds. *If we keep the boggy ground to our left, we'll come to a small clearing and a raised rocky ridge that will do as a causeway. Once we start following that, we'll make better time.*

Cobar forged ahead once more.

Andel could hardly think for the sound of the countless small creatures that clung thickly to the lower branches. Through their connection, she could feel Lind's sharp focus searching out possible predators, animal or vegetable, but so far they had seen nothing larger than a hand-span.

How do such tiny bodies make such a volume of noise? she said.

Hey! Lind called to Cobar and Casco, *remember on Belanze? On the trail with Huldar? Those tiny eel-things that made a piercing shriek every time they detected a footfall? Took us a day just to work out where the sound was coming from.*

The sound had a psychic component, Casco said to Andel. *Awesome camouflage. Couldn't believe they were so tiny when we finally dug one up. Huldar formulated a counter-song to neutralize their cover … brilliant really.*

I heard about that, Andel said. *Didn't he get Imperial recognition for it?*

Certainly did. Huge honor. The other teams have been scrambling to catch up for several rotations now.

Let 'em try! Cobar growled. His shoulders bunched as he pushed through the wiry chest-high scrub.

When they finally reached the clearing, Andel slumped with relief. Even Lind appeared tired.

The rounded patch of rock seemed a lost and lonely island, surrounded by a grey-green sea of shrubs. Lind pulled a tripod and kettle from stores. Cobar conjured a flame, and soon there was hot tea with a dab of honey and kanth. Andel sighed as the mild stimulant eased the ache in her legs. Walking was one thing, but stepping around, through and over tangled vegetation on sodden ground was quite another.

She looked down at the boulder beneath her and felt the surface with practiced hands. "This rock's different from the others we've seen."

"It's just a rock," Lind said. "If we studied every one …"

"But look at it," Andel scraped away some of the lichen, "the texture, the color … when you clear away the debris on the surface, you can see it's spotted – crystal intrusions – quite pretty really. Maybe it was flung out by one of the volcanoes we've come to study."

"How can a rock this size fly through the air all the way from there? You're just making this up."

Andel paused, a little shocked by Lind's rudeness. "I know it's a long way," she said levelly, "but I've seen it happen. On Parsay there was a massive eruption – I saw rocks as big as houses fly through the air as if they weighed nothing."

Lind's next comment stalled when Casco frowned.

"We've made good time so far," he said. "Better than expected." He looked hard at Lind then said to Andel, "We'll watch your back if you want to do a little divining."

"Thank you," she said.

With a deep breath she placed her hands firmly on the rock. Its meager warmth eased the chill in her fingers. Close contact was not necessary for her exploration, but it was a comfortable habit. When divining, she would connect to a specific stratum and often walk for miles, following trails laid deep underground during millennia long forgotten.

She closed her eyes. The flaring spiral Mark on her forehead warmed as she pushed her spirit into the boulder. Its structure sang of strength and time, and beneath it she found evidence of impact, proof that the boulder had exploded from the volcano's maw in a massive, long ago eruption.

All around, deep under the waterlogged soil, layers of ash and pumice gave further evidence of that mighty event and many lesser ones before and since. There was also evidence of vast floods and even a massive fire. The local ecology must have been routinely devastated. Then, while scanning for more indications of the frequency of eruptions, she sensed the unmistakable vibration of gold.

With her eyes still closed, she stood and scanned for the strongest signal.

What have you found? Casco asked.

That way! she said, pointing south. *Gold. It's quite strong.* She paced to the edge of the clearing. The deposit pulled with a physical force, but the thick vegetation around their small stone island prevented her from following.

Casco's gentle touch brought her mind back to her body.

He said, *This place will be easy to find again, and the gold is going nowhere.*

Andel shook her head to clear it.

"Gold so soon," Lind said brightly. "You might be worth something after all." She filled Andel's mug with more tea. "Here. Some kanth. It's a stimulant."

"I know what kanth is, Lind."

"Good for you!" Lind retorted.

The excitement of the find lifted Andel's spirits despite the other female's unfriendliness. As the team continued toward the ranges, it seemed there was new purpose in their step. That night, they camped on the opposite side of the plain, gazing over at the plateau toward the rest of the team at base-camp. With a little farsight to sharpen their vision, they could see the glow of the marquee.

"At least it's warm in here," Andel said. "Thank you, Cobar."

Casco reached for more tea. "Gold on the fourth day!" he said. "That's a record. This'll lift Huldar's spirits."

Cobar nodded, as if thinking deeply, then rumbled, "But where are the predators? Not even the evidence."

"Well, that means the inland sea's got to be a giant impact crater," Lind said. "Must be. Killed off all the bigger species. And the eccentric orbit of the planet just goes to prove it."

"But the geology argues a huge eruption at some point," Andel pointed out.

"'The geology argues'," Lind repeated scornfully.

"Yes!" Andel said. "And the area is still active. Look at the ranges around us, the conical peaks –"

"I do know what a volcano looks like!"

Cobar rolled his eyes and whispered a precious bottle of Lethian Besh from Qalān. He lifted it toward Casco, who answered the offer with an empty mug. He tried to catch Lind's attention with a wave of his hand, but she was not ready to let the argument go.

"I think the inland sea is more likely a caldera, not an astrobleme," Andel said.

"'Astrobleme'," Lind echoed, but after a second glance at the opened Besh she placed her mug beside Casco's.

When Cobar offered the bottle to her, Andel hesitated. She was not much interested in alcohol – but if she didn't drink with her teammates …

"Have you ever even tried the stuff?" Lind asked her.

Andel looked at the other two. Casco winked and offered her a small glass.

"Maybe just a little," she conceded.

Lind took a swig. *Astrobleme!* "Might loosen you up," she muttered.

Andel chose not to hear. She sipped the dark brown ale, which tasted better than she'd thought it would, and pulled an official report form from Qalān.

As she settled down to write notes, Lind made an incredulous face. "You're doing that now? You sweet on the Gok or something?"

Cobar chuckled.

"Seems as good a time as any," Andel replied, and soon lost herself in labeling the rock samples she'd picked up and the recounting of her day.

———

Casco sat back and enjoyed his ale. Soon he would activate the strong psychic link he shared with Huldar and make his own report. He could sense his friend's impatience, but it was best to approach such a meeting with his thoughts organized into words and phrases. Imagery was infinitely more useful if attached to conscious meaning.

A short time later, he smiled to see Lady Andel had nodded off with stylus and paper still in her hands, and that Cobar was also fast asleep – but Lind lay awake, waiting for him to connect with Huldar. The yearning in her eyes made him sad.

JUST TALK

Huldar lay in his tent and tried not to scratch his healing skin while he waited for Casco's scheduled contact. The efforts of Ubaid and Alis had restored circulation to his extremities. Now it was just a matter of waiting for his skin to repair itself, but the healing of his injuries had taken great energy and it would be some time before his reserves were fully replenished.

He wondered where the team had made camp. Had they made it all the way across the valley, as Casco had hoped? He hadn't received word of any danger or incidents through the day, so he had to assume they were all going well. Again, he pulled his hand away from his face. It seemed to have crept toward an itch all of its own volition.

At last he sensed the familiar presence and Casco asked, *How you feeling?*

Much better, thanks, Huldar replied. *Good of you to finally find the time. Besh, is it?*

Casco smiled, sympathizing with his friend's frustration. *Yes, Besh it is. Sorry you're not here to share it, but you know what they say … all the more for me!*

I see you've crossed the plains? How's the new diviner working out?

She's good … maybe the best we've had. Found gold already.

He studied Casco's sending of events with great interest. A lucky find, or was it? Andel of Trianog seemed to have had an instinct that there was something there.

Needs work on her leadership skills, Casco said.

That will come.

Maybe you should take her under your wing – Casco sent a virtual wink – *give her a few lessons.*

No time for that ... Huldar was careful to hide his attraction to their new team member. Such emotions had no place on assignment. *Duvät Gok is pushing for me to start on local Qalān tomorrow.*

Bit soon isn't it? What's up his ass?

Huldar winced as his sudden smile reopened the scabs on his lips.

Usually spends the first year sulking, Casco continued, *then the last few months it's tantrum time. Same every assignment.*

Well, he's ahead of himself, Huldar sighed. *Won't let up. Hobbles in here to berate me personally, even though he's every bit as burned as me. He's vowed to never set foot beyond camp again – or at least not with me. Says I tried to kill him.*

Congratulations! Let's hope he means it. What are you going to do?

Huldar sent the mental equivalent of a shrug. *I'll get back to work tomorrow. He seems fixated on the inner sea. I'll make my way there first. Short hops: shouldn't be too taxing. Maybe work toward you lot on the way back.*

Casco's disapproval was a mark of their friendship, but Huldar ignored it. Besides pacifying their Overlord, he hated lazing about convalescing while a whole new planet waited to be explored. No, it would be good to be working again.

Don't push yourself for our sake, Casco said. *Tsemkarun Andel is more than up to the physical strain ... much to Lind's disappointment, I must say.*

Two strong individuals getting to know each other. They'll work it out. Huldar frowned momentarily, then his connection cleared. *I'll tell Duvät about the gold,* he said. *That might cheer him up.*

Casco sniggered. *A big rod of gold in his hand might cheer him more, but we can be pretty sure he hasn't got one of those!* He sent a new image of Overlord-as-a-cake, now with a thin yellow grain of hamarsi sagging between its legs.

After their conversation, Huldar tried to put Casco's image aside, but the next morning when he reported to Duvät Gok, he found it hard to keep it from surfacing.

––––––––

After speaking with Huldar, Casco opened his eyes and gazed around their tent. Andel's report lay unfinished by her side and Cobar was lightly snoring, but Lind was still awake. Her haze seemed troubled, and Casco thought he knew why. He drew her attention with a subtle mental query, then hushed his voice so as not to wake the others.

"Why do you dislike her so much?"

Lind looked at Andel with distain. "Trianogi are weak. She's unreliable. At the first sign of trouble she'll freeze up and say 'It was foreseen ...' or some such rubbish. They're all the same. I don't know how she even made it onto the team."

Casco shook his head. Despite his initial reservations, he had seen great promise in Lady Andel. "She was the highest ranked candidate available for this mission. One refused just because of the communications issue, but even when she knew, Tsemkarun Andel was still keen."

Lind shrugged. "So what if we can't communicate with the Realm while we're here? What's there to say?"

"For you, maybe – you have no family. But what of the others? And if Huldar had died out there in the snow ... what then?"

Lind looked away. "You would have led us."

"Huh! Do you think our Overlord would go along with that? A half-breed in charge?"

"If Huldar had died, he'd be dead too." *And no one would miss him.*

"Aloud, please," Casco said. He waited for Lind to continue. Her thoughts needed to be vented, and for that, speech was best.

"Archangels!" she hissed at last. "... Except for Huldar, of course."

He motioned for her to lower her tone and she continued in a forceful whisper. "Pure arrogance in a bigger bundle. Duvät Gok nearly killed him. You heard him! He wouldn't take no for an answer, wanted that work done straight away even though he knew how dangerous it was. Thought he'd choke when Huldar made him go as lookout. 'I'm related to the Empress *Ishiquel!*'" she said, imitating Duvät Gok's pompous tones. "How many times have we heard it? What did he think? The cold wouldn't affect him because he's Tiamäti? Because he's an archangel? That it wouldn't dare?"

"I am half archangel," Casco said.

"And look how they treated you!"

Casco sighed. It was true that things were difficult for half-breeds, especially on Giahn, the Tiamäti homeworld. Angels and archangels – both races looked down on him. But off-world with the Uri'madu such bias no longer applied.

"The prejudice comes from both sides, Lind, but not here, and definitely not from Lady Andel. Both of my parents were honorable people."

"I've seen how she looks at you," Lind snapped.

"She's curious, is all," said Casco. "You underestimate her."

"Oh – and she's pretty. You should look at her with your eyes for a change!"

Ah, Casco thought to himself. *Here is the heart of the matter.*

Lind looked away. "She's a phony, stuck-up little … You'd think she was royalty the way she goes on. Did you see her in the scrub? First sign of trouble, she'll cave."

"Don't think I don't see you, Lind," he said gently. "I know what the problem really is. You can't force someone to love you – it's there or it's not. It's nobody's fault."

Lind fiddled with the edge of her blanket and would not look at him. He suspected her eyes might hold unshed tears.

"Try and keep an open mind about her; that's all I ask," he said. "I think she'll surprise you."

Andel's soft snore was broken as she muttered in her sleep. She turned over and snored again. In the silence, it seemed over-loud. Lind looked at him, a plea for understanding.

Casco shook his head. "What, that little whimper? That's not snoring! Now, when Gento gets going …!" He smiled. "You're looking for things to dislike, but we're a team, Lind, like it or not. Negativity won't help. She may be inexperienced, but she's doing her best. You should respect that … and keep an eye out. We don't want her to end up like poor Joumelät. Now, go to sleep. Another long trek tomorrow."

He pulled his bedding over his shoulders and settled down to sleep. A distant chorus of cheeps and rattles emanated from the swamp far below. He could feel Lind's continued attention in the prickle of his neck hairs.

"Casco?"

"Hmm?"

"I didn't mean to disrespect your parents."

He rolled over. "Well, think before you put the words – or the thoughts – out there."

Lind's attention withdrew. He hoped she was considering his advice. The calls of nocturnal creatures merged with the crackle of the fire and the keen of wind in the tent's rigging, sounds that sang to him of a safety he would always treasure.

THE LAHAR

After a full day's climb, frozen snow blasted against Andel's waterproof jacket and congealed in the fur lining that edged her hood. Tired from the long ascent, she paused and gazed up at the looming conical summit held fast in its carapace of ice and snow. The thin plume of vapor they had noted when the climb began was invisible now from the mountain's flank. Sunset glints dulled and faded into deep blue shadows. A tremor juddered her legs. In the distance the ongoing crash and crumple of an avalanche generated a storm of low frequency rumbles. Snow crunched underfoot as she resumed her climb.

Step by step, Cobar led them up a snaking ridgeline to the lee of a curving outcrop, where they pitched camp. Gradually the tent warmed, but the rock beneath them groaned and shuddered with alarming regularity and the team huddled in their bedrolls, unable to sleep.

"Can you do your assessment now, Tsemkarun Andel?" Casco's voice was hushed, as if any sound might wake the slumbering peak. "I don't like the sound of that."

Or the feel, Lind added.

Andel nodded and pushed herself upright. With little further preparation, she began to push her senses downward. Beneath layers of pumice and ash sandwiched between contorted beds of solidified lava, she discovered a volcanic chamber with welling magma on the rise.

Heat shimmered through her senses. Molten rock roiled and popped. Her mind tasted the oily stench of sulfur dioxide and seething gouts of super-heated steam. The eruption would be explosive. Peripheral vents were already unstable, and she sensed multiple fine fractures in the rock-face to the north-west.

When she returned to herself, three sets of eyes fixed on hers.

"We have to leave here soon," she said.

"How soon?"

"Tomorrow."

So, it's imminent then?

"I think so." Andel shrugged self-consciously, aware of the inadequacy of her reply. "Volcanoes are like the Breath of a planet," she said. "The only rules they follow are their own. However, whether the volcano blows or not, the ice above us may be ready to slump. We're too tired tonight, Casco, but in the morning we should link to examine the mountains around us. Ponds may be forming in the ice. You and I are strongest in farsight, and together we can achieve this more quickly."

Casco nodded, but his eyebrows knit.

"I suggest we leave as soon as our survey is complete," Andel continued. "Lind, we'll need a high-energy breakfast in the morning, please."

The wiry Lethian seemed on the verge of a retort, but Casco silenced her with a look. "High energy breakfast it is." He hesitated, as if trying to frame his words. "Lady Andel, you are Trianogi, and your House is often gifted with foresight. Is this true of you? Can you see a safe path?"

"Lies and illusions," Lind growled. "Superstition and a glib tongue. Trianogi can no more see the future than I can!"

"That's not true," Andel replied sharply. "My mother is a gifted foreteller but she can't choose what she sees, only as the Breath allows."

"Convenient –"

Lind! That's enough! Casco barked.

"Why do you dislike me so?" Andel cried. "I have done nothing to you!"

"We are all tired, Lady Andel," Casco said. "If you do see something, could you please let us know?"

"Of course," she answered, proud of the steady calm she projected once more, but on the inside, her heart beat high in her chest. She took regular breaths and hoped her hands would stop shaking before anyone noticed.

Casco glared at Lind. "You and Cobar take down the tent after breakfast. Be ready to leave as soon as we're done with the survey."

Cobar nodded and without a word, rolled over and returned to sleep.

Casco and Lind soon followed suit, but Andel stayed awake listening to the mountain for long into the night. Every time the ground beneath them shook, or a giant hammer pounded in a distant, volcanic forge, her hand strayed to her brother's gift – and when at last she dreamed, it was of a strange mish-mash of fiery rings and a baby, her baby, hidden and crying in the darkness.

———

The team woke early and ate quickly. As soon as they were finished, Andel asked Casco to join her outside the tent. She held out her hand. "Take it, Casco. It will make our meeting easier."

She closed her eyes and waited.

Casco hesitated. It was not that he was afraid, but to touch someone skin to skin, to invite them into your inner self, these were privileges he had seldom granted.

Come, she smiled, *I won't bite, I promise.*

Her hand felt small in his, fine textured and sensitive. He let his mind flow through but steered clear of her inner self. Although it was well screened, the only archangel he had ever worked with in a similar way was Huldar, and he wasn't sure how close he could come without causing offense.

He returned her smile as naturally as he could and tried to relax. As their minds swirled together, he quickly recognized her ability for farsight vastly outstripped Huldar's and made even his own seem work-a-day.

Your power ... he said. *Are you sure this isn't ziquarra? Why didn't you say something?*

It is not much really, she said. *Like all abilities, it's strengthened with use, but I'm usually looking downward into rock, not searching out terrain. This is new for me, and with your help, I think I might enjoy it! A bit like flying must be.*

Well, I'll let you direct us, he said, and with a nod they were on their way.

Before long, Casco was sure he would never look at simple rocks in the same light again. *I'm used to finding paths,* he said. *I don't really understand the way you see these things. All a bit geological – beyond my simple mind.*

She gave his hand a gentle squeeze. *I don't believe that for a moment, Casco. You've a fine mind. You just need more practice, that's all.*

Lady Andel admired him? He paused for a moment to digest this. It was difficult to lie when inner veils were relaxed. Now it was his turn to blush.

After some time wandering, she directed his attention to the southern face of an alpine peak.

Can you see that? she asked.

He strained his mind to focus. A dark space amid the shadows of a snow-covered hillside revealed itself to be a cavern of some sort. *What is it?*

An ancient lava tunnel, she said. There's quite a few of them scattered about. Must be like honeycomb in there.

Casco blinked. Part of him could still see Cobar and Lind. The campsite had been dismantled as requested and they sat in the shelter of the snaking ridgeline, waiting. Andel stood beside him, holding his hand. With the other she pointed as if it would help him see, although the space they were looking at – the lava tunnel – was well beyond anything they could view unaided.

Interesting, he said, *but I think we should go back.*

He shared an image of the ponds they had found in the mountains surrounding them, a growing volume of volcanic melt-water held back by ice dams. At any moment one, in particular, might shatter and send a deluge surging through the gullies and ravines. He had scouted a return path of high ground and ridges, but they would not be completely safe until they were back at base-camp, two full days away.

I'll forget where I was, Andel protested.

A shame, Casco agreed. *Have you seen enough?*

Yes …well, no! She smiled. *There can never be enough!*

This was something Huldar might have said, and Casco returned her smile. He sensed in her a fierce exultation in this use of her power, and a longing to know all the answers – but despite this, she was ready to take his advice. The self-contained Trianogi was different from any other diviner they had had on the team … more present, but her spirit somehow more elusive.

They relinquished their farsight and he let go of her hand. The ground rumbled again. Fresh snowflakes caught on Andel's lashes. Her gaze turned eastward. From where they stood that most precarious dam appeared to be no more than another blue-white ridgeline.

"So you're back," Lind said. "About time. The tremors are getting worse."

"Casco, could you show Cobar the path you've decided on?" Andel said. "It makes sense to stay out of harm's way if we can."

"What path?" said Lind. "Shouldn't you show it to me too?"

"I'm sure lady Andel intends you to see it as well," Casco said.

Andel took a soft breath. "Casco assures me you have sharp eyes, Lind." She pointed to the east. "Watch that ridge for us, please. There's water behind it – a kind of igneous slurry. If you see any changes, let us know immediately."

Igneous? Lind rolled her eyes. "I can't walk and watch," she said. "The going is too rough!"

"Try, please," Casco said.

"I'll be watching it as well," Andel added, "but these two will be occupied with guiding us down."

I don't care whether you like her or not. Casco said to Lind's mind alone. *Do as she says.*

Lind didn't answer.

C'mon, Cobar. He put one hand on the burly Rukh's shoulder. *Let's get us down from here and home safe.*

They wound gradually downward via the ridge-tops until they came to a steep-sided gully lined with a carpet of snow. Casco didn't like it, but this was the quickest route back to higher ground. While he searched the terrain with his mind to sense the stability of the descent, a vigorous tremor shook them and he was dismayed to see stones moving freely beneath the snow.

Lind scowled. "Why've we stopped?"

"I don't like the look of that," Casco said.

"The look of what?"

Casco ignored her. "Can you see beneath the snow, Lady Andel?" he asked.

Andel closed her eyes for a moment. When she opened them again, she looked worried. "A moraine … and before you ask, Lind, it's a slide of loose rocks dumped there by a glacier."

Lind sneered. "Then why not just call it that? A rock slide!"

Andel's reply was cut short by a fresh quake. Cobar pointed to the scree.

Casco nodded sharply at something Cobar had shared. "We'll need ropes."

A deep crack reverberated down the length of the gully, as if something distant had broken.

"The ridge has given way!" Lind cried.

A low rumble came up through their feet. Casco felt his reflexes sharpen, his mind step up a gear. It was no good going back the way they'd come, and they couldn't afford to wait for the flood to pass – it could be days before the path was clear again, or longer.

"Quickly! We have to cross. Ropes, Cobar!"

Stones began to jitter. Cobar uncoiled a length of rope.

"It's coming," Lind said. "I can hear it! Can't we just cross?"

"No! Wait until we can rig a safety line. Cobar, quick as you can – see that rock on the other side there? To the left? Anchor it there."

"Hurry!" said Lind.

Cobar tossed the rope end to Casco. "I'll go first. Make sure the others are ready."

Casco turned to Andel, "Hold on to this!" but she was standing unnaturally still. Her eyes were closed and she seemed not to have heard him.

"Look at her," Lind said. "I told you this would happen!"

Casco studied her for a moment, unwilling to believe Lind was correct or that he would have to physically carry her to safety – then he noticed something else.

"Her Mark!" he said. "It's glowing!"

"I can hold the path stable," Andel said evenly. It was as if she forced words from her mouth. "I've got it! Just go!"

Lind tested the gravel with her foot then scrambled across without incident. From the opposite ridge-top she craned her neck, searching for signs that the water was coming. Cobar followed at a run.

The rumble became a low roar, filling their ears. Casco hesitated.

What about you? he said to Andel.

"Throw me the rope!" Andel muttered. The formation of words seemed difficult.

"Hurry!" Lind cried. "It's coming!" She shared an image of the lahar snaking down the valley, thickened by rocks and mud scoured from its channel.

With movements rapid and sure, Casco tied the rope around Andel's waist. *Are you ready?*

She squeezed her eyes more tightly shut. "Go!" she breathed. *Just go!*

He paid out the rope as he ran. When he reached solid rock he turned.

Now! he cried.

Andel's Mark dimmed as her mind released its grip on the shingle. Casco kept tension on the rope, and as she started down to the shaking floor of the gully he willed her to keep balance. The roar of the approaching waters grew deafening. Air stirred, pushed before the flood. The rope jerked as icy pebbles rolled beneath her tread. There was no time!

Give me the rope! Cobar called.

In an instant, he saw what Cobar intended. *Hold on!* he yelled to Andel, then the two ran away from the gully in tandem, towing her behind them.

Andel scrambled as a black wall of water filled the gully, eating everything in its path.

Lind screamed.

Casco ran as he had never thought he could, but the rope jerked taut: Andel was caught in the deluge. He braced himself as the powerful current tore at his arms. His feet skidded against the stony ground. Then came a jolt from behind him as Cobar wedged himself against an outcrop. Time slowed. His thoughts raced. How could she survive? Archangels were tough, but the diviner was small and slightly built. He fished for her mind in the maelstrom. They had been close during the survey – they had held hands – that must count for something …

There she was! He didn't know if she felt his presence – her awareness was focused solely on survival. Somehow she'd had the presence of mind to push a bubble of energy between herself and the onslaught, enough to keep her limbs from being broken. She held the rope in a death-grip. Her need to breathe gripped Casco's lungs as if it was his own. *Hold on!* he cried. She must not pass out. He willed her to survive. Her strength and bravery had saved them from the lahar. Surely she would not lose her life because of it!

PULL! he shouted to Cobar. *PULL!*

The rope slewed toward the mountainside and at last Andel's head broke the surface. She rolled and gasped for air but was unable to find her footing. Then as suddenly as it had arrived, the flood passed. Andel was left like a stranded fish, still holding tight to her lifeline. Casco threw himself back the way he'd come and slipped and skidded to her.

Andel! Lady Andel! he cried, and swept her semi-conscious form into his arms.

Snow fell on her face. She shivered with cold. He stabbed his forefinger toward a small plateau above them.

Tent! he yelled. *Fire!*

He wrapped her in a blanket and held her while the shelter went up and the fire was lit.

Huldar! We need help! he called, but their leader was absorbed in Qalān and unable to hear him.

Once inside the tent he laid her on a rug as close to the flames as he dared.

Let me see! Lind pushed him aside. *She's in shock. Get her something to drink. Tea – not too hot. Quickly!*

She closed her eyes and hugged Andel close. Warmth emanated from her body as she activated her healing talent. "Andel, Lady Andel," she murmured. "Stay with me."

Casco blinked, but obediently prepared a mug of honeyed kanth and held it in readiness while he and Cobar anxiously looked on.

Andel's eyelids fluttered. He held his breath until her eyes slowly opened. "Lind?" She focused on the face above her, then her brows drew together as she looked around. "I survived?"

Casco sighed with relief. "That you did," he said gently. "Because of you, the way you held the stones, we all did."

Andel's brow furrowed. "I underestimated the danger," she whispered. "I couldn't hold on." *It's my fault.*

"Nothing is your fault, Lady Andel," Lind soothed. "No one could have done better!" she added stoutly, but even so, Andel's face crumpled. Tears dampened her cheeks.

"Reaction," Casco murmured, but in Andel's exhausted state her veil weakened and the face of a young Trianogi leaked through. He had the same hair color as she and the same light-brown eyes.

The image faded as she lost consciousness, but they'd all seen it.

Her brother? Lind asked.

Casco shrugged. He knew nothing about her family. "Will she be all right?"

"She's in shock, but no broken bones." Lind studied her face. "Does Huldar know what's happened?"

"Enmeshed in Qalān. I'll try again."

He crouched as the tent pole rattled and swayed. The ground beneath them groaned. When the tremor passed, he was able to contact their leader and send an appraisal of their situation. Almost immediately the connection broke off, and he knew that Huldar was in Qalān once more, negotiating a path to their rescue. Hopefully he would reach them before the eruption did.

Inside the tent, Cobar held Andel's hands in his meaty paws and Lind watched over her as tenderly as if there had never been animosity between them. Would the truce last beyond this crisis? It would certainly make things easier if it did.

Cobar looked up expectantly. "Did you get to him?" Lind asked.

"He's on his way," Casco assured them. He picked up the remains of the tea he'd made for Andel and took a sip. It was a little sweet for his taste, but comforting just the same. Then the terrain shook in a fresh bout of fury and warm liquid spattered his hand. If Huldar didn't get there soon, he might be too late.

ERUPTION

It was nightfall. Huldar stared across the darkening plain, entranced by the fiery red sparks and glowing blobs of molten rock that spurted from the now distant mountaintop. The dull boom and crack of explosions jolted his higher senses. Billows of ash leveled into a dense plume blowing away to the east.

The hairs on the back of his neck tingled and a quick scan showed Casco's familiar haze approaching. Soon he heard the light crunch of gravel above the endless chirruping from the swampy plain below.

For a while, his friend stood with him, watching the fireworks. They both gasped as a huge bleb of lava belched from the summit. Clouds of dust and rock exploded from the mountain's side. Seconds later the soundwave reached them.

Casco rubbed his ears. *A warm welcome to the new planet*, he said.

Huldar snorted. *I hadn't thought of it like that.*

Truly! The God-Emperor himself would be envious of such a display.

I can't believe the noise. I doubt we'll get much sleep. And them! Huldar waved his hand toward the swamp. *It's as if that wave of mud started a party down there.*

Casco's mood darkened. *If you hadn't found us …*

It was Breath's design, Huldar replied. *We are woven into its pattern with a fortunate degree of strength, my friend.*

Casco grunted. *It must be so. The lahar was terrifying.* He replayed his memory of the event, and Huldar had to admit it was remarkable they had survived.

He tried to picture the small diviner holding the path. *How did she do it? Each individual rock and pebble held still? The complexity of such a thing – and in such a short time, under such pressure? I tell you, Casco, her Tsemkar was well earned.*

She's very strong, Casco agreed. *And in more ways than one.*

Huldar sensed something pressing on his friend's thoughts. *Out with it*, he said.

A strange thing happened not long before you found us. Lady Andel regained consciousness for a moment …

Huldar tilted his head a little, inviting Casco to share, and received the image of an archangel, another Trianogi by his look.

His brow furrowed. *She was weakened. This image was not intentionally revealed.*

I know … Casco did seem a little ashamed for sharing what he had seen … *but if there has been tragedy in her life, it's best we're aware, isn't it?*

Huldar spent a few more moments examining the image his friend had shown him. *The face is a bit like hers …*

Does she have a brother? Casco asked.

I don't know. Although he tried to dispel it, the image resonated in his mind. Even second-hand it seemed charged with emotion. *I'm sure she will reveal her story, if and when she is ready. It's not for us to pry.* But the picture wouldn't go away ... he was so like her, even to the unusually dark hair and the thick, dark eyelashes. *Maybe she does have a brother,* he said, *and the trauma of the flood reminded her of something?*

Casco remained silent, but Huldar sensed in him a touch of amusement – and wry speculation.

"I hardly know her!" Huldar sputtered. He looked around hoping no one else was near enough to hear.

Casco leaned closer. *Well, now you know a little more.*

And even if I did find her attractive, Huldar stressed the 'if', *such feelings might not necessarily be returned. What if I approached her and she told me to go sing another song ... Breath! Three years can be a long time.*

Three years of not knowing either way can be a long time too.

Irritation puffed from his lips. *What if we get distracted, and it all ends badly, like Joumelät?*

That was not your fault! Casco said.

It might have been. Huldar shared his darkest fears. *I was talking to her. Neither of us saw it.*

Casco shook his head. *You were on the other side of the river! I was closer. Was it my fault?*

Of course not!

"She made a mistake, Huldar," Casco said. It was as if by giving his thoughts voice he could give the truth greater strength. "A terrible, complacent mistake. There was nothing we could do."

"I am our leader," Huldar countered. "Her parents were distraught."

"I'm sure they were. Maybe they even said that they blamed you, but that was their distress speaking." Casco looked him in the eye. "You did nothing wrong! You take your position seriously, your responsibilities, and we are all proud of you because of it. The Uri'madu ... you heard what Lady Andel said. She felt honored to have been accepted onto our team. She had heard of you, she said. Dwell on that if you must dwell on something. That is a good thing."

Reluctantly, Huldar nodded. Above them, the moons made an arc across the sky. High in the firmament a tight cluster gleamed like bright jewels strewn in a nebulous cloud of purple and orange. To the west, stars descended right to the horizon; to the east the volcano's power had banished the stars all together. It was beauty that Joumelät Enna's eyes would never see, and no amount of regret could change that simple fact.

He nodded again. Perhaps Casco was right. "I'll try and let it go."

"Good," Casco said. Warmth passed between them. *But you'd be less of a leader if you didn't care.*

SPRINGTIME

Through the weeks that followed, exploration progressed in fits and starts at the mercy of climatic conditions. On one bleak morning, as Huldar walked past the marquee and prepared to call off another day's efforts he heard Arko talking to Tam.

"How long have we been here now?" Arko said. His voice was muffled by the relentless patter of the rain.

"Thirty-five days, I count," Tam answered.

"Thought it'd be warmer by now."

"It is! Every day, less frost, and it's been a week since we had one of those fogs."

Huldar pushed aside the door-flap. "Morning all!"

Most of the team were already inside, lounging near the fire. He stepped between them with his hands held toward the warmth.

"Urmahji in the pot," Tam said. "Nothing like good thick tea to warm your bones."

"Aye," Sari said. "Warm your bones it will, and we could all do with a bit of that this morning."

Huldar sighed. "And another day lost to the weather."

Heat from the ceramic mug seeped into his fingers as he mused over projects placed on hold once again. Nachiel had already made changes to the map unfurled on the work-room table, but there was a whole world waiting. They would focus on the central continent, forays moving outward with the edge of the thaw until the next continent became habitable – he'd learned that lesson the hard way. Duvät was keen for portals around the inland sea, but there was a massive delta to the north and thermal vents to the south where the ice had already gone. The planet was coming to life before their eyes and each stage was critical.

The chatter in the tent was interrupted when the doorway opened with a dull slap and Duvät Gok stamped the mud from his feet. Annoyance cloaked him like a blanket. He aimed his scowl at Huldar.

"Why aren't you working?" he demanded. "It is vital that the portal system around the inland sea be completed!"

"Yes," Huldar answered, "and I have been. Only yesterday I discovered a series of straits on the north-eastern edge. The sea's not closed off, as we suspected. You should see it! The waters bulge between the gaps. Rocks like teeth, narrow and sharp – they comb through the foam like fingers. Come with me next time."

Duvät Gok's gaze narrowed suspiciously. "Give you a fresh opportunity to kill me? No, thank you. I'll be staying right here!"

And Breath be praised for that! Huldar muttered to himself. "I'll work on the eastern quadrant next."

"Why aren't you out there now? It's raining water, not lava!" The Overlord glared at the rest of the Uri'madu. "The lazy lot of you! And to think it was I who approved the very best of charm-sung waterproof jackets for you; that's more coin on your backs than you could ever be worth!"

"The weather is too bad," Huldar said, "and we can expect more sleet and snow by nightfall. Seriously sub-freezing temperatures. But perhaps if I had done more work on areas other than the inland sea ..."

"Hah!" Duvät turned on his heel and strode off, but as he swept aside the tent flap a pool of water spilled from the roof and dowsed him in an icy cascade.

In the deep silence that followed, even the creaks and crackles of the fire seemed overloud. As his squelching steps continued toward his own tent, the Uri'madu followed with their minds. Andel flashed around a cheeky glimpse of rain dribbling from his sodden hair, his expression red-faced and furious.

"Oh dear! He does look cross," Sari said.

"Lady Andel!" Tam gasped with mock outrage. "Is that polite?"

"How's the hair!" Arko sputtered.

"Breath of El!" Casco laughed. "Face like that could curdle milk at twenty paces!"

"I shouldn't have shared," Andel stammered. "No! I mean it! Don't tell him."

Gradually the laughter died down. From across the room, Casco met Huldar's gaze and lifted his mug. When he nodded, Casco came over with a fresh brew in either hand.

"So," Casco asked, "have you done *any* work on the inner sea? You were north-side near the delta yesterday."

Huldar smiled mischievously. "I've done some," he said, "but you won't be safe until there's a network of usable portals in place over the entire continent. When that's covered I'll turn my fullest attention to completing the Overlord's pet project. In the meantime, might as well enjoy the time off. Breath knows it'll be over soon enough." He looked at his team. "Bush? Topper? Must be your turn to tell us a story."

"Yes please!" Andel said. "I've heard you two sometimes work as spinners for the Navigators' Guild, and that's why you have nicknames."

Tam sported a wry grin. "What about that trip you did for the Faythans – the one where you ended up on Haas, or one of its moons ..."

"DuMah!"

Sari clasped her hands together. "Oh yes! Tell us about DuMah, and the fire in Lady Lamät of Faytha's pants!"

Topper shook his head. "Again? Cobar, Gento, you all right with that?"

Gento dug Cobar in the ribs. "Still funny."

"Well!" Huldar said. "The floor is all yours."

―――――

Some days later, when Huldar entered the work tent he found the Overlord poring over the map on the table. It was folded so that only the central continent was showing. He was turning a small glass globe in his hand and looked up with a guilty start, so engrossed he hadn't even sensed Huldar's approach.

"Yes?" Duvät shoved the globe quickly into his pocket. Huldar couldn't be sure, but he thought it had flashed a prism of color.

"The portal system around the inland sea is complete," Huldar said.

Duvät frowned.

Huldar hesitated. He had expected a more positive reaction. "I'll assign a team to study the straits," he said, "then progress to the southern quadrant and so forth until the entire shore-line is mapped."

The Overlord's frown deepened.

"… If this is what you want," Huldar added. Surely this was why he'd insisted on the portals?

Duvät pursed his mouth as if Huldar had made an offensive smell. "It would be unwise, as I'm sure you agree, to spend time lazing on the sea shore before we have a little more by way of potential riches to show the God-Emperor, don't you think?"

Huldar spent a moment studying the grain of the tabletop. "But what of the question of whether the sea is the result of a crater or a caldera?" he was eventually calm enough to ask. "Our diviner tells me that unusual minerals may be formed by the heat and pressure of such an impact; valuable substrates, rare gems … surely this warrants our attention?"

"Ah, yes. Tsemkarun Andel." Duvät nodded, smiling as if the new diviner was an affirmation of his own genius. "Gold has already been found quite near here, at the base of the ranges." He scowled again. "Go south. Find more."

"South?"

"Yes. It is on the landward side of the ranges where Tsemkarun Andel sees further promising signs. Then north. We have several months yet before the climate on the Eastern Continent becomes more benign, so make each day count."

"You don't want me to explore the inner sea?"

The Overlord glared ferociously. "South! I want you to go south! Is that clear?"

Huldar strode from Duvät's tent and headed toward the marquee. His lips compressed as he struggled to understand. In truth, it didn't matter where their exploration started, but he had worked hard to make the extra portals and to hide his delays. Now it seemed that the orders he'd followed had been arbitrary. The work had been for nothing. It didn't make sense.

As he pushed aside the door he saw several of the team huddled close to the cookfire. Tsemkarun Andel had already been dispatched to the western plains with Cobar and Casco to hunt mineral deposits and continue her volcanic versus meteoric impact study. Ronnin, Sari and Arko were preparing to research the volatile ecology of the vast delta system that emptied onto the outer northern coast – it's life-systems constantly adapting to changes in melt-water level and chemistry. The remaining Uri'madu looked up at him, awaiting new assignments.

"I'll be taking a small party south to the granite ravines," he snapped. "The snow there has melted and Duvät thinks there may be more gold."

"I'll come with you." Lind smiled brightly.

His frown deepened. It was not for Lind to decide her own duties. "You go with Alis, Topper and Bush," he said. "Secure the water sources and support Alis of Naghar as she searches out edible and medicinal plants."

Lind's face fell. He immediately regretted his gruff tone, but she did have healing talent and it was logical for her to assist in this work. She had never minded before.

"Gento and Nachiel, come with me. Tam, you and the healers will be stuck here with the Overlord. I wish you luck. Stay in touch. I'll let you know when to start packing for the move to the east. Ubaid, if anyone calls for your healing skills, let me know immediately."

He turned to Gento. "Get the kit we'll need. I'll meet you by the southern portal in two hours." He pointed to Topper. "Come with me. I want to be sure you know the relevant songs."

His teammates glanced at each other.

Topper's eyebrows lifted. Huldar's scowl turned inward on himself. Topper was a highly competent explorer, an ex-spinner, and more than capable of hearing a portal's tuning without being shown, even a semi-wild one – but now the words had been said, he could not take them back.

"The Gok strikes again," Tam muttered.

Huldar sighed. "My mood will improve as soon as I'm away from … Got any of that urmahji left, Tam? I think I need one."

SLUGS AND GOLD

They arrived in the ravine country, and Huldar's attention was immediately gripped by the sight of the rugged cliffs. Within the deep canyons over which they stood guard, rapidly growing forest reached for narrow slots of sky. Here, hot springs and geothermal vents supported a mist-shrouded ecology more advanced in its seasonal development than other regions where the thaw still proceeded at a more leisurely pace.

At his feet, bright yellow worms lurked like a child's forgotten ribbons beside a soggy pond. When a bubble-headed tadpole crept to the surface in search of air, one of the worms slid forward and wrapped it in a death-grip.

He looked up as a flock of iridescent creatures fluttered through the canopy. They landed with a spatter and a thud on a stand of pole-like fronds and folded their glassy wings neatly before lumbering off between branching, red-fingered fungal growths.

"Flying slugs?" Nachiel muttered. "Now I've seen it all."

Feeling truly alien, the annangi made their way to a place where the crags were cut through by a winding swath of grass that ran like a pathway from north to south. Opposite the clearing, a forest of young strap-trees waved in unison – for all the world like an underwater kelp garden captured by the breeze. Beyond this, more ravines combed downward as if clawing for purchase on pillows of plant-life.

Huldar looked from the forest to the grass and said, "We'll set up here."

"Right you are, boss," said Gento. He whispered and several large bundles appeared beside him.

Nachiel looked up and down the grassy site. His brow pinched. "I don't like it. We'll be right in the path of every big and nasty that comes this way!"

Huldar waved his hand at the forest. "It's better than in there. There's no slugs and no fungus."

Nachiel still hesitated.

"We'll set wards," Huldar said, "same as we would anywhere else, and the portal is right there!"

"I still –" Nachiel started.

"Are you volunteering to chop a hole in that?" Gento shrugged toward the strap-trees. "Give it up, Nachiel. This looks like a fine enough place to me."

Nachiel chewed his bottom lip doubtfully. When the fronds rustled he spun toward the movement.

"It's nothing," Huldar said. "Probably more slugs." He watched Gento creep up behind his teammate. For such a large figure he was remarkably quiet on his feet.

"I hope so," Nachiel was saying. His head bobbed as he searched the vegetation.

"I'll take a closer look later on," Huldar continued, "and if I find any rampaging, flesh-eating monsters –"

"RAAARGH!" Gento roared.

Nachiel squeaked in terror. "Big brute!" He put his hand over his heart. "Nearly frightened the life out of me."

Huldar left them to set up camp while he went to assess the feel of local Qalān. When a sudden thunderstorm darkened the skies, he hurried back to find a fire already burning and all their bedding in order.

"Ah! Just in time!" Nachiel said. "Kettle's on the boil."

"Thanks!" Huldar gazed around the inside of their new domain. "This looks very comfy, and see, oh ye doubters, we're sheltered from the worst of the winds by mountains on either side."

Gento tossed his head toward the weather. "Pink hail?"

A drift of it had followed Huldar inside. "Volcanic fumes?" he ventured, kicking it back out. He'd never seen hail that color before, but he thought he'd read about it somewhere.

The noise of the storm increased. A ferocious gust made the leathers creak. Nachiel paused mid step. "Oh no! What if this clearing was made by tornadoes?" He glanced apprehensively at the ceiling. "Regular tornadoes! I don't want to get sucked up into the sky and torn apart!"

"Relax, Nachiel," said Huldar. "It's not that bad, and, as to what made the track – I saw no broken trees or debris further down. I don't know why it's there, but it goes a long way – right down to the sea, I think. If Casco or the new diviner were here, they could tell us more."

Guy-ropes hummed as a fresh squall buffeted them.

"Now, how about a quiet ale to celebrate the absence of the Overlord?" Huldar said. "And what have we got to eat? I'm starving!"

———

The next morning, Huldar ducked beneath a curtain of icicles hanging above their tent flap. Droplets of melt-water reminded him of salivating teeth, and despite yesterday's jokes he made a quick scan for predators.

On his way back in, he didn't duck low enough. Nachiel looked up from his bedroll, startled by the fall of as broken ice.

Gento stood over a bubbling pot of porridge. "Just a little more," he muttered, "and a pinch of that salt from Parsay." He stirred it again and the aroma of little attar wafted through the room.

Nachiel rolled his eyes. "It'd be nice to think he was muttering charms to improve the flavor."

"Hmm." Huldar grinned. "Unlikely."

"It is what it is," Gento growled. "Here, tea should sweeten you up."

Huldar turned to Nachiel. "If you could take your gear into the forest today and do some sketching? I particularly want images of those flying slugs."

"Slimy things!" Nachiel grimaced. "But at least they won't eat me."

"They'll look good for the review when we go home. Nothing like novelty to keep the guild's patrons happy. And the orange fungi … you know the ones … the top explodes when you touch them? After that, whatever else takes your interest."

"I'll start as soon as the fog lifts," Nachiel said. "Assuming it will lift! I have some lovely new paper I bought in the Imperial City just before we left."

He cracked open a flat leather case and smoothed his hand over a creamy sheaf of paper. "Doesn't it smell divine? Hmm ... like silk ... or clouds on water."

"Clouds on water!" Gento sniggered.

The case closed again with a snap. "How's that breakfast coming along?" Nachiel said.

Huldar grinned. "Ah, yes – Gento, since you're on kitchen duties today, for the evening meal I'm thinking wild talemgal fried in crosin oil with stremon patties and a nice, red-karientos sauce? What do you think, Nachiel?"

"Ooh, yes, please!"

"Then a big slice of easanberry tart with saroo cream cheese, and all washed down with a glass of finest casset liqueur." He looked up at Gento. "What do you say?"

The Rukh snorted. He shared an image of exotic dishes served on a gilded platter, presented by himself in the uniform of an Imperial servant.

"Looks like he's going to tip the food over your head," Nachiel chuckled. He turned to Gento. "Imperial colors suit you. Watch out for the Gok! He might fancy a nice big Rukh, especially in a costume like that."

"Do you think?" Gento slopped a ladle of little attar into Nachiel's bowl.

"Hey! Watch the case!"

Gento smiled as Nachiel wiped a blob of warm, gluey seeds from the leather.

"Anything else, my lordling?" he asked sweetly.

Leaving Nachiel and Gento with strict instructions not to venture too far, Huldar set out through the fog to follow the broad clearing and hopefully get more of a feel for what it was. Prints or scat might tell him something about the animals thereabouts, but the whole area seemed clean and clear – very strange.

He came to a raised hummock a little drier than its surroundings and kneeled with his palms against its surface to let the local song seep into him. After a time, he began to hum in tune with what he sensed and when he found the right pitch, the inner life of nearby ecosystems began to course through him … first a trickle, then a flood … the joy of renewal, the ecstasy of rebirth, trunks grew, leaves reached for the warmth, mites burrowed and flowers took shape while underground creatures prepared to emerge from their long, dark sleep … He smiled with joy. This was why he loved what he did.

But when it was time to narrow the focus, he found that he could not. In a silken surge the song gained force and took him with it. A powerful drone thrummed in his soul, rushed him through mountain and stone into deep green oceans then deeper still until he thought he would finally see the mysteries at a planet's core.

Then a voice murmured like the hush of wavelets on a gentle shore. He strained to hear it.

They come … They are here! Breaker and redeemer as one …

The contact broke and Huldar lay gasping in fresh sunshine. Elements of his experience slipped away as the waking world exerted its influence, but he remembered the words. In his mind there remained the image of a starry circle and the sense of a path unbroken … and in his heart, a feeling that the Great Design had brought him there for a reason: that his fate was now sealed and fixed in the pattern of time.

Huldar? Shamkarun Huldar!

Nachiel's voice drove the last trails of vision from his thoughts.

Over here! he replied. He felt as if he'd been trampled by a herd of beasts. As he rolled to his feet, he glimpsed a small patch of orange beneath the turf. He bent to see what it was and found a brightly striped pebble, curiously out of place. As he prized it from the ground it resonated against his fingertips. Was it *charmed*? How could that be? He looked at the barren circle, where a ring of vegetation had grown up around it. It must have been there for ages, yet that was impossible.

The sound of running footsteps came closer.

"Huldar!" Nachiel called.

He peered up at the sky. It was almost midday. He must have lain for several hours, caught in the planet's song, yet time had passed so quickly.

He pocketed the charmstone before Nachiel could see it.

"Are you all right?" Nachiel panted. He imaged Ubaid's seamed Naghari face.

"No need," Huldar assured him.

"What happened?" Nachiel insisted. "We lost you. Your voice was gone for so long and it didn't come back. Gento's still searching …" He paused to message his team-mate, then continued almost in the same breath. "I looked here – I *thought* I looked here, then I saw you just lying. Why were you gone for so long? Were you in Qalān?"

Huldar let him talk. How could he explain? Eventually the inquisition stalled, but he just shook his head. He needed more time to digest his experience.

Nachiel seemed close to tears. *It was as if you'd left with a navigator, or got lost in Qalān … or died.*

"Well, I'm certainly very much alive," Huldar said, "and I'm sorry to have worried you. I'll explain later, but truly, there's nothing to be concerned about."

As they turned for the campsite, Huldar couldn't stop wondering – what did it mean when the planet said he had come? *Breaker and redeemer …* Was it a prophecy? How was it that a planet could speak, and that he could understand?

The remainder of the day was spent walking through forests and wrestling with local Qalān, then, after a speedy evening meal where Nachiel and Gento were uncharacteristically quiet, he put his questions to rest as they set out on a nocturnal survey.

They chose to explore territory they'd already covered in daylight. Although the bitter cold pressed down on them there was no snow – compared to what they'd experienced at base-camp the conditions seemed almost temperate. As they made their way along the broad floor of a steep ravine, the clacks and whistles of thousands of creatures filled their ears.

When Gento pointed out a small lizard with a phosphorescent crest, they paused to see what it would do. Tiny bugs drawn to the light battered against it, but the lizard waited motionless beside a small pile of dirt and appeared to ignore them. A sudden trickle of grains slid down the side of the mound. The lizard's upper arms folded slowly back like springs ready to strike. As an insectoid burrower pushed through the crest ignited with flickering bands of color, and they caught a brief glimpse of something little more than eyes and abdomen before the glow-lizard pounced.

"Well!" Huldar said as the lizard munched its prize, "Beauty is as beauty does – but Breath, it's cold!"

"Time to get back?"

"Certainly is."

By the time they returned to their campsite, the fire had all but gone out and a lace of brittle hoar caked the guy-ropes.

Huldar stamped his feet to warm them. "Can you pass me one of those shawls?"

"Here, one each!" said Nachiel. He held the last one to his face. "Mum knitted it for me. Blue kressie-wool makes it extra warm." He scowled at the blackened fire-pit. "Gento, do something about that will you?"

Gento rolled his eyes. "Why is it always me?"

"Because you're the best at fires," Nachiel replied. "It's a Rukh thing."

"And nagging?" Gento teased. "That must be a Nhadu thing. Perhaps the repetitive jaw movement helps you stay warm."

Nachiel turned. "Tell him to stop, Huldar … Huldar?

But Huldar barely heard them. He sat and watched fresh flames kindle then sipped the tea Gento gave him without tasting it. Leth was a House of ecologists. Since the dawn of archangels, this had been their role in the Realm, and yet he knew of no one besides the leader of their guild who had ever communicated with a planet – and even then, had it been a conversation? He didn't think so. Perhaps it was not the planet that had spoken … perhaps it was something else. And what of the orange stone? Was it mere coincidence that he'd found it at the same time?

"You're very quiet," Nachiel said.

"I'm fine, really!" Huldar reassured him. "Have you noticed the eye-placement of the life-forms here? Many we've seen have multiple eyes, or occasionally just one. Have we seen any with just two eyes?"

"No, come to think of it," said Nachiel.

"I'm too tired to think at all," Gento muttered. "Ready to turn in."

Huldar nodded. "I won't be far behind you. Good work today, my friends, good work." He sat in silence and listened to the flames, and when the crackle had been joined by muffled snores he reclaimed the orange stone from Qalān and held it cupped in his palm.

"What have you got to tell me?" he murmured. "I wonder where you come from?" When he picked it up between his fingertips to hold it closer to the fire, he noticed a faint hum. "Ah ha! A beacon stone? But you've lost strength over time and your call's nearly faded away." He turned the pebble in his fingertips. *If I can identify the exact charm, I might even know who sung it.*

Gradually, enough notes surfaced and Huldar recognized an older style of song no longer in common use. With gentle voice he refurbished its power, but not enough of the original remained for him to discern who had made it. Maybe the pebble's planet of origin would be a further clue, and for that, he would need to ask Tsemkarun Andel. The thought made his heart beat faster and he put the stone away.

The next morning, he crunched across the frost to where he had found it. If someone else had been here and used Qalān, there would be traces.

When he placed his palms against the ground and concentrated, he found that, sure enough, there had once been a portal close by. It was old and decayed now but proof of a former Annangi visitation! Although the resonance was faint, he sensed the jangle of work done without proper negotiation. The singer must have been quite powerful to use Qalān in this way, he thought. Definitely a Shamkarun, maybe even a navigator. No self-respecting Lethian would force a portal so.

He attuned himself to its path and found it exited onto a long sheltered bay on the shores of the inner sea, not too far from the straits. He frowned as he recalled how adamant Duvät Gok had been about having portals on the inner shores, yet now he was just as determined they should stay away.

With a whisper, he connected to the husk of the decayed portal and prepared to re-establish it, this time with proper respect, but Gento's call to breakfast cut his efforts short.

"Never fear," he whispered, "I'll be back soon to patch you up. Have you working smoothly in no time!"

————————

Many days later, the team had established that the area was free of dangerous predators and, although still watchful, they felt comfortable increasing the range of their individual journeys. However, the slug population seemed determined to make their own explorations and found the campsite particularly intriguing. Huldar set the usual critter-deterrent wards, but although the onslaught slowed, he had yet to find a song that would keep the more adventurous from coming inside.

On a bright spring-like morning, as he followed a flock of them through the strap-trees, hoping to find a natural defense, Nachiel called, *Huldar! Come quick!*

He squinted to the north. The summons seemed urgent, but there was no sense of danger.

On my way, he said, and a few minutes later he stepped through one of his newer portals into the gloom of a slot-like ravine, as close as may be to where Nachiel and Gento were working.

Over here! Nachiel called.

The narrow space opened into a broad keyhole canyon with towering walls. Huldar pushed through the forest, careful not to step on any slugs or damage too much foliage. His hand waved to fend off a cloud of buzzing wings that burst from their roost in a wide pink flower. Vines coiled and un-coiled, sensitive to his touch. Many plants already bore fruit, and he made a mental note to have Alis or Ubaid test their properties.

Through the dense trunks of the understory he glimpsed the flash of a shirt.

Lady Andel's going to love this! Gento said.

At first he thought it was shadows, or a trick of the light, but as he got closer, he saw that the striped lines on the ravine walls were seams of quartz. Nachiel waved, urging him to come quickly. Excitement made their hazes bright.

Gento pointed. *Look at this!*

Huldar paused as the sight sank in. Within the shining bands of crystal ran yellow veins of gold that ramified like Qalān on a planet. He ran his fingers over rivers of metal. This would surely bring a smile to the Overlord's face. As he sighted along the glittering seam, he realized it was aimed more or less at the area where he'd found the beacon.

Maybe it was left behind to mark a potential gold mine, he thought, *but if that's the case, why the portal to the inner sea?*

It was Gento who found it, Nachiel said, and the big Rukh beamed. *I thought it was more slug trails, and then he called me over and I nearly dropped my stylus!*

"Let's get some samples," Huldar said. "I'll start a feasibility study right away. This should keep the Gok happy."

"He'll say, 'Told you so.' I can hear him now!" Nachiel raised his shoulders. "So annoying. What would he know?"

Huldar smiled. "Well, it was Lady Andel, actually. She thought we might find more gold here and she was right."

VISITATION

In the weeks following the discovery in the ravines, time for relaxation became scarce. An initial study of key environmental elements was required, but identification of ecological corner stones took time, patience and a keen ear for the song of the planet. In addition to this, Huldar had to make scheduled visits to other groups and write regular reports.

On an afternoon of sunshine after a morning of storms and rain, the humidity within the canyon was on the rise. Huldar sat on a rock and brushed a cloud of gnatish creatures from his face as he checked his notes.

"Ah, yes," he muttered to himself. "The yellow moss and the strap-trees ... synchronous reproduction linked by a pheromone." He blew to dislodge a gnat from his lips and drew a line on the parchment sheet. "But there seems to be a connection between the moss and the slugs and the fungal gardens. Are strap trees part of their cycle too?"

With a sigh, he plunged his senses back into the local biome. Once more, the vibrations of the area filtered through his mind and he sifted through their myriad small songs, searching for links and correlations.

Shamkarun Huldar! The Overlord's call jangled him from his study. It came from the direction of their campsite.

Huldar groaned. "And the song unmissed returns," he muttered. "What does he want?"

With great reluctance, he released the last shreds of connection, then, brushing leaves and dirt from his clothes, made his way to the nearby portal and stepped through.

Duvät Gok faced him with his back to the hearth. His arms were folded. One foot tapped the ground. Gento hovered by the fire, unsure whether he should stay and continue preparations for their evening meal, or make a hasty exit.

Huldar tipped his head toward the door. Gento bowed and hurried away.

"It is time to move," Duvät announced. "We have been detained on this continent for long enough."

Huldar frowned. "The east is still frozen."

The Overlord shrugged. "It was cold here when we arrived, and we all survived."

"But I haven't finished my assessment," Huldar said. "There are several key relationships I have yet to decipher, and I'm sure you won't be happy with an incomplete report."

"Then work faster."

"The planet cannot be hurried!" Huldar frowned slightly. "The thaw is just beginning. I assess as factors unfold," he said, "as you know. How can it be otherwise?"

"You're the ecologist. You tell me!"

Although the Overlord was often overbearing, on past assignments his decisions had not been so capricious, and again it seemed he was in no mood to be reasoned with. Huldar shook his head and tried to think of a compromise. "Very well," he said at last. "It's possible I could finish this initial segment of my study within ten days."

"Five."

"Within ten days," Huldar continued smoothly. "Then I will assess the progress of the Eastern Continental thaw."

"Assess all you want." The Overlord scowled. "We're leaving."

Fatigue spun behind Huldar's eyes. He felt his anger rising, but was incapable of quashing it. "I am a leader in my field," he snapped. "The best you'll get. It will take ten days, no less!" He battled to keep his veil smooth. "This reef of gold is an important find. The Guild will expect a thorough impact assessment over the entire time of the thaw before they can even begin to think about the possibility of a mine. I don't understand the hurry."

Duvät's chin jutted. He pulled himself up to his full height, roughly level with Huldar's nose. "I am the Overlord," he said haughtily. "The Imperial representative. You are of House Leth, second of a minor lineage – where I am of House Tiamät, the Imperial House and First of my family. My grandfather is related to the uncle of the Kaskarudjan Kariiel Enna. My ancestry may be traced to the Empress Ishiquel Enna herself!" He paused to draw breath. Unseemly anger oozed from his every pore, but Huldar sensed an oddness to it – even desperation.

"I am Overlord!" Duvät said again. "You will do as I say."

Huldar steeled himself. It would be impolite to show anything but absolute calm, but despite this, he couldn't help leaning forward just a little. "And I am team leader ... responsible for our safety," he flicked his finger between the two of them, "yours and ours. You know the protocols as well as I do. Accordingly, if I deem the move to the east ill advised, we will not go."

"Then deem it wise!" Duvät snarled. He turned and stormed to the exit, almost tripping over the rug. "Ten days!"

There was a flutter of wings as Gento hurried a slug from his path.

Huldar found his teeth clamped together so hard he had to make a conscious effort to relax his jaw.

Gento peeped around the door-flap. "What's wrong with him?"

They looked around as Nachiel came in. "I saw him wandering up and down as if he was looking for something," he said. "I don't think he found it. Put him in such a mood!"

"He wants us to go the Eastern Continent, even though we know it's still frozen," Gento said.

"Why would he want that?" said Nachiel. "We'll all be killed!"

Huldar shook his head. "Ten days, I told him."

"But it's your decision, Shamkarun Huldar," Nachiel said. "He might be the Imperial representative, but you have the say in this. Guild rules." He paused, then recited, "*If the team leader deems that a direction of the Overlord unduly threatens the safety of the team, the team leader will advise the Overlord of the situation and the Overlord will defer to the team leader's decision* ... Well, that's more or less what it says."

"Guild rules," echoed Gento.

Sounds of the forest filtered in as Huldar tried to think. He picked up a stick and fed it to the flames. "We'll do what we can to finish up here," he said at last, "then I'll go to the Eastern Continent as I said I would and see if there is anywhere we can survive."

"And if there's not?" Nachiel asked.

A cloud of sparks crackled from the fire as Huldar jabbed the stick into the coals. "We stay here until there is."

He had meant to visit Casco tomorrow. Andel was entrenched in determining the extent of a tin deposit, and he and Cobar were supporting her. He'd hoped to spend at least half a day with them, reviewing data and research patterns – and watching Andel while she divined. She was by far the best practitioner he had seen. But now he would have to check in remotely.

The other team was west, of course. The thaw was gaining pace and they were trying to see as much as possible of the delta system before it was completely flooded. They'd discovered many wonderful wetland species, including a predatory vine. If one brushed against the leaves, it sprayed its victim with a malodorous substance that was very difficult to remove. The smell lingered for days. He thought of bringing one home and planting it in the Overlord's tent …

IN THE TENT OF DUVÄT GOK

Ten days later, Huldar returned from the Eastern
Continent and set out for Duvät Gok tent. He dressed
formally for the occasion, hoping to remind him that
the team leader had the final say in the matter in
question. A floating seed landed on his shoulder and,
as he brushed it away, he felt a brief sense of wonder at
the insignia of House Leth embroidered on his lapels.
The jacket had been presented to him by Arien Leth,
the lord of his House, in recognition of his services to
the Explorers' Guild – it still embarrassed him to think
that he should be singled out for such honor. He
smiled, remembering Arien's craggy face, so solemn
and proud on the day, but behind the Leth's cool
demeanor lay a passionate nature always ready to
defend the lives of El's Design – especially those beings
who could not defend themselves.

There was no one nearby, so he cleared his throat
and began to rehearse for the coming ordeal.

"The move to the Eastern Continent is …" *No, let's
not even mention the word 'move'. How about* – "The
Eastern climate is still dangerously cold, and I need
more time to complete the assessment – *no* – the initial
feasibility studies on the newly discovered gold in the
ravines."

He looked up at clouds racing across the sky – forerunners to the advance of the front. With any luck he would speak to the Overlord before the rainstorm hit. He resumed his murmuring – "It is my duty to be sure that future mining activities will cause no harm to the planet's ecological balance, and to do that I must make an accurate assessment of the local ecology. When the area has been properly assessed, I will work with the diviner to devise strategies of utilization. That's how it's always been done. How it *should* be done. We are the Uri'madu. There will be no cutting corners ..."

An image of Andel as he had last seen her came to mind. Walking with her eyes closed while she divined, she seemed so vulnerable, yet she moved with confidence, as if she had intrinsic knowledge of the path ahead ... extraordinary. It wasn't as if she was shy – it was more that she was guarded ... afraid of being hurt. He wondered what had happened. Every once in a while she would smile, or laugh, or share some absurdly convoluted insight, and he would glimpse her soul, shining and beautiful. Then she would close again like a flower touched by frost. He cringed inside, remembering his gaffe at their very first meeting. To be fair, getting to know the opposite sex was not the greatest of his gifts.

He stopped before the overlord's tent and brushed down his sleeves, then he squared his shoulders and scratched the leather door-flap politely.

"Duvät Gok?" he said. "Duvät Gok, are you there?"

There was no answer.

Huldar laughed at himself. *All that speechifying and I didn't think to check if the Overlord was at home.* He cast about with his mind, hoping to sense Duvät close by, but he was nowhere near.

An early gust was the only warning as a sheet of freezing rain swept the camp, quickly plastering his hair to his head. The Overlord's door was unsecured, and with barely a hesitation he stepped inside. The impropriety made him uncomfortable, but rain beat hard against the leather and he decided that the shelter was worth the moment or two of awkwardness. Then a powerful gust lifted the door-flap and made the tent-walls billow. Papers scattered from Duvät Gok's rather plain desk and Huldar gave chase.

He picked up an invoice clipped together with several others. It was stamped with the rune of House Faytha. Huldar's eyebrows lifted when he glimpsed the amount outstanding. How could the Overlord possibly owe so much coin? Beneath this, he found a chit for a gambling debt and then another scrap that looked like a map. His cheeks flamed. He had heard that gambling was a problem for Clan Gok. With hasty movements, he returned the papers to the desk and went back to his position just inside the door.

The moment the squall subsided he stepped outside again. Damp hair and clothes did nothing to improve his mood. How was he to face the Overlord now, knowing that he was a gambler? He decided to leave his visit for another time, but had walked no more than a few paces when he sensed him heading his way.

"Duvät Gok." Huldar nodded a bow and noted sand on the Overlord's shoes.

"Shamkarun Huldar?" the Gok replied. He sniggered at Huldar's wet jacket. A brusque hand-sweep told Huldar to follow. As the overlord swept his door aside, Huldar rolled his eyes. His fingernails were freshly painted with the Imperial blue of the God-Emperor's court, but he doubted Duvät had actually been there.

The Overlord halted beside his desk and glanced down at the papers Huldar had returned. His eyes narrowed. Beneath the shelter of firm mental screens, Huldar cringed. The Overlord's gaze followed damp footprints leading to and from his desk, then arrowed back to his.

"What were you doing in here?" Duvät Gok demanded. There was flint in his yellow Tiamäti eyes.

Huldar showed him an impression of the rain squall, the reason he'd entered. He indicated the papers. "They blew from your desk. I replaced them."

Duvät's gaze bored into his. He felt the Tiamäti trying to pry beneath his veil and was shocked by the force of the intrusion. Duvät was not Marked, but he was an archangel of House Tiamät and, like many of his brethren, strong in powers of the mind – especially secrecy. With a sharp word of song, Huldar closed him out. Overlord or no, such rudeness could not be tolerated.

The papers are your business, Gok, not mine.

What did you see? Duvät demanded.

Gambling debts.

Despite the grave dishonor the Faythan invoices signified, Huldar was surprised to see a look of relief flicker across the Overlord's face.

"Your private amusements are of no interest to me," he said. "I came to talk about another issue."

Duvät released a sub-audible sigh. "Go on."

"The Eastern Continent. The Uri'madu will not be able to relocate until the snows have cleared. One month, no less, before we move."

"It must be sooner!" Duvät slammed his fist onto the table. "What is wrong with you people?"

"There is nothing 'wrong' with us," Huldar snapped. "Unless you've discovered a major weather-working charm, that is how long it will take."

"Two more weeks, no more."

"Whatever you hope to achieve there, it cannot be accomplished by a team who are dead of exposure!"

The Overlord paused and seemed to consider. "Very well, I will allocate extra coal for the fires."

"Coal? You have coal?"

"Yes. I brought it with me as … a contingency." Duvät's crafty smile sent Huldar's irritation levels soaring. "You can have some to keep your delicate little toesies warm, provided you relocate as ordered."

Huldar considered this. There was no wood for burning while the ground was still covered in snow, only what they'd brought with them, and as the thaw progressed it seemed less and less likely they would find anything resembling an average, ligneous tree. Coal might solve that problem, but the gasses it emitted could be dangerous in confined spaces.

"How much do you have?" he asked.

"Enough," Duvät admitted. "In case the navigator is late to return – I brought ten sacks or so – enough to survive."

"All right," Huldar said. "We will need three bags. Give them to Tam."

"Three? I was saving them for the north!"

"Give us three," Huldar insisted, "and we'll leave in two weeks. Why was this not noted on the cargo manifest?"

"Because they are mine!" the Overlord snapped.

He signaled Huldar to follow him through the door, and once they were outside he dragged two large lumpy bags from Qalān. They plopped heavily to the ground, staining the slush with coarse black dust. Huldar waited, and Duvät produced another.

"There!" Blue fingernails flashed as Duvät dusted his palms. "Two weeks! No more." He scowled. *Are we understood!*

Without waiting for Huldar's reply, he returned to his tent and was swallowed into its secrets.

Huldar hefted the grubby bags into his own Qalān. His head was spinning. That someone as fastidious as the Overlord would have a secret hoard of coal was strange to say the least – and he was a gambler? What other secrets was he hiding ... and what would Casco make of this turn of events?

He took a deep breath and turned toward the marquee. Even with the fuel as a sweetener, he was not looking forward to telling the team they would soon be working in frigid conditions again.

THE EYES OF BEL NISHANI

Duvät Gok watched from the cover of his tent as Huldar stowed his bags of fuel and headed for the marquee. Who knew what he'd tell the team – and did he care?

"At one with the planet? I accept it? Bah!"

He stalked over to his desk and snatched the damning documents from under the stone. "Just because it was raining? What was he really doing in here? In *my* domain, my inner sanctum!"

He collapsed into the chair before the desk and laid the papers out before him. "He's lying – I know it!" he muttered. "Snooping around! He's an ecologist, for Breath's sake. He's not going to melt in a little rain." He flicked the group of dockets with one blue-varnished fingernail and the Faythan invoice skated lose. If Huldar made free with the knowledge of his debts or of his entertainments, Duvät's authority would be eroded, his honor decidedly tarnished.

Tack, tack, tack – his fingernails danced a rhythm of annoyance against the desk top. With a brusque gesture, he shoved the papers aside, then swore as the map fluttered free and fell to the floor. As he recovered it, his heart rate steadied. The Great Design still favored him. Lethians were intensely moralistic which, although irritating, meant they rarely gossiped – and, more importantly, Huldar had not seen the map.

He smoothed his palm across the rough diagram and felt the tingle of unseen messages in the paper. This unpretentious scrap was his greatest secret, the key to his future fortune. His gaze flickered to a locked drawer at the back of the desk, where the gem, the amazing crystal globe lay hidden. It seemed, at first glance, to be completely transparent, but if you looked closely, there was a rainbow inside it that altered and re-formed whenever it was turned. The Eye of Bel Nishani – his finger traced the characters scrawled on the map then followed the curve of a long beach on the inner sea. He already knew where he could find more.

He imagined his wife. "The rooms are too small," she scolded. "There's no fountain in the courtyard!" She waved her arms theatrically. "This is little more than a dingy shack!"

No matter how well she hid it he knew this was what she thought, and it made him angry. But now he saw she was right all along. He didn't fit in there and it was his grandfather's fault. His grandfather had been of Clan Enna, a navigator no less, and related to the Empress – the chosen of the Chosen. Why would a high status Enna select a lowly Gok to be his bride, and, even more confusing, why raise his daughter as a Gok, not an Enna? So selfish! He'd done it for love – or so the story went, but because of his grandfather's short-sightedness, Duvät had been born to the clan of the bureaucrats. The flunkies. All his life, he had paid the price, but now the scales would be evened.

His grandfather had been to this planet before – in secret. He had found the gem, made the map, and hidden them both in a drawer in this very desk. The piece was all he'd left to him when he died. Those hints were meant for him to find.

Duvät tapped the wooden surface again. Why his grandfather had come to this dreadful place then hidden his fabulous souvenir from sight was beyond his comprehension, but he was thankful, whatever the reason.

"It's so ugly. Where are we going to put it? Throw it away," his wife had yelled. "Unless you can get enough for it to buy tomorrow's meal!"

Now she would regret her angry words! The gem and the map were his security, his opportunity. Maybe his grandfather had understood the shame he had caused, and this was his way of atonement.

After a sure bet went bad, he had been left with barely enough coin to buy food, and the Faythans more than keen for payment. But then, by the greatest of luck, his grandfather had died. When he found the gem, his first thought had been to sell it then and there. It was only when he'd looked more closely at the paper the globe was wrapped in and realized what it was that he'd seen the opportunity. Although a part of him had enjoyed the fantasy of his wife sold off and enslaved, under the circumstances, the find had seemed like Breath's design. His very last coin had gone into the Faythans' coffers, and the promise of more when he returned had been enough to keep them at bay.

He closed his eyes and ran his hand over the paper again, reading the impression of the snowball planet sung into it. He smiled when he remembered the moment he'd recognized this very same planet on the Explorers' Guild's list. Even now the turn of good fortune amazed him!

With a little prompting and a few hidden strings, he had ensured this planet for the Uri'madu. And, as if it was a sign, there had been a Trianogi on the list of potential new diviners. The ancient scryer, Ulisharu of Trianog, had been first to see the planet, and having another Trianog apply for a place on the team seemed like El's blessing on his venture. It was all falling into place.

Now all he had to do was to be on the beach when the creatures described on the map emerged from the sea. His grandfather had found a dead one and discovered the gem-like quality of its eye. Now, it was Duvät's turn. This was no time to be squeamish: he would kill the creatures and take their ornaments for himself.

Such rare and beautiful gems would be greatly sought after. There would be plenty of coin to pay out his gambling debts. He imagined the surprise on the Faythans' faces when he paid them all in full. With his accounts paid, his wife would look at him with admiration again or, at the very least, a lack of loathing. He would purchase a fine manor in Sadir, or even Al Bayut, where he could see the Imperial Palace. Because of his forethought and planning, they would want for nothing and he would never have to exile himself on a frozen, Breath-forsaken planet again!

Huldar was the only concern. The plan involved unnecessary killing, as the ecologist would see it, though the deaths were certainly necessary for him! His insistence on an early move to the east had caused a great fuss, as planned. Everyone was distracted and would be for some time. Duvät nodded – he would make sure of it!

In due course, the creatures would emerge from their watery home, and Duvät Gok of Tiamät would be there to greet them. Briefly, he wondered how big they were, but that moment passed. There had been no other large animals found on the planet so far, so why would the sea-creatures be any different?

He looked at the map again, the crude drawings and rough notes. *Eye of Bel Nishani* was written near a pale circular blob – no doubt the name was some gibberish in the language of navigators, but to his mind, the sound had the ring and tinkle of coin about it.

His gaze moved to the Djan'rū symbol. His grandfather had left markers leading from there to the inner sea, or so the map said, but although Duvät had searched, the charms had long since faded. However, since Huldar had obligingly made new portals all around the shores of the inner sea, this no longer mattered. The place he had to find was clearly marked, and one thing he'd become good at over the millennia was reading maps.

Following in his grandfather's footsteps? He sniggered at the thought. His grandfather had been an arrogant boor, Enna to the core. No, this was *his* time. His new life had begun, his own path to riches – and even better, no one else knew it ... yet.

EASTERN CONTINENT

Huldar stumbled in from the shrieking wind and tossed a bag of coal toward the center of the marquee. Frost clung to his eyebrows. He should have covered his face.

"Get the fire lit! Quickly, Tam!"

Tam and Arko grabbed the bag. Black lumps of fuel spilled onto the rug. Huldar pulled on a fur-lined balaclava and turned for the exit again. Outside, billowing tents huddled around the marquee as if looking for warmth. Dark leathers faded into dull white, swallowed by the blizzard. The wind was a malevolent force, whining among the guy-ropes as if it resented their presence.

Huldar saw a loose rope on Lind's tent and ran to sing it tight before the flapping leather could fatigue and tear.

Lind emerged from the tent door, her face framed by the thick fleece of her hood.

Thank you, she smiled. *My hero!*

"It shouldn't have come loose!" Huldar yelled. "Be more careful!"

Lind's arms hugged her chest, keeping her heavy coat in place, but the collar was loose. She seemed to have little on beneath it.

I'm sorry, she said, *I thought I had everything in place.*

The smell of smoke eddied faintly with the dull, wet scent of snow. Despite the appalling cold, she loosened her arms and opened the fur a little more. Huldar glimpsed her cleavage.

"Dozy shuna!" he cried. "There'd be nothing in place if your tent had ripped!" But the wind swirled into his open mouth and snatched the power from his words.

After the scorn you heaped on our diviner, what right have you to be so careless? he said. With a snarl, he continued into the teeth of the gale to check on the other tents, just to be sure.

Further on he saw a dark figure staring into the blizzard and recognized Andel. She stood as if trying to absorb the storm's secrets, as if she wanted to be part of it. A particularly heavy blast rocked her on her feet. Her head moved and he knew she had felt his presence. Despite the conditions, warmth flushed his cheeks.

When he came to the space reserved for the Overlord, his scowl deepened. Duvät Gok had taken one look at the woeful weather and decided to remain at the base on the central continent. "Inform me when the wind has dropped," he'd said.

Breathless Tiamäti bastard!

As he emerged from the lee of the marquee, flying snow assaulted his face. Recalling the Overlord's smile as he'd stepped back to the warmth made Huldar seethe. Ice crunched as he stumped on.

By midday, the blizzard had cleared. As he searched the horizon for the next storm coming, Casco appeared beside him in the freezing slush. He could sense no immediate disturbance, but the planetary systems were changing rapidly and it was impossible to predict the weather with any accuracy. "Seems clear for the moment."

"I wouldn't be in too much of a hurry to tell the Gok," Casco sniggered. "He might come back."

A slow grin crimped Huldar's eyes as he peered up at the crisp blue dome of the sky. "You're right. Might turn again at any instant." He clapped Casco's shoulder. "Let's take a look at the map and see if we can get some work happening nearby. Come watch my back while I get started on local Qalān?"

Casco nodded. "Someone's got to keep you out of trouble."

————

Within a few weeks, Huldar had zigzagged a sparse but adequate network of portals across the great Eastern Continent, and made the first link across to the Southern Archipelago. Since they had already found promising gold and mineral deposits on the central landmass, he felt no hurry here, anticipating a steady examination of key terrain features and interest points.

Over the next several months as the long warming season rolled through its various processes, their sense of time became harder to reconcile with Giahn time – the standard of the Realm. Most inhabited planets had day-lengths and yearly cycles that were within comfortably similar ratios, but here, as winter blended through spring, the slow increase in daylight hours was barely perceptible.

Signs of a lasting change came as warm winds arrived to tease the barren snowfields. Snow and ice were transformed into mighty rivers that churned in a muddy race to the sea. A green haze emerged to cover the great plain where they were camped. It thickened then was swallowed by a riotous flush of flowers. Colorful carpets crept like rising waters between long corrugations of rubble stretching to the horizon – all that remained of the icy tides. Along the ridgelines' northern flanks, tiny white flowers heaped like the glacial drifts they replaced, and the Uri'madu enjoyed a period of peace, at one with the vast open skies and wide natural beauty of their temporary home.

But when Duvät Gok met with Huldar and Casco in the sturdy tent that was their designated work area, the harmony ceased. The Overlord stabbed his finger at the map laid out on the table. "… And I want this cliff examined, here, here and here." His list of "key terrain" seemed endless and arbitrary.

"May I ask why?" Huldar's irritation bubbled beneath his veil. If the Overlord had not delayed being there, he would have known of this list and made portals accordingly. Again, it seemed much of his work had been wasted.

Duvät glared as if his enquiry was open mutiny. "The God-Emperor wishes us to search for rare substrates! These places seem likely. Is it my fault you were too hasty?" He jabbed the same finger at Huldar's face. The air in the workstation congealed. "You've established portals in all the wrong places. Start now, and maybe we will get something useful done before it's time to leave!"

After a brief struggle with the door-flap, Duvät Gok stormed from the tent.

Casco released his breath in a plosive sigh. "What's wrong with him?"

Huldar thought he knew. "A while back, before we left ... It was sleeting. I went into his tent when he wasn't there."

"And?"

Casco paused as he shared his memory of what had happened. "He was right to be angry," Huldar admitted. "We had a chat, I asked for more time, he gave us the coal."

"No ... there's more to it." Casco narrowed his eyes, considering.

Huldar hesitated, but Casco deserved the truth. "I found some papers ... things he'd rather I hadn't seen."

"What things?"

"Gambling debts ... He's a gambler."

"Gambling?" Casco exclaimed. "We're not that well paid. Where does he get the coin?"

"I'm not sure," said Huldar, "and I'm even less sure where he'll find the resources to pay what he owes.

"And we thought it was just trouble with his wife!" Casco half laughed. "I can't believe it! I know he's unpleasant, but gambling! How can he make all these stupid demands, as if he's the God-Emperor himself? How can he look us in the eye?"

Huldar shook his head. *He's angry with me for knowing.* "If the Imperium found out he'd be lucky to keep his job. Shifty kalla must have veils within screens within veils."

They studied the map in silence.

"Best get started then," he said at last. "You call the others. We'll meet in half an hour."

"Right," said Casco. "You're not going to tell them, are you?"

"That the Overlord's a gambler? Course not!" Huldar frowned at the map. "I'll start work on the portals he wants, but can we organize a team to start on this bit." He indicated to a mountainous region to the north.

"Might still be snow," Casco pointed out.

"Well, here then." Huldar pointed to a stretch of coastline. "The coast should be fine – this area here? I saw some caves. Could be something there that'll keep him off our backs."

After Casco had gone, Huldar continued scowling at the map. Charms of preservation tingled in his fingers where they touched it. This was the original map made by Ziquarudjan Ulisharu of Trianog; the notes at the top had been hand-written by the great scryer herself. Because of this, he believed it was a reliable representation of the planetary landmasses as they had been, but it was a few thousand years since Ulisharu had retired, maybe more, and terrain changed over time, climate altered, continents moved. How long had it been since this planet had actually been discovered? How long since this drawing, the record of a shared remote viewing, had been made? Huldar had been a child when the old God-Emperor, Zohrät Ashik, had died, but he remembered that when the new God-Emperor took over, many stalwarts of the previous reign had resigned, Ziquarudjan Ulisharu among them. He wondered if she still thought of the many planets she had discovered, or if she was even still alive.

With a sigh, he re-rolled the chart and replaced it in its long leather cylinder. It was here for all to use, details to be added as they were discovered. At the other end of the table was a tray of reports left for Duvät Gok. He began to flick through them but paused when he recognized Tsemkarun Andel's flowing script. It was her volcanism assessment. His blood boiled afresh. She had saved her team from certain death and nearly lost her own life, yet there it was, still unread.

He shoved the papers back into place. Processing these was the Gok's one useful task, and he'd failed to complete even that much.

EXPLORATION

Hunkered down on a low hill in a sea of rolling blue-green plains, Huldar shaded his eyes and gazed east toward barren tundra and the glare of a crumbling ice-shelf. On the other side of the continent, where the Uri'madu were camped, warm ocean currents had accelerated the thaw. Here in the west, the ice retreated more slowly, but every hand's-breadth of change was just as exuberant. At his feet, new vegetation grew so quickly he could almost hear its progress with the naked ear.

After a last look, he clapped loose grains of dirt from his palms, freed his legs from a clinging vine, and stepped through the new portal to the foot of the long range of chalk cliffs Duvät Gok had placed on the list for urgent exploration.

His head tipped slowly back as he studied the massive rock face, almost as white as the ice, and sheer but for a long underscore, rounded like the curve of a breaking wave. He squinted over his shoulder for a glimpse of the sea. The oceans would rise to the level of this formation and stabilize there, possibly for a full year, before the freeze began to lock them away again. He should assign a team to study the transition, but doubted there would be time on this first foray. Maybe next time.

The next portal took him to the cliff-tops further down, and he rested for a while with his legs dangling over the precipice, watching distant breakers glint in the sun. Although the wind was chill, the biosphere sang with the need to feed and grow; but curiously, the urge to reproduce was subdued, as if the planet knew its summer would be long and there would be time to do things properly.

He lay back and looked up at the cloudless sky, enjoying the warmth and solitude. It was raining where Andel was. He pictured her as he had seen her that morning, wet and miserable, yet determined to continue her work. She and Casco had found several serendite deposits associated with a seam of fiery red opal. Serendite was highly sought after by leather-workers as a substrate for superior waterproofing charms, but the opal was far more beautiful.

She had handed him a rounded lump of yellow stone to examine. He closed his eyes and pictured the smile on her face as he discovered the delicate opalized seashell hidden within it. She'd been surprised how quickly he found it.

He kept the stone. Little by little he would remove the outer casing until the fossil was revealed. Maybe he could make a plaited leather clasp for it, the way his father had taught him, then he would give it back to her.

He was still smiling when he returned to Qalān. The next major branch in the planetary web would take him to more decaying snow-fields, but before that, there was possibility of a portal set on the very edge of the precipice. They didn't really need it, but from the outside it would seem as if one were stepping into thin air!

As he made his way along the cliffs, he saw no creeks or rivers; there were no lakes, not even a pond. But there were caves. Perhaps Bush and Topper would find water below ground. It was uncanny how reliable the brothers were. He'd never asked them how they did it, but their campsite was only a few steps from where he intended to finish the day. Perhaps it was time to pay them a visit.

That evening, Huldar sat with Bush and Topper swapping stories by their fire, but as much as he enjoyed their company, sharing their evening meal was an ordeal. Despite the once-tangy local herbs Topper had added to the pot, stoic chewing yielded little flavor from an over-cooked lump of krale.

"So, Topper, where did your talents came from?" he asked.

Bush poked at the gluey substance in his bowl and said, "I'm assuming you don't mean 'is cookin."

"No, indeed!" The brothers had slipped into dialect, and Huldar's eyes crinkled in a smile as he sensed their shared laughter.

"Family tradition," said Topper. "We learned bout findin water at our parents' knee, we did … or knees, I spose. They could both do it, but Mum was better at it than our da."

"At least our da could cook," said Bush.

"So this …" Huldar waved his fingers over his bowl "… is your mother's fault?"

"Hopeless," Topper admitted. "Still is. We try and eat out when we get home."

"Unless Da's a'cookin," Bush chuckled. "It's all about survival, see – even in the family nest."

"No," Topper went on, "I've no idea how it works, really. We just listen to the land, let it talk."

Huldar nodded. That, he could understand.

"But there's something I can tell you, Huldar," Bush said, "if you don't know already. These plains, see em now all green and lush? By high summer all be desert."

Topper agreed. The corners of his mouth leveled.

"We found fresh liquid water, deep underground," Bush continued. "Take time to bring it to surface, but glad of it afore too long."

"Should move somewhere less open," added Topper. "Move now afore weather turns."

"Starts a'burnin," Bush added, "like me brother's cookin!"

"Thanks, lads." Huldar smiled thoughtfully and added *find a new campsite* to his already extensive list of things to do. "I'm afraid I hadn't thought that far in advance."

"Probly too busy thinkin bout the Lady Andel an all." The brothers exchanged a knowing wink.

Huldar peered into his bowl, not sure how to respond.

"Now, now, don't be gettin upset," Topper said. "But we water-finders, we see which way the wind's blowin, and say nowt about it, if that's what's wanted."

"Does anyone else know?" Huldar asked.

"Well, no, not everyone." Bush turned to his brother. "There's lord Duvät Gok, now. Bet he don't know, eh Topper?"

"Probly not."

"An the Lady Andel herself?" He elbowed his brother's ribs. "Think she'd be knowin?"

"Probly not." Topper slowly shook his head. "Be obvious, don't it. If she did, she'd be all over following the lord Huldar here like a nasca-fly for glitter!"

"Glitter!" Huldar shook his head. "Here," he said, and fished a bottle of Lethian Besh from Qalān. "I've just the thing. Is this glitter enough for you?"

"Sure got some sparkle!" the brothers agreed.

As the fire dimmed, the night sky and its unfamiliar patterns crowded down as if willing him to make sense of them. Low in the east, the main part of a great circular constellation had arisen. If he stayed awake long enough, he was sure he would see the bottom of it, shining like a huge wheel in the dark. But as he drifted off to sleep, it was the bottle of Besh and Topper's toast that still sang in his mind … "To diviners! May we always see more than the rest."

CATCH THE RAINBOW

Duvät Gok stood on the lonely beach, watching for signs of schooling fish. All was as his grandfather had described – the moons were rising in the correct sequence, the sea was at the right level, and this morning, blue crustaceans had washed up on shore. He had been vigilant, seen all these signs fulfilled, all but the one-eyed sea-creatures that were central to his plans.

Small waves lapped the shore. A whiff of rotting shellfish teased his nostrils. Sand stretched away on either side as far as he could see. His robes flapped, playthings for a light sea breeze. Behind him, rows of dunes arched gracefully toward a green forested strip, then to an unbroken wall of snow-covered mountains. Far away, across the curve of the waters, dark ridges clawed through the snow, gaining ground as the thaw intensified. Huge rivers of ice-melt gushed and gurgled to the sea, but not here. Here, all was calm … waiting.

He wondered what the creatures would look like. Were they big or small? Would they be slimy? Would they scream? He rubbed his thumbs over his manicured nails. How would be the best way to end their lives? What if they fought back? What if he got hurt? The prospect of fish-scales and blood on his skin made him nauseated.

The sun drew perspiration. His feet weighed holes in the sand. One by one his outer robes were shed, but the signs his grandfather noted had occurred and he dared not leave his post.

After an eternity of squinting at the sea, an anomalous ripple crested beyond the breakers and his body stilled. Was that a fin, knifing through the furthest waves? Gaze anchored to the locus, he hardly dared breathe. Finally his great patience was rewarded with a second sighting – Breath of El, and a third!

Soon, the water was alive with roiling fins and long, eel-like bodies and a sound began to throb from the waves. His heart pumped as he made his way to the edge of the water. The alien voices swelled above the sigh and crash of the seas until he could hear little else – and the mass circled over and over, as if finding the courage to do what they must do … as if they knew he was waiting for them.

He grabbed his long knife from Qalān. A breaking wave ruined his slippers, but he hardly noticed. His robe slapped against his legs, but the discomfort was forgotten as the first silver bow-wave shot through the waters and a dark head surfed ashore.

The sea-creature's single eye gleamed upward, a refractive orb even more beautiful than the gem in his pocket. Duvät was transfixed by the sight: the culmination of his expectations. It surged past him, close enough to touch, twice as long as he was tall, and thick through the trunk. Filled with purpose, its silver-striped body undulated toward the dunes, blue-tipped dorsal fin waving back and forth like a tethered wing aloft in the breeze. Its mouth was open, still singing as if calling its brethren to follow.

Duvät shuffled awkwardly beside it and brandished his knife. The smell of salt and seawater filled his nose. His robes clung. Slippers squelched. Deep sand sapped his strength. He stopped and the creature forged on. His grandfather hadn't said how big they were.

More sinuous bodies wriggled from the waves, flaunting their eyes. He meant nothing to them. His glorious future, it was right there! Yet after all this effort, he had failed. His grip on the knife wavered. Shame filled his heart. Was he so weak? Then one of the creatures made a shrill squeal, and some long-buried memories flooded back.

He had killed a barbet once when he was small. His mother had beaten him for it and his father's disgust had stung his mind – but the joy, the thrill of power, that had been good. The barbet had been a stupid thing: stupid to trust him, stupid to get in his way. Even with its legs cut off it had still tried to get away; even with its head smashed, its body had kept twitching, trying to run. He remembered now.

Another sea-creature wriggled past. It didn't even notice him or his knife. It didn't recognize the danger. It was stupid, like the barbet. It deserved to be killed.

With a cry, he launched himself at its back and stabbed down hard. Flesh parted. Slimy blue fluid oozed from the wound, but the creature wriggled on. Its song continued without pause.

Stupid thing! Stupid, stupid, stupid! He clung to its back and stabbed it again and again. His chest and arms were sticky with blood and slime. Its movement flung him from side to side, but he drove his knife in hard and used it to haul himself toward the head.

With a last great effort, he took aim and plunged his blade at the creature's skull. Its spine severed with a gritty crunch. The creature flopped helplessly, unable to proceed. Slime clogged beneath Duvät's fingernails as he fought to hold it steady, and all the while, it continued to sing. Finally, he straddled the head and pounded his blade down.

The creature jerked and lay still. Its voice faded at last. Others continued their advance on the dunes as if nothing had happened.

He clambered to his feet. Sand stuck to him. Juices seeped through his shirt, warm and tacky against his chest. Their slow tickle downward excited him. He'd done it! He'd killed the beast! Adrenalin thrust through his veins. He turned to the next creature that came toward him, and with a manic howl leaped astride its head and killed it with a single blow. The dying eye stared up at him and its rainbow began to dim.

"No!" Duvät cried. The prize was losing value as he watched!

With the edge of his knife, he sawed around the fading orb, trying to excise it before the color fled completely, but the flesh was hard and rubbery and the stench clogged his nostrils. In frustration, he threw the knife aside and clawed at it with his fingers. To his surprise, he reefed the orb from its socket quite easily. It was firm to his touch and hardened quickly into crystal. There were score-marks where his blade had scraped it: a lesson for next time. He put the damaged eye into a rough bag and looked around. More creatures writhed up the sand, each one housing a spectacular prize. He would have to work fast to kill them all.

His arm rose and fell. His fingers plunged beneath more shining trophies, each one a donor to his future fortune. His legs tired from clenching victims' heads. His knife-hand was blistered but there was no healer to soothe the sting or mend the soft skin of his palm. Anger flared in his soul. It was not fair! He was no Ashik warrior. Why should he have to wield a blade? With a snarl, he launched himself at the next of the beasts and simply gouged its eye from its socket. Blood spurted from the hole in its skull. Its thrashed aimlessly, leaving trails of blue ichor as life slowly faded. Other sea-serpents blundered into it before changing direction.

"Stupid!" Duvät snarled. He turned from one suffering creature and captured another.

His new method was much quicker. Soon another bag was wet with ooze. As he moved across the path of the swarm he left a trail of sightless creatures that bumped from body to body. Their song was disrupted by cries of agony that turned the ether to chaos, yet ever more of them squirmed from the sea, forging trails through the maze of the dead and dying in their efforts to reach the dunes.

By late afternoon, Duvät was exhausted. As he wandered back to the portal, he weighed a last bag of orbs in his hand. He'd killed an astonishing number of animals today, but next time they beached he would be ready, and the next. His future was assured, so long as the Uri'madu did not find out, nor the guild.

He paused before returning to camp and took a last look at the scene below. Sightless creatures lingered on, crying in confusion. Although many simply gave up, one long silver-striped body made it through the tangle and burrowed into the face of a dune. Why it would do so with such urgency, Duvät Gok neither knew nor cared. Then the sands of the hinterlands seemed to shimmer as packs of small sand-colored lizards swarmed from beyond the dunes and quickly submerged the dead and mortally wounded as if the beach itself had swallowed them. His one worry had been how to disguise the physical evidence of what he had done, and it seemed the Breath was with him even in this. Would the scavengers be a danger to him? After a short time he relaxed. They attacked only carcasses or those too weak to continue. He'd seen and dealt with far worse on his travels to other worlds.

Back in his tent on the central continent, clean again and somewhat refreshed, he laid out the gore-encrusted bags to examine his treasures. The contents of the first two bags were much as he'd expected; clear, palm-sized spheres, each with a rainbow inside. In subsequent bags, the orbs taken 'live' had shrunk to one third of their original size, but, as if in compensation, their color had intensified to nothing less than a droplet of liquid rainbow. A simple polish with a soft cloth was all it took to bring them to their full glory. More amazing still, when he placed the gems together, their auras combined in a cohesive show of light that turned his tent-walls into a palace. When moved, the rainbow fractured and shimmered until a new resting point was found, then it healed itself back into a cohesive whole.

As he poured the orbs into a fresh bag, light flared through his fingers. After he tightened the drawstrings, he had to open them again, releasing the rainbow to flood his jaded goals with hope. When he closed the bag for good, his hands shook so much with excitement that he fumbled the knots. His voice croaked, barely able to sing the charm that would prevent anyone but himself from opening them.

"My grandfather was a fool!" he murmured. "The eye he left me must have been taken from a creature long dead. Trash! Not like these living ones … gems incomparable." He stroked the smooth fabric as a plan swam through his mind. "I could pay the Faythans off with the dead eyes – they're larger, and wonderful enough when one hasn't seen the real thing – then, just when they think they've gained the advantage, when they think I've been forced to surrender my greatest prize – and they'll sneer at the lowly Gok, the gambler and fool – ha! Then I'll show them the real prize, *my* prize, the true Eyes of Bel Nishani, and then they'll see I'm no weak-minded shuna for them to milk. Ha! Then we'll see the tables turned!"

As he lay down to sleep, he cuddled a lumpy bag close to his chest and breathed in its fishy, ocean-fresh odor. The blisters on his knife-hand throbbed and his legs and shoulders ached. Although there was no healer to tend them, he took heart that the indignities suffered would be well worth the outcome, and just for now, he could hold his winnings in his arms and dream of pleasures to come. When he returned to the Uri'madu, all knowledge of the Eyes of Bel Nishani must be shut away, not even the slightest hint available for scrutiny. But perhaps tomorrow, there would be more creatures to kill.

He must be vigilant.

He must be ready.

THE FIVE LEGS

After months camped on the vast plains of the Great Eastern Continent the Uri'madu moved to the foothills of the coastal ranges to escape the baking desert that the grasslands had become. Work continued, and the map in the workroom was slowly fleshed out as teams surveyed, cataloged and made notes. If Duvät Gok had been more reclusive than he had been on past expeditions, no one complained. The atmosphere in camp was decidedly better in his absence. However, when at last the Overlord settled into the Eastern foothills with them, he made his presence felt by calling a meeting at which all were required to attend.

That evening, Andel entered the marquee and made her way to the table.

"Ah! Lady Andel!" Tam said. "I see you've managed to divine your way to the honey-cakes."

"Tam!" Andel grinned and reached for a golden-brown treat. "It's good to see you too."

"Tea?"

"Thank you, Sari." Andel smiled. "That would be most welcome."

Sari turned to Lind, who was closer to the tea-things. "While you're there, could you make one for Lady Andel too?" Sari brushed the top of a large cushion, one of a pile they had arranged near the hearth. "Here, you sit with us. Nice and close to the fire." She looked over to see how the tea was progressing. "Lind! Lady Andel prefers galano, not dar-leaves."

Lind rolled her eyes and reached for a jar of galano twigs. With great ceremony, she arranged three of them one by one in a ceramic mug with the rune of Trianog emblazoned on the side.

Satisfied, Sari leaned closer to Andel. "Now, tell me – is it good to be home?"

"Home?" Andel looked around the marquee. Gento and Cobar stood chatting; Gento met her gaze and saluted with his mug. She doubted it was simple tea that sloshed from it. Ronnin smiled gruffly over a bowl of Tam's best aromatic stew. All wore light clothing but the fire still smoldered in the hearth. On the plains where their former campsite had been, temperatures were baking hot. Here in the foothills, the summer days were only slightly cooler, but in the evenings a misty sea breeze kept the heat at bay, and at night the temperatures could plummet.

Bush and Topper pushed through the door, laughing. They wore bright shirts with swirling botanical patterns as if to mirror their playful mood. Behind them, Huldar seemed tall and strangely graceful. His plain loose shirt was unlaced at the neck. Worn khaki pants fitted well over narrow hips. He looked at her and smiled. She gave a small wave but when Ubaid signaled for his attention he seemed almost relieved.

Andel turned to see a mischievous glimmer in Sari's eyes.

"What?" she asked. Her cheeks flamed.

Sari merely grinned and looked up as Lind arrived with the tea. "Oh, that's lovely," she said. "And this one's mine? Thank you."

Lind passed the mugs but didn't sit down.

"You're not going to join us?" said Andel.

"I'll be back later," she said. "Save me a spot for when the fun begins."

As the rangy angel sauntered toward Ubaid and Huldar, Andel felt a touch of hostility in her mind, although it was slight and quickly veiled.

"Perhaps it was the fuss about the tea?" she said to Sari.

"The tea?" Sari shook her head. "She's always been keen on him."

"Keen on who?"

"On who? Lord Huldar, of course." She smiled. "But you needn't worry, Lady Andel. He's never shown her the slightest interest – not in that way."

"Why should I worry?"

"Worry?" Sari's brow lifted. "Why, there's no need to worry at all."

As if sensing their conversation, Huldar flashed a glance their way. The intense blue of his eyes halted Andel's thoughts.

"Not at all," Sari repeated. A secret smile curved her lips.

"Have you a husband, Sari?" Andel asked.

"Husband? No, not me."

"Family?"

"Sister back on Lentath," Sari said. "Old and stringy now, like me. Married to a fine Nhadu spell-singer, Dursin. Blessed three times, no less."

"Three children? El's blessing indeed."

"Yes, and two grandchildren now as well." She paused to stare at the glowing fire-pit. "Makes up for me, I suppose."

Andel glimpsed a deep loneliness in Sari's heart and reached out to touch the angel's arm. "What do you mean?" she said gently. "You might find someone. El may bless you yet."

Sari shook her head. "Thanks to our peculiar biology, there's no blessings for we Annangi without marriage, and that's not likely. Still, it's not that I ... What of your family, Lady Andel? Who waits for you back in the Realm?"

Andel smiled. When she got home her mother would be difficult to face, but that was nothing new. On the other hand, her father would want to hear every last detail of every assignment on the wild planet. "Would you like to see them?"

"To see them?" Sari nodded. "That would be lovely."

Andel took Sari's hand for ease of contact and shared images of her mother – short yet imposing, her hair neatly bound as always while she tended the garden; and her father, taller, with brown hair like her own and warm, yellow-brown eyes that were kindly and enquiring. But then her imagery faltered.

I had a brother too, she said. "… I'm sorry. It's too difficult." She broke the contact. Tears prickled beneath her eyelids. Her hand crept up to her breast pocket and the small memento she kept there.

Sari smiled encouragingly. "But your parents look like fine people, archangels of course, and well to do – and they love you very much. I can see it in their eyes."

She was grateful when Sari turned to watch the fire again, giving her a chance to adjust her inner veils and return her aspect to its customary calm.

"My own parents died long ago," Sari said.

"Tell me."

Sari's lips compressed. "It's hard to know where to begin. I wasn't there when it happened, but there was a terrible storm … we lived in the northern plains of Areesh. Nothing fancy. They grew little attar, a herd of shuna. Mother always had cakes in the cupboard and a kettle on the fire. She liked galano, just like you. And father, he was a Rukh, you know – but always out walking with the herd. He loved the wild moors. On the day it happened –"

"Meeting's about to start." Lind plopped down beside them and tipped her head toward the hearth.

"Oh! The Overlord's here already?" Andel said. "I didn't realize! Sorry, Sari. Another time?"

Sari hesitated slightly, then settled back into silence.

Duvät Gok cleared his throat. "Good evening, all!" An uncharacteristic smile played across his mouth. "Yes, very good." He bowed his head for a moment, as if lost in thought. When he lifted it again, his eyes glittered in the light of the coals. "I have been looking through our target summaries and we are well on track," he said. "Well done."

He smiled again. Andel had never seen him smile. She was unsure whether he'd noticed the stunned silence. Someone disguised a laugh as a cough. His face returned to its habitual scowl.

"But of course, there is plenty still to do," he said brusquely. "We are nearly halfway through our contract and yet to visit the northern continent and the far southern archipelago." He swept his hand back toward the work tent. "Our reports must be kept up to date! I notice that several are yet to be completed." He lifted his chin. "The God-Emperor despises laziness, and so should we."

"That's more like it," Lind muttered beneath her breath.

Andel heard Casco's faint snigger.

"I want those reports by tomorrow." Duvät Gok glared around the room. "You know who you are!"

"Faking," Lind murmured. "Hasn't read a report in months."

Duvät made a curt signal and swept from the marquee. Huldar stepped forward, frowning as he watched the Overlord's departure.

"For a moment I thought he'd been exchanged for someone pleasant," he said quietly, "but it seems not."

When the Uri'madu had settled, he continued.
"Now, the minimal tilt of this planet means there are no
seasons, as such – only one long cycle from freeze to
thaw and back again. The southern islands are at a
higher latitude than the northern polar landmass, so
they're bare of ice sooner and habitable for slightly
longer – slightly longer," he emphasized. "We'll have
four weeks at best before we have to take what time we
can for our visit to the north polar regions."

"Where there'll be even more snow and ice," Tam
muttered darkly. "Can't wait."

"Yes," Huldar agreed. "It's been quite a feature,
hasn't it?"

"Could call the planet 'Snowball'," said Arko.

"I'm sure we'll find a much more original name,"
Huldar said. "But that's something for another time.
We'll have to wrap up here soon, within six weeks I'd
say, seven at most. I've already made a portal to the
edge of the southern archipelago, so that should keep
him happy, but no further infrastructure as of yet."

"How many islands?"

"Not so many as there were when the thaw began,"
Huldar said. "Some have been drowned by rising
oceans. However, the waters have reached their peak
and a number remain well above sea level. Some are
quite large, so there should be plenty of interest – and
the cool will be refreshing after the heat of the deserts."

Andel's pulse quickened as he looked right at her.

"Tsemkarun Andel?"

She nodded.

"We'll need a rapid assessment of the volcanic
potential down there. An eruption could be
devastating."

"Of course," she answered.

"Is it possible for you to head south with me before the rest break camp? Let's say four weeks from now?"

"'Never blind yourself to the song ...'" Andel's voice petered out when she noticed the faint smile creasing Huldar's eyes.

"It's something my father says," she stammered. "It's better to know the dangers before you take risks, but the risks you take define you."

She saw Huldar's eyebrows creeping upward. "So, four weeks ...?"

Sari nudged her very softly in the ribs.

"Yes, of course," Andel replied. "That's quite possible."

She looked down, hoping her blush would be mistaken for the glow of the firelight. Why did she always say the wrong thing? Casco's head shook slowly from side to side, but she could feel his inner smile. Sari's gaze was warm, but Lind's expression seemed ... was it triumphant?

She tried to pay attention to Bush and Topper's report on the water situation, but it would be her turn soon and already she was nervous.

"Lady Andel?"

She started. Was it time for her to speak already?

"Umm ... Hello everyone," she began. "I'd like to begin by saying how lovely it is to be all back together, it's been months since we met like this, and thank you, Tam, for the magnificent feast you've prepared!"

She waited for the smatter of comments to finish. "Now, Casco and Cobar and I have covered a lot of ground, mostly to the north and north-west so far, and I am happy to report we've found this continent bountiful indeed. On the edge of the western desert we have found a wonderful bed of blue calcite, which, as you know, is favored by potters for glazes and also its properties as a substrate which will survive the high temperatures of firing, and also light-singers for its ability to hold light for long periods of time. And also, there is a charm that can make it invisible, so, an interesting find, and –"

"Tell us about the nacrite!"

"Arko!" Sari said indignantly. "Manners!"

"No, it's all right, really." Andel smiled at her friends. She could understand their impatience. "Yes, the nacrite – I was going to make you wait, but ... well, remember when we were all on the cliffs? Well, while we were all sitting around waiting to try out Huldar's 'sky step' –"

Nachiel chuckled. "And Gento was flinging those spongy fungus-balls around! Ugh!"

"I copped one right on the head!" Arko said.

"Yes, well, perhaps the mysteries of Gento's sense of humor should be discussion for another time," Andel said firmly. "Anyway, as I was saying, while we were waiting there on the sky cliffs, I couldn't help having a little feel for what was there, and there it was – the signature of nacrite. It's rare but unmistakable, and it was coming from somewhere beneath us. Casco and I returned the next day, and in a cave under the cliffs we found –"

"*You* found," Casco interjected.

"– a wide cavern where nodules of nacrite bob about like yellow bats on the ceiling!"

Sari shook her head in amazement. "Stones floating like bats? Amazing!"

Nachiel clasped his hands together. "More precious than anything, even the fire-opal you found before we moved to the foothills. Though that's gorgeous!"

Gento agreed. "Every sword-maker in the Realm will be beating a path to that nacrite," he said. "A weapon with that in the alloy... forged by a Sajhar, you have a blade that's flexible yet strong – light as a feather and sharp as a bento's tooth."

"Congratulations, Tsemkarun Andel," Huldar said. "And having since investigated the site, I can say that, better still, the nacrite is easily accessible through a network of existing caves and tunnels, meaning it can be harvested with minimum disruption to the planet. The Uri'madu have never found such potential riches before, so well done, everyone."

"Where's the smiling one?" Tam asked. "Does he know?"

Huldar shrugged. "He would if he'd read the report, but sadly, I think he's been too busy."

"Busy making our lives miserable," said Casco.

"Not so miserable that we can't enjoy a good feed!" Tam spread his hands above the feast he had prepared. "Come and get it! Spicy krale casserole served on a bed of purple ground-nuts harvested from the newly famous sky-cliffs region." He paused as Duvät Gok reentered the marquee. "Ah, Overlord. Joining us for dinner?"

The Overlord grunted. "It's amazing what hunger does for one's tolerances."

Later, Andel sat chatting with Sari and Gento while she finished her meal. After scraping out the last, she saluted Tam with her bowl. "Very nice!"

"Not bad, eh?" he replied.

"Not bad at all."

"How about a story?" Gento said. "Huldar?"

"Someone else should have a turn." Huldar's gaze settled on Casco. "What about you?"

"Yeah, Casco," Topper called. "Tell us a story!"

"Casco! Casco! Casco!" They all took up the chant until Casco grinned and held up his hands.

"All right!" he said. "As it happens, I do have a story. How about –"

"Lord Marachel the Weaver!" Arko shouted.

"The Iskilatu Gates!" Lind cried, her hands clasped together like a child's.

"No," said Casco. "How about –"

"The Five Legs," a deep voice rumbled.

"Exactly," said Casco. "Cobar, my friend, you know me too well."

"Haven't heard that one for ages," Gento said.

Andel leaned closer to him. "I haven't heard it at all," she admitted.

"You'll enjoy it," said Sari. "It's about explorers, like us." She looked at Tam. "The shawl?"

Tam reached into Qalān and pulled out the storyteller's mark of office, a wide shawl, once white but now yellowed with age. Sari took it from him and arranged the soft kressie-wool over Casco's back, then returned to her place beside Andel.

Casco shrugged his shoulders to settle the folds, then waved his fingers for drink and honey-cakes.

Tam groaned, but brought a bottle of Besh and a plate of cakes anyway.

"Get on with it, Casco!" Ronnin muttered.

"Wants his moment with the shawl to last, he does," said Topper.

Bush laughed. "The only time we'll all be listening."

Finally, Casco held up his hand and everyone fell silent. Beyond the tent, a chorus of nocturnal creatures filled the vacuum with sound. Within, coals creaked quietly in the hearth.

"The Five Legs," he announced, and bowed his head. "We honor El with this story of discovery.

"This is a tale from the time of the God-Empress Karuzät Enna," Casco began. "Thirty-fourth God-Emperor of the Realm, and grandmother of Tsemkarun Ishät Ashik, who is, as you know, the thirty-sixth God-Emperor."

"Makes sense, doesn't it?" Nachiel said. "The ... *ow!*"

"Quiet!" Ronnin whispered. "He's got the shawl!"

"Toward the end of Karuzät Enna's reign," Casco continued, "the apprentice scryer, Ulisharu of Trianog, discovered a new planet; a cool world, but none the less green and welcoming."

Lind sat up taller. "The same Ulisharu who discovered *this* planet? Made our map?"

"The very same," Casco said. "Karuzät died only three hundred years after Ulisharu of Trianog began her apprenticeship."

Duvät Gok cleared his throat. "The God-Empress Shamkarun Karuzät Enna," he corrected. "May she rest sweetly in the Breath."

"Of course. Thank you, Duvät Gok." Casco smoothed the tasseled edge of the white shawl. "Anyway," he continued, "as Ulisharu studied the new world, she noticed a strange feature on one of its continents. There were clusters of domes like balls of twine clumped together, rising high and spreading low, as if they had been knitted from the grassy plains around them."

He looked expectantly at Huldar, who answered with a small nod.

Tam emptied a pile of nuts onto the ground in front of Casco. Huldar muttered a charm beneath his breath and the nuts began to move.

"Look at what he's doing," Andel murmured. She watched in fascination as Huldar guided the nuts to form into domes.

"Just like in the story," said Sari. "Clever, isn't he?"

Casco continued. "Imagine the young scryer's surprise when rolling from the tubes came dozens of furry five-legged creatures."

Andel was delighted when a ball of groundnuts rolled across the table and raised itself up into a star shape. Another joined it, and another then the three shapes linked to form a single mass.

"With much appendage-waving," Casco went on, "the creatures formed into groups and set off across the plains, rolling along in communal balls. Ulisharu realized she had discovered one of El's greatest blessings – a new sentient species.

"The God-Empress Shamkarun Karuzät Enna was keen to make contact with the new race, so scryers and navigators worked together day and night to develop a chord of translation. In due course, a team of Imperial Explorers set off, and high in the Palace Of Winds, Ulisharu and the God-Empress watched constantly, waiting for their arrival on the unknown world."

Huldar sang again and the ball of groundnuts reformed into a miniature cupola. The ghostly image of two women appeared, standing beneath the pillars of its roof.

"Now, as we know," Casco went on, "every team has a Shamkarun, and in this case it was Shamkarun Okriien Enna who was chosen to lead.

"The honor of first contact is rare indeed and each situation is different. Would the new species be aggressive? Would communication be possible? There are no rules or guidelines beyond the need for peace. We Uri'madu have not yet been in such a position, but we can all well imagine the excitement and trepidation that Shamkarun Okriien Enna's team must have felt."

Casco paused as Huldar rearranged the groundnuts into two piles. One became a small group of Annangic shapes, from the other a ball pinched off and rolled toward them.

"When they were ready," Casco said, "Shamkarun Okriien left his team close by and walked on alone to stand by the open end of a tube. After some time, a star-creature rolled from it. When it saw the annangi it stopped and froze like a fur-covered stone.

"Okriien Enna sang songs of gentleness, hoping the creature would respond with curiosity rather than fear, but the world of the Terric – which, as you have no doubt guessed, is the people this story is about – is also a world of fearsome predators. Quick as a wink it fired its slingshot straight at Okriien's head.

"Now, Okriien Enna had been chosen, in part, for his ability with screens, and the stone was easily deflected, but this did not stop the furry Terric from trying again, and again. When it realized its sling was ineffective, it retracted its limbs and laid still, a knee-high ball of fur, and started to shriek for help.

"Have you ever heard that cry?" Casco asked them. "The distress call of a Terric?"

Huldar winced. "Yes, I have."

"Terrible," Nachiel agreed.

"Certainly is," Casco said. "Soon, more Terric came rolling from the tubes, summoned by the call."

Andel watched the tabletop, where several more balls of groundnuts rolled toward the annangi and surrounded them.

Casco nodded. "Shamkarun Okriien waited, his veil calm, his haze open, while his team stood back, poised on the edge of their half-wild portal, ready to come to his assistance or help him escape.

"The largest of the Terric stood up like a hairy star, all five limbs extended, her long manes flowing in the breeze, and approached the Shamkarun. Three dark globular eyes pushed out from her middle. They swiveled on their pedicles and examined Okriien Enna from head to toe. She came closer and poked Okriien's waist with long, sharp claws.

"Others of the Terric began to unfold. Their eyes turned. Their claws clattered. The leader stood as tall as he could be. Her olfactory organs wobbled. Her mouth chittered in commentary as she walked around, and her eyes rotated, absorbing the sight of the strange new being from every angle.

"After several circuits, the Terric grasped Okriien's shirt in her claws and pulled. Okriien realized she wanted to see what was beneath his clothing.

"Slowly, he took off his shirt … The Terric raised their arms and clacked their claws. The leader's chittering grew more aggressive. She pulled at Okriien's pants.

"Okriien hesitated, but as the leader's agitation increased he saw no other option and removed his trousers.

"At that, the Terric lowered their limbs, their chittering smoothed into chirps and their gestures became soft and friendly. The rest of the annangi came forward, food was offered, and the creatures went wild with excitement. No one else was required to remove their clothing, and perhaps that was just as well because it was only after fluent communication had been established that the truth was discovered. When Okriien Enna had removed his pants, the Terric believed his penis was a retractable fifth leg and accepted him as one of their own.

"But one has to wonder," Casco said, "would they have greeted us so warmly if Shamkarun Okriien Enna had been female?"

With a cheeky grin, Huldar made the groundnuts on the table grow into a single male annangi with an improbably long penis, then he let his creation collapse.

ON THE SOUTHERN ARCHIPELAGO

"Andel, could you stand a bit closer, please," Huldar said. "Cobar won't bite, and I believe Casco had a wash this morning."

"But did you?" Casco said wryly.

With a muttered song Huldar stepped the four explorers through to the rocky shore of a small bay on an island in the planet's deep south. Andel was almost knocked sideways by the unexpected force of the wind. Beside them, a wild grey ocean heaved against a long headland. Giant waves swept foam across the shallow reef in an endless cleansing roar. Small shrubs dotted the stony dunes behind them, pressed low and westerly as if extruded by the savage polar winds.

Portal needs a little tuning, Casco said.

"Sea levels won't begin to fall for several months," Huldar yelled against the wind. He pointed to the breakers. "Over here, before the seas rose, this reef terminated in a cliff. There's a great chasm."

Casco waggled his finger at his head.

Sorry! Huldar said.

There's no need to yell now!

Sorry, he said again, and proceeded to tell them about sea levels and cliffs more quietly. His mind-voice had a lilting quality that Andel always enjoyed, but today she noticed a more personal aspect to the sound, as if they stood closer together. When he squinted seaward, Andel followed his gaze and saw a row of tumbling black clouds massed on the horizon.

We'd best move on, he said. *Big island further south – it'll be cold, but there are colonies of sea-dwellers on the shores and this may be our only opportunity to see and assess them. And besides, that's as far as my portals extend so far.*

What of Andel's survey? Casco asked, reminding Huldar of their earlier experience of volcanism. Their narrow escape was clear in his mind.

Time for that tomorrow. I know there're no portals yet, but Andel, if you and Casco can far-sense where you need to go, I'll make sure you get there. Cobar –

– will keep us safe, the muscular Rukh finished for him.

Huldar clapped him on one ample shoulder. *Let's go then!*

As they stepped through the next portal, the tearing wind cut off. The roar in their ears was replaced by a cacophony of staccato grunts, and a pungent, salty smell assailed their nostrils. Before them, a vast colony of huge worm-like creatures basked on the sand just beyond the waves. Their blubbery bodies were covered with fluff-tipped scales in broad dagger patterns of turquoise and white. Long muzzles lifted vaguely. Faceted eyes moved lazily toward the annangi then back to the waves as if they could not truly see what they did not understand. Shiny nasal flaps opened and closed as the creatures breathed. Four dark flippers splayed from beneath their front ends, followed at the rear by a pair of vestigial limbs that looked for all the world like large annangi hands, and their streamlined tails were long and whippy, hinting at a far from lazy life beneath the ocean.

So, we meet some larger creatures at last! Casco said.

Huldar showed them an image of the demure, furry worms he had seen there only months before, apparently a larval stage of these behemoths.

They look more like huge, roly-poly cushions than living creatures, Andel said.

Cobar drew their attention to a substantial scar that broke the markings on one worm's side. *And look at that one to the left there. Predators to match their size.* He pointed to the torn grey flesh of another creature's tail. Bluish ichor still oozed from several long gouges.

Andel winced as she noticed white cartilage exposed. *Those teeth-marks are huge!*

We must be cautious, Cobar said.

"'To feel the Breath of El so close makes a friend of every breath'," Andel murmured.

Your father again? Huldar asked.

She looked up into Huldar's gentle smile. *Yes,* she replied. *And Cobar's right. Somewhere nearby there must be creatures with huge mouths, sharp teeth and appetites to match.*

They scanned the horizon. Low hillocks rose and fell as if the ocean continued inland, frozen in the landscape. There was little exposed vegetation, but hardy plant-life utilized the meager soil in the dips. The south-polar ice sheet was a fine thread of white glimmering on the horizon. To the north-east, a chain of drowned mountain peaks faded like ragged stepping stones into sea-mist and distant spume. Closer to shore, ice floes and slush filled the sluggish waters.

Andel turned toward the distant roar of startled blubber-worms at the far end of the beach. Blue and white bodies rippled toward the ocean. The Uri'madu crouched low. Andel closed her eyes, craning her mind to see what had caused the creatures to flee. She searched the network of hollows.

There's movement! Her mind gave chase.

What is it? Huldar asked.

Andel shared the image of a pack of red, six-legged lizards flowing like a river parallel to the shore. The agile creatures kept low in the gullies, running with their two front legs arched above their heads as they darted among the ropey plant-life. The injured blubber-worm moved restlessly. The river of red changed course.

It's the blood, Huldar said. *They're after the wounded one.*

They're coming closer … fast! Andel said.

We should move, said Cobar.

Huldar raised his hand. *No, wait! Stay still!* The thrill of finding predators and prey thrummed in his voice. *The portal is close. If we move they may sense us.*

Cobar and Casco glanced at each other, wary of his decision. *I'll screen us,* Cobar said.

Casco frowned. *They perceive the world differently from us. We can't rely on screens to keep us hidden.*

We'll be fine, Huldar said. *Lethians know these things.*

Andel wished she shared his confidence. *Here they come!* She crouched low with the others, almost afraid to look.

There was chaos as the lizards crested the dunes. Worms roared and thundered toward the sea. Flippers beat against sand. Blubber rippled with effort. Enamel-red lizards streamed between the heaving bodies, faster by far than their prey.

As the first of the predators fastened itself onto the raw wound, the injured worm made an eerie scream. Its tail thrashed against the sand, but for every attacker dislodged another latched on, and another, until its rear end was a mass of seething red.

Andel looked away.

Well, Casco said. *Not the jaw size we expected, but serious predators nonetheless.*

I can't watch this any more, Andel said. *Please, can we go now?*

Huldar nodded. *Aye, let's go.* But as they stood, one of the lizards turned.

Andel gasped. *It's looking straight at us.*

Skeins of blue fluid dripped from the lizard's jaws. It had two large eyes as red as its body and a third, jewel-like eye in the center of its forehead. It cocked its head. Horizontal pupils narrowed to slits, then expanded as they locked onto a new prize. Others looked up from their feast.

Huldar spread his arms in front of his team. *Slowly now: just back away. The portal is right behind us.*

A small group of lizards left the carcass and rushed at them, their heads the still point in a flowing tangle of limbs and tails. Andel huddled close to the team, afraid to look away. She tried not to stumble as they backed another step.

Now! Huldar said, and with a whisper of song they were returned to the wind-swept beach. As one, they turned their backs to the gale.

Casco wrapped his arms across his chest. *Isn't this where we first arrived?*

I told you, Huldar said. *I've only had time to make two portals. It was nothing like this when I came before.*

At least we're away from those red things. Andel shuddered with more than the cold. *When they looked at us, all I could feel was hunger.*

We could stay here, Huldar said, *but I'm sure I can find somewhere better.*

Most places would be better, Casco grumbled.

While Huldar braved the wind to commune with Qalān, Andel crouched in a low depression with the other two.

"Any sign of them on this island?" Casco asked her.

"No, but let's not assume we are safe. Something else made the wounds that drew them in the first place."

"Let's hope it lives in the briny deeps."

"And stays there," Cobar said.

Eventually, Huldar stepped them through to the base of a barren plateau on the far side of the same island. The wind still howled, but they found a small cave where they could shelter.

Andel thought it might be a sea-cave formed eons ago when this platform had been at the shoreline. Her eye came to rest on a rounded, knee-high boulder, pale against the slaty shingles of the ancient headland. Curious, she knelt beside it. The surface felt rough beneath her fingers.

What is it? Huldar asked.

She closed her eyes and a maze of calcified tubules filled her senses – salt, algae, biological detritus. *This stone is from the seabed*, she said. Her eyes opened. Not far away was another boulder of similar size, and another. Then she noticed mounds of smaller stones wedged in the lee of every crevice. They were too high above sea level for them to have been deposited naturally.

I think it was washed here by a giant wave.

She stared out to sea, trying to visualize the enormous wall of water necessary to have swept this material from the sea floor and deposited them here. What had such triggered an event?

Huldar joined her. *Perhaps Lind was right about the central sea being an impact crater.*

Hmm, maybe, she said, *but even if that were so, this is more recent.*

We know the sea rises no further than it has already, but could they have been carried in the ice? asked Casco.

Not in this case. See, there are no score marks – no scraps or fragments caught beneath it. She scratched at the boulder with her fingernail. It was soft and easily marked. *No, this has happened sometime in the recent past – since the current thaw began.* She removed a leathery strip of seaweed caught at its base and looked up at her teammates. *I'd say within the last few months.*

Huldar raised his shoulders. *How could such a massive disturbance have had no impact anywhere else? Why didn't I feel it?*

Maybe it's natural, Casco said. *There's plants in the gullies, life on the shores. Maybe it's an expected part of the planet's cycle, not a catastrophe at all.*

Then where are the rest of them? The other rocks from the past events?

Andel looked at the barren shale of the cliffs. The answer seemed obvious. *Deposits from older cycles would have been crushed by the ice and the remains washed away or dissolved in the thaw.*

Will it happen again?

No way to tell.

Cobar craned up the cliff-tops. "Should move higher," he rumbled.

"Good idea," Huldar said. "I don't want to be drowned in my sleep by a giant wave!"

Huldar searched Qalān again and took them to a sheltered niche below the snow line of an inland hilltop where they could safely set up camp. After they'd eaten, Andel left the tent and lay back with her head in her arms, staring up at the night sky. The great circular constellation that rolled by increments across the inky dome seemed born of the silver line of the ocean. Above her, moons made a scattered line from horizon to horizon, some round and full, others shadowed, and some no more than bright dots moving in concert with their larger siblings.

Huldar joined her and pointed out a dark breach in their path. "See how the moons are bunching, leaving that gap there?" he said. "Might cause changes in tidal activity."

"Could there be a link between the giant waves and the moons?" Casco offered. "Do they align with the sun? What if there are times when the moons and the sun are on the same plane … an eclipse?"

"There was an eclipse, months ago now," Huldar said. "A major one with all of the larger moons bunched up at once."

"Would that be enough to generate a tidal wave?"

"Perhaps," Andel said, "but for some reason I keep thinking of nacrite."

"Nacrite?"

"It seems strange, I know, but I've never seen so much nacrite in one area as I saw in the cave near the sky-step. Maybe there are other deposits trapped in a cave under the sea, or a system of caves. It's mobile. What if the pull of a large eclipse makes the nacrite surge …" she fanned her hand up and down "… displacing the ocean?"

"A localized event," Huldar said thoughtfully. "Predictable ... not the result of an eruption or quake at all."

Andel grinned. "If we could find the extent of the wave and its apparent epicenter, I might be able to locate the nacrite."

"If that's what it is!" Casco poked the fire. "You're taking a bit of a leap."

"Hmm." Huldar scratched his head. "I must admit, it's an unusual theory."

"But we could test it," Andel insisted. It was a good theory; she knew it! And to find more nacrite would be beyond sensational. She watched Huldar thinking, but he was too well disciplined to give anything away.

"All right." He smiled at last. "We'll keep your hypothesis in mind while we explore the islands. There might be further signs ... although I've never heard of a nacrite deposit so large it could generate a destructive wave."

———

Andel awoke after a surprisingly refreshing sleep to find the morning sun shrouded by mist. They had been on the island for several days now, and this was the first let-up in the gale. Their elevated campsite was an eyrie above the island's plains. When the fog lifted, she would be able to see how far the rapid greening had progressed. Down on the steppe, thick pillows of emerald moss made a pockmarked surface for shrubs and succulents to find shelter and grow. Whole flocks of pale pink nuts crept on animated roots until a suitable hollow was found, then they nestled in and sprouted almost overnight with large mottled blooms. As these died back, a new generation of wandering nuts ripened and began their journey.

While Cobar made breakfast, she clutched a steaming mug of tea. "I wonder how the others are getting on?"

"Warmer than here!" said Casco.

She ran her fingers over the rune of Trianog on the side of her mug. "What did you make of Duvät Gok?" she asked. "At our meeting, before we left?"

"The smile threw me," Casco agreed. "Thought I was seeing things."

The sound of rustling paper as Huldar smoothed their copy of Ulisharu's map cued Andel toward their makeshift table. He placed a pebble on each corner to hold it flat.

"So, where are you sending us today?" She shared an image of the hat-shaped island they had seen to the south-west. From the information they had found so far, she was certain it was close to the generation point of the wave. "It's in the right place ..."

He traced his finger along the chain of islands in the center of the archipelago and stopped over the island's position.

"Promising?" she asked.

"Hmm." He studied the map. "If that's sandstone, there might be some fossil records there. Could tell us a lot."

"Oh, it is," she assured him. "Sandstone, limestone, chalk – similar geology to the sky-cliffs –"

"Where you found the nacrite." He sighed. "You're not going to let this go, are you?"

She shook her head.

"All right," he said. "I'll see what I can do. If we go to the portal … here," he pointed to an area on another, more westerly island, "I think it will open into that region, maybe directly onto that island you've called The Hat. No harm in taking a look.

"Casco and Cobar, you go back to Long Island. Learn what you can about the fault-line there."

The two nodded. "The rift escarpment looks interesting," Casco said. "Might be fossils there too."

By the time Andel and Huldar arrived on top of the broad sandstone mesa that gave the island its distinctive look, it was already near midday.

Huldar's haze glowed with excitement. "Look at this!" Beneath their feet were lumpy beds of fossilized bones. Andel saw a huge spiraling indentation where a long-dead creature had left its mark. She wandered toward another, smaller collection of mineralized remains.

"Huldar! Over here! Can you see this …? Yes! It's a skull with three distinct eye-sockets."

"An ancient ancestor of the lizards? This will keep us busy for ages," he said.

They walked from find to find, calling out to compare notes. Each new fossil seemed more intriguing than the last, and Andel almost forgot that they had come to The Hat to find a point of origin for the giant wave. But then, wedged in a crevice close to the edge, she found a skeleton that was far more recent.

She straightened up and shaded her eyes. The sea spread like a glittering gown around the island, the swells mere ripples today and shining in the summer sun. It seemed impossible that a wave could be so big as to engulf The Hat entirely, but that was what must have happened. There were no predators on this island big and strong enough to have carried such a large fish so high.

Huldar, she called. *You should see this.*

Shreds of desiccated flesh still clung to the bones. Bleached scales fell away as she touched them. *How did that get there if not because of a huge wave?*

I don't know, Huldar said. He too gazed thoughtfully at the ocean. *Such a wave … can you imagine?*

Terrifying, Andel agreed, but she was too excited to feel fear. The nacrite was there. She could feel it as if the planet spoke through her bones. A second major discovery – surely she had earned her place among the Uri'madu.

Huldar shook out the map. *We found your first boulder here*, he pointed to an island in the eastern chain, *then seabed gravel on this one …*

She ducked under his shoulder to look. With the three points to work from and The Hat as the central marker … *It must be along here somewhere*, she said, indicating a region between islands.

Huldar leaned so close she could feel his breath on her cheek. *We'd better find a way down to the shore so you can get a closer look*, he said.

She straightened quickly. Her heart was pounding. "Yes, that would be quite wonderful."

––––––

Late that evening the four explorers sat inside their sturdy mess-tent and stared into the campfire, warm mugs of spiced jhavo nursed in their hands. Andel sipped the thick, sweet liquor and appreciated the burn as she swallowed. Inner warmth met the radiant heat of the fire and the bitter cold of the Antarctic night faded. She wiggled her toes inside her boots. It seemed ages since she had run barefoot on the moss of Frith, her homeworld. She pictured her home, Aventhe – the moss would be fruiting by now, a soft fuzz of amber over the verdant green that carpeted the hills. Sweet white rayno blooms would hang from the archways, tinkling in the rain. In her mind's eye she saw the vesa arrive to cloak the north-facing walls of the old stone manor with flamboyant red and blue, their wings a-shimmer as they soaked in the sun. For a few weeks, the strident buzz of their all-pervading mating call would drive her parents mad, but the beauty of their delicate rituals made the period of annoyance seem a small price to pay.

"… lines of erosion," Casco was saying, and something about tides, but small flames flitted across the coals, the jhavo warmed her belly, and she found it hard to pay attention.

She murmured a reply when he said good night, then a cold blast of night air drove her lethargy away. Both Casco and Cobar had gone. She looked across the fire into Huldar's eyes. He smiled and fed another small piece of coal to the flames.

The silence stretched on.

He lifted his mug. "These nights … they remind me of home."

"I didn't know it got so cold on Lentath." Andel took another sip of jhavo.

"Hmm," he nodded, "it does … in the highlands where my family live."

"I was thinking of home, too," said Andel. "The sun, the moss … barefoot and warm."

Huldar smiled. "Oh, yes, barefoot and warm would be nice." He poked the fire. Sparks swarmed up and vanished through the smoke-hole.

"Did you camp out often, as a child?" she asked.

"We Lethians rarely stay indoors," Huldar nodded, "especially those of us who dedicate to the life of the Breath. We want to feel it all around and listen to its songs. There is always more to learn." He gave her a quick glance then returned to the flames. "It must be different for you Trianogi." He looked up again. "You must miss your home and your family."

Andel thought for a moment, comparing her gentle early life with the more rigorous one he'd described. "It *is* different," she said. "I was not raised for a life of environmental challenges or dedicated at an early age to my studies, but my family were perhaps a little bit Leth-like. Rain or sun, we were often outdoors. Sometimes Father would take us on weeklong hiking trips through the wild places of Frith. And there was our uncle, Shamkarun Roshu, the navigator. He took us all over the known. My brother loved it, loved the chime. He wanted to be a navigator too – an explorer."

"What happened to him?"

Huldar's voice was gentle, but when she tried to tell him about her brother's accident, her throat closed over. Her hand went to the small stick she still carried.

"I'm sorry," he said. "I didn't mean to upset you."

"No, no. It's just that …"

His mind radiated calmness and peace, but underneath she sensed his concern.

I have lost loved ones too, he said.

She took another sip of jhavo and let it slip down her throat. "It was late," she whispered. "We were on Germane, the Trianogi world with the twin suns?"

Huldar nodded, *I know it.*

"Then you know the dangers. There are rocks that form there, minerals that can be found nowhere else. They say that the planet will be habitable one day, that its orbit is changing. A strange world. Mystical. That's why we Trianogi love it so. But it's harsh."

His eyes were on the flames, but she could feel his care like a warm cloak, ready to listen, wanting to know.

"My family went there." She bowed her head. "Father thought we would enjoy the experience of sunrise from the high plateau. We arrived after dark, when the tides had passed. Camped not far from the Djan'rū. Uncle Roshu said he'd be back before sunrise. We would shelter as the dawn passed over us, then leave before the winds began. We pitched our tent near the remains of a stone hut someone had built, but the gravitational surges had been too much for it. My brother, Aan– Aanjay – isn't it silly? After all this time I still have trouble speaking his name.

A strong memory of Aanjay's face came back to her. She could almost hear him. *Look, sis! Come and look!* It was never fully dark on Germane. In her mind's eye she saw it again as if it were yesterday.

They scrambled down a crevasse together and into a narrow cave.

It was dim and musty.

"I want to go back now," Andel said.

Don't be silly. There's nothing here. I scanned it.

I want to go back, she said again. The premonition of danger hung like a storm cloud. She could almost hear the thunder. But Aanjay scrambled further in. *Here*, he said, and handed her a small piece of stick with rounded ends. *Beautiful, isn't it?*

She studied the intricate designs. *Did bugs make these?* She smiled and tried to hand it back.

No, you keep it, he said. *Explorers need specimens to study!*

Her fingers played over its satiny surface as she followed him deeper into the cave. *I wonder how it got so smooth*, she said, *and why the ends are all rounded.*

There's rocks here, Aanjay said. *Shiny ones with green streaks. You like rocks!*

On the far side of a yawning fissure there was a pile of pebbles, each one almost perfectly spherical with a surface like polished green glass. He stepped delicately around the hole, then picked one up and threw it to her. They were cool and slick to touch. The green was banded like layers of moss frozen in ice. How did the stones get so round, she wondered, like the stick?

The sensation of danger escalated.

The cave shook. Dust and rubble fell from the ceiling.

"We have to get out!" she cried. "Aanjay, come on!"

Andel felt her mother's call and started for the opening, but behind her Aanjay screamed. His mind clutched onto hers – a tumbled blur as he fell through the fissure, then striations of worn rock-face as he landed in a tunnel underneath. Agonizing pain came from his leg.

It's broken, he cried. *Help me, sis!*

The thunder in her chest increased, and she realized it was not her heart, but the cavern itself. The spherical stoned shivered. Grit shuddered from the cave walls – and then she knew. Water! Water had shaped the stones!

She ran to the edge of the fissure and teetered on the edge. Aanjay looked up. His leg was all wrong. If she lay down, she could almost reach him. Air blew against her face.

Take my hand! she cried.

She remembered his touch, his desperate grip, the feel of his skin slipping, her fingers stretched, then left cold as the flash flood boomed through the tunnel. Then there was only the thunder. Spray blasted her face. She screamed when his death-cry came – *My brave little sister. Take care of Mother. She loves you so much ...*

As if from nowhere, her father snatched her up and sprinted for the opening. Behind them, a churning spume filled the cave. They barely made it to safety before the water jetted past them and arced to the canyon floor so far below. Aanjay's body was never recovered.

"How old were you?" Huldar asked.

She wiped tears from her eyes. "One hundred and sixty summers. He was five-ninety, almost of age. Our uncle arranged an interview for him with the Navigators' Guild, and he had been accepted. The trip to Germane was supposed to be a celebration."

Fresh tears blurred her eyes. *He wanted to explore, to see everything.*

Aye, he did. And now you are seeing it for him. Huldar's soft brogue washed through her mind.

"If I had left when I knew it was dangerous, if I had stopped him ... I didn't make him listen." ... *Didn't listen to myself.*

It wasn't your fault, Huldar said. When she didn't respond, he gave a gentle smile. "*What can we say to those whose song is no longer heard,*" he recited, "*to those whose charm was silenced, loose threads unfulfilled? Breath blows and carries desire ... sorrow and joy, the twins, each in the other's shadow.*" He made a small bow. "Kaskarudjan Imahtara of Trianog."

Andel blinked back fresh tears. "Thank you," she sniffed. "Imahtara was a great poet, revered by all Trianogi. I read her works as a child - Aanjay and I - we both did, but I don't remember that piece. It's very beautiful," she added.

Huldar reached into Qalān and retrieved a small book bound in soft suede. He stroked the cover fondly. "My mother gave me this," he said. "Maybe it was handwritten by Imahtara herself. If not, someone has gone to a lot of trouble to preserve her works." He handed it to her. "You'll find it in here."

She held the leather bindings to her nose and breathed in a faint perfume. *Samarkala?*

Huldar smiled. "Borrow it, if you like. It has often comforted me."

Really? She clasped the book in wonder. *But it's priceless - irreplaceable!*

He nodded. *I look forward to hearing what discoveries you make in its pages. Keep it as long as you like.*

Thank you!

My pleasure. Huldar inclined his head. Andel watched his long legs unfold as he climbed to his feet. "And now, I'm off to sleep," he said. "Tomorrow's a big day. We'll go back to The Hat and see if your unique theory has substance."

"Good night …" She held the book to her heart, close to the keepsake Aanjay had given her so long ago. *And thank you again.*

The tent flap closed. Andel explored the book's cover with sensitive fingertips. Slipped between two pages was a red ribbon: she opened the book at that point to find detailed drawings of flowers and creatures intertwined against a starry night sky. Had Kaskarudjan Imahtara made the illustration herself? Among the figures was another poem with characters written in red-gold ink – perhaps it was his favorite passage. She held it to the firelight and read …

… Time is all we have,
Love is all we are,
Time and love,
El's boundless gift.

RESCUE

The smell of warm grain and fruit drew Huldar from sleep. He pushed aside his snug furs and pulled on clothing as quickly as he could, guilty for having slept late. With a rueful smile he remembered his late-night conversation with Andel. His impulsive gift had seemed right at the time, but now he felt awkward.

He wrapped his jacket tight and followed his nose to the cookfire.

She was next to Casco, eating already. She smiled at him and he returned it with what he hoped was a suitably casual greeting, comradely – yet warm. He accepted a breakfast bowl from Cobar. The fruit was one they had collected in the east, fragrant and sweet, but the taste barely registered. He was supposed to go with her to The Hat today to examine that trace she'd found, but perhaps he should go with Casco. He needed time to settle his stomach. He waved his bowl toward Cobar.

"If you go with Andel to The Hat, me and Casco will be on the –"

"Nope." Cobar shook his head.

Huldar blinked.

"Remember?" Casco said. "We discussed this last night. I need his help to examine the Long Island escarpment, unless you fancy a day or two being an anchor while I scale cliffs?"

He glanced her way and hoped she hadn't overheard. It would seem as if he didn't want to be with her – but he did. It was just that …

With her empty bowl held by her side, she stood and looked out to sea. A loose plait tumbled from beneath her fur-lined hood. He remembered the book again and emotion zinged his haze. He saw her turn and quickly looked away.

"Yes, yes," he said. "Yes … Andel and I will go to The Hat." She nodded. "Stay in touch, you two," he added. "In a few weeks the others will join us, then a few more and we'll be away again and off to the north. We'll come back here after that, so no tearing rush, but I'd like to get study fields collated before they get here."

"North pole? Can't wait." Casco rolled his eyes. "Come on, Cobar, got your climbing gear sorted?"

Cobar grunted. "Two more weeks of peace."

Huldar watched as they stepped through the portal, then turned to Andel. "Ready?"

On the fossil plateau, the weather was calm and sunny and they soon had their jackets off. Below them, the sea stretched onward beneath an azure sky.

"It's like an endless bowl of blue cream – islands like lumps of fruit," Huldar said.

Andel looked at him. "And you think I say strange things?"

Huldar tried to suppress the laugh building in his chest. "The islands … don't they look like fruit to you?"

"Fruit and cream?" She peered at the ocean. "Hmm." She pointed at some small cottony lumps just below the horizon. "Are those clouds, or perhaps a spun sugar confection waiting outside the bowl of the ocean for a giant invisible hand to sprinkle them over the top?"

"Definitely!"

As he released his laugh, a swarm of lizards flitted like a green shadow across the rock shelf below. They were smaller than varieties found on other islands, but still something to be wary of.

They made their way over the fractured surface. He glanced at the fossils embedded in the stone, treasures that would have to wait for another time. Today was Andel's day. It would be up to him to protect her while she scanned the ocean bedrock for possible nacrite deposits.

Low bushes and shrubs grew in sheltered fissures, and when their legs brushed against them, showers of small, hopping insects scattered, bright as jewels. He indicated a larger, fluorescent green beetle, and Andel smiled with pleasure.

Look, she said, and shared the image of the lithe pink lizard that stalked it. Its head was motionless, three eyes measuring. Its front two legs were tipped with large serrated claws and cocked above its head like those of the voracious predators on the northern island. With no more warning than a flick of its tail, it leaped at its prey. Andel gasped. Its forearms wrapped the green carapace in a death grip and after a brief struggle the beetle went limp.

Venomous? she asked.

Must be, he replied. *Let's not try to pick it up.*

Down on the reef, the air was still and humid. The sun blazed down, and they squinted against the glare.

"It was there," Andel said. "By that outcrop, the one that looks like a weyfal, or, if you look at it another way, a piece of fruit." She turned to him, her eyes bright. "Race you!"

He let her run ahead, thinking it would be easy to catch up, but soon discovered she was much better at running over the uneven surface of the reef than he was. She glanced back as she neared the target, eyes alight with excitement, and laughed aloud, but when she stopped her haze settled back around her like a cloak. She stroked the weyfal rock thoughtfully then opened her palm toward the sea and closed her eyes, preparing to feel for the nacrite she seemed so confident was there.

Wait, Huldar said. *Let me scan for lizards first.*

Oh, of course. When she smiled, he felt the corners of his mouth curl and he sighed inside. When he was with her, he could think of nothing sensible to say, and now he was smiling like an idiot just because she had smiled, and out of breath because she had invited him to run faster. What a fool he must seem! He settled his breathing and let his senses range, searching for the collective sparkle of a lizard pack. He found the dominant group foraging on the other side of the plateau. Several smaller groups were scattered to the west, kept occupied by a hatching of grubs.

All clear, he said.

She nodded and closed her eyes again. After a moment, she kneeled on the reef and put her palms against it in much the same gesture as he would use when feeling for Qalān. Her mind was still in light contact, but she was processing through talents he lacked and the information made little sense.

Her head tilted slowly as the interaction grew more complex. Light from her Tsemkar glimmered on the slick surface of the rock.

There! she said, and with the word came a sense of direction, south-east. Her voice rang with suppressed excitement. *Nacrite has no physical connection to the rock around it – and that usually makes it hard to sense – but there's mountains of it! This could be the cause, just as we suspected!*

Her sense of triumph gusted through him, a feeling so wondrous that he almost laughed aloud, but when she saw him react, the sensation was quickly pulled back beneath her veil.

My apologies, she said. *I should be more disciplined.*

Please, don't apologize. Such an exciting moment, and I am pleased to be sharing it with you. His heart raced. Had he said too much? Would she think him too forward? He kept his questions firmly lidded and smiled into the middle distance in what he trusted was a leaderly way.

If she sensed his turmoil, she shared nothing of it. He prepared to stand guard as she divined deeper into the rock. The exact location of the nacrite was vital knowledge. He was every bit as keen to find answers as she was.

She stood up and, with her eyes still closed, set off across the reef, walking with complete assurance on a steady trajectory heading for the sea. He followed, ready to guide her around any obstructions she may not sense.

Two paces from the edge of the reef he stopped her.

He waited, one arm held out to keep her from falling into the sea. Her head turned as if scanning. A wave sloshed over their feet. Foam hissed and bubbled. *Lucky the waters are calm today*, he thought to himself. Had the swells been bigger, they may have been prevented from accessing the reef at all.

At last the images she shared with him slowed and he received something that made sense – a dense cluster of nodules bobbing in the lightless waters.

Excitement surged between them. *It's trapped beneath a layer of basalt!* she said. *A vast slab that extends to either side of where we are now. The formation … it's as if an enormous shelf – miles long – has fallen into the sea. The friction of the nacrite has caused erosion, a series of domes on the southern edge, and it's trapped there, concentrated. When the moons are in alignment and have their greatest tidal pull, the rock must be destabilized. A giant fulcrum! When the balance is tipped the whole assemblage suddenly tilts …*

… Causing the wave!

Yes!

Amazing!

But the nacrite can't escape beyond the lip of the dome, so it stays there, and then the weight slowly pushes it down again.

Andel stood motionless, her mind enmeshed in rock and nacrite. No part of her physical body betrayed the excitement of the spirit it contained. Without thought, he stepped closer. Their hazes almost sizzled when they touched. She remained statue still, but he knew she was acutely aware. His arm drifted closer as if drawn by her infectious energy.

HULDAR!

He blinked, stunned by the force of the call. Like a startled bird, his moment with Andel fluttered and was lost.

HULDAR, HELP ME!

Lind? What is it? He tried not to sound annoyed. It must be important if she had called to him from so far away.

I'm trapped! she cried. *There's wasps; they're swarming! I may have broken my ankle. I don't know what to do!*

Where are you?

Near the sky-step. I've fallen into a sinkhole or something. Hurry!

Where is Alis? Weren't you with her?

I ... I'm on my own.

Why? What's happened? Is Alis safe?

Yes! Lind said. *Of course she is! Just hurry!*

"Trouble?" Andel had withdrawn from her exploration. Her sandy-brown eyes were fully present.

He nodded. "Lind. She's hurt." Of all the moments for someone to need him! *I have to go.*

"I'll stay here," Andel said. "I'll be fine."

"The lizards?"

She shrugged. "They're busy with the bug outbreak, you said so yourself. They won't worry me today."

"No. We can't risk it." He put his hand up, asking her to wait while he extended his thoughts toward Casco and Cobar. Within moments he saw a close-up image of layered sandstone through Casco's eyes.

Lind's in trouble. he said. *Can either of you come to watch over Andel?*

Going to take some time, Casco replied. *If you hadn't noticed, we're halfway down a cliff!*

Andel touched his arm. "I'll be fine, truly. I have a feeling about this."

He peered across the rock shelf toward the portal, then up the sheer cliffs to the edge of the plateau. The portal was the only escape from the reef, and too far away for her to make a rapid escape. He pointed to the bluff directly opposite them. *If the lizards come, see that ledge there?*

She nodded.

It's defensible, he said. Then with a flash of inspiration, he whispered the mysterious orange stone from Qalān and put it in her palm. "It's a beacon charm," he explained. "If you keep it close, I'll always be able to find you."

She rubbed the pebble with her thumb, feeling the charm within. When she smiled, he knew that, incredibly, he'd done the right thing. As he hurried to the portal he felt weightless, as if his body had been imbued with Andel's nacrite. But as he drew near to the sky-cliffs, the distress call came again, urging him to hurry, and his buoyancy faded.

Before the final step Huldar paused. There was no room for error. The fate of Joumelät Enna was testament to that – and he had to have the song ready to bounce them through the portal if need be. Qalān and emotion did not mix. There could be no mistakes. With mind and body in hyper-drive, he stepped through.

Green grass and warm sun, but on the breeze he heard a whirring sound and a faint clacking – perhaps a call of some sort? It was coming from the forest's edge.

Lind! he called. *Where are you?*

Over here! I've fallen into a pit of some sort. There're wasp-things. Be careful! They're dangerous.

As he drew near, he could see where the noise was coming from. Above the hole a cloud of angry insects with long green bodies darted to and fro. Flashing orange wings beat with blurring speed. Banded antennae sprouted like gaudy spears from armored heads.

Huldar backed slowly away. He focused on the pitch of their call, but the staccato clicks left no room for his voice to take control. When he turned his attention to the thrum of their wings he found the space he needed and began to sing, trying to fill the tiny intervals with enough sound to form a counter-chord that could be manipulated.

With an orange flash the swarm turned to face him. They had no eyes!

He pushed the shock aside. The Shamkar on his cheek warmed as he pushed his voice forward, but he was not quick enough. Without warning the insects flew at him, each antenna aimed like a weapon. There was no time to form a protective shield. At the last second, he ducked and the dazzling horde flew over his head.

They swept back for another try, wings flared in the bright glow of sunset. The time for delicacy was gone. He made the notes hard and forceful, and as he readied himself for the next onslaught, the sightless army hesitated. For a moment or two they milled as if they had forgotten why they were there. He felt a brief, alien connection with one-mind-as-many, then watched their sparks disband like shooting stars into a universe of living things, each unique vibration absorbed back into the overarching song of the moment.

He found Lind among the roots at the bottom of a pit, sheltered by a canopy of fronds. She ran her hand lightly over her swollen ankle and struggled to her feet.

"I landed badly," she said. Her face was a pale oval in the gloom.

He looked doubtfully at the steep sides of her enclosure and said, "Don't worry, I'll have you out of there in a moment." He pulled a rope from Qalān.

"My ankle hurts too much," Lind said. "I can't climb."

Huldar eyed the tangle of debris at the bottom of the pit. "A sling, then. See that old root, the twisted one? That's it! Do you think it could hold your weight?"

Lind tested it and looked up at him. "Should do."

Huldar threw the rope and watched as she tied it to the center of the short length of wood. He whispered a charm to keep the knot firm, then winched his end around a sturdy trunk and started hauling. When she was just below the lip he tied the rope off and took her hand, dragging her to the surface. Her tattered shirt revealed arms that were scratched and covered in welts. The angry scrape on her cheek needed the attention of a healer, and also her ankle, which seemed quite swollen.

"Shame you healers can't heal yourselves." He held out his arm and she clung tightly. "Is the ankle broken?"

I'm no healer, she said. *Not really.*

Huldar gave her a small squeeze. "Yes you are!" She was clearly in shock. "You might think of yourself as Leth, but your mother was Naghari. Your skills are growing every day." He smiled. "Come on. Let's get you back to camp. What happened to Alis?"

I came out here alone.

Alone? "Lind! You should know better."

I wanted to see the sky-step again. It's so amazing ... and the sunset. It's beautiful, isn't it?

He could hear the lie in her mind.

She turned inside his supporting arm and suddenly his gesture seemed like an embrace. He stepped back in confusion. Her hand came softly to his chest.

Thank you, she whispered. *I knew you would come.*

Sadness welled in Huldar's heart. Through her touch he could feel her desire, her high hopes for the moment – and also that she had upset the insects on purpose, not realizing they would actually sting, then fallen as she ran in genuine panic.

He smoothed frazzled hair from her forehead. "Of course I came," he said. "I would always come to any of you who needed me." She did not resist as he took her hand from his chest. He could feel her courage wilt, like a soft-petaled flower cut from its stem. "I am an archangel and your team-leader," he said quietly. "It is my duty."

But I love you! She threw her soul open. *Does this mean nothing to you?*

He stayed silent.

She turned away. "It's Andel, isn't it?" she said numbly. "I knew that. It's just that I …"

He looked into her face. Her eyes were huge and dark. "Lind, we have known each other for a long time … hundreds of years … seven new planets, or is it eight? In all that time we have been friends, you and I, good friends, colleagues, but nothing more. I care for you, I respect your intelligence, your resourcefulness; I enjoy your Lethian nature, stubborn as my own, even your prickly humor." He gently squeezed her hand. "But I am not in love with you."

I know … "I know that. I'm sorry."

"Don't be sorry." He released her hand. "But please, don't do this again. Now," he said, "if we could return to camp?"

When she hesitated he felt his anger rise. He'd left Andel alone on the reef. What if something happened to her – or anyone else on his team, while he was attending this circus?

"I'll take myself home," Lind said. Her frozen expression did nothing to hide the moisture trapped against her lashes.

"Of course I'll take you," he said gruffly. She gave no more than a token resistance as he took her elbow.

She limped determinedly toward the sky-step portal. "You want to get back to her. I can feel it."

"Yes!" he said. "I left Tsemkarun Andel unguarded in a dangerous place so I could come and save someone who had made a safe place dangerous!" He gritted his teeth against the snarl in his voice. "I hope, for your sake, that no one else needs rescuing today."

"I'm sorry."

"Good," he said stiffly. "So am I. Now let's go."

"You won't tell her, will you? You won't tell anyone?"

Huldar took a deep breath and kept walking. Lind hobbled beside him, her haze a clot of misery. Her ankle was badly injured and he felt sorry for her pain, inside and out, but he would not relent. He needed to get back to Andel. The thought of a marauding lizard pack preyed on his mind.

Minutes later, Lind was safely with the healers. Huldar waited until he was certain she would be all right, then started back to The Hat. He made his way rapidly over the fossil-beds on the plateau and looked down from the edge. Small breakers smashed against the weyfal rock now the tide had turned, but there was no sign of Andel. She hadn't called out and he sensed no danger – but nevertheless his heart began to pound. Then he remembered the charm-stone.

He stepped down to the reef. Soon the rising tide would cut off their escape. His heart raced as he followed its call across the broken surface, and as he rounded the headland he saw her in the distance, draped over a broad outcrop that projected from a sandy beach. A quick scan told him she was completely calm, sunning herself. It took several moments to bring his aspect to order, then he continued casually as if he were merely returning to the job. When he got closer, he saw Casco and Gento and laughed at himself for not noticing them all at the same time.

Andel! he called. *Still hard at work I see? And you two layabouts?*

Right here, boss! Casco and Cobar were sitting on the edge of a rock-pool with their shirts off, dangling their feet in the water.

Andel climbed from her boulder and hurried across the sand. "Is she all right?"

"She'll be fine," Huldar said, but his sadness for what had happened lurked close to the surface. "She was attacked by insects and fell into a sinkhole." Casco and Cobar joined them and he showed them a rough approximation of what had happened.

"Hmm," said Cobar. "The sling was good idea."

"Lucky the hole wasn't too deep!" Casco added.

Huldar nodded. "Deep enough."

"And you sang those things to calmness?" Andel said. The admiration in her gaze rinsed much of the sadness from his heart. "That's amazing!" she went on. "They look so ferocious."

"They *were* a bit of a challenge," he admitted.

"Have you done that sort of thing before?" she asked. "How did it feel to be in touch with another creature's mind? But not just one being … all of them acting as one!"

"I hadn't thought of it in that way." He paused as he tried to remember the event more clearly. "There was no feeling of a 'mind' such as we'd know it," he said. "There was a single will, but it was bubbly, like foam. I had no inkling of any thought patterns, and when they left, the foam fragmented, sort of. They just fluttered away and I was glad my charm worked."

"And Lind is all right?" Casco asked.

"She must have been relieved to see you," Andel added.

"It was mainly her ankle – and a few bites," Huldar said, "but nothing Ubaid can't fix. Now, how did you go with the nacrite? Found anything new?"

"Come and I'll show you." She danced away toward the cliff face. "Over here …"

Casco and Cobar shared a resigned sigh and hurried to keep pace.

"It's all right for you," Casco muttered to Huldar, "but we've been traipsing up and down these rocks for hours now. It was easier climbing cliffs."

"Casco!" Andel laughed. "You know that's not true!"

The weathered rock towered above them, chill in the shadows. She turned to Huldar. "You know how nacrite is often associated with calcified sediments?" She paused to gauge his interest.

He looked at her blankly. "Calcified sediments?" He hoped he didn't seem too clueless.

Her small hand caressed a pale formation sandwiched between darker layers. "A whole seam of exquisite, pale yellow marble," she said. "It's just down here! Worth a fortune on its own. And … you'll be amazed! Really, you will!"

Casco winked at him. *Really, you will …*

"It goes right underneath the basalt fulcrum, and …" Andel hesitated, her eyes shining "… the largest deposit of nacrite I've ever heard of!" She laughed with joy.

Huldar laughed with her. "Truly, I am amazed! Such a series of finds – no wonder you're so happy!"

"There's no doubt now that we'll be returning to this planet," Casco said. "The nacrite here may not be mineable – and we'll have to take into account the ecological significance of the wave – but the other nacrite probably is and I believe that some of this marble might be too."

They looked up as a shadow crossed the sun. The weather was turning. Shredded clouds flew across the sky, harbingers of change. Andel pulled her coat on, and the others followed suit.

"Time to head back," Huldar said, "before the tide cuts us off. You've all done unbelievably well! I think a little more jhavo is in order, don't you?"

"Ha!" Casco nudged Cobar's ribs. "Told you he had another jug of that stuff stashed away."

INSIGHT

Alone on a craggy northern island of the Southern Archipelago, Huldar hunkered down beside a mighty waterfall and watched the dawn light flood beneath a pall of inky dark clouds. In an instant, squalls of rain were transformed into shining capes. Wildlife filled the air with chirps, wails and ratcheted clacking. The roar of the falls thundered through his body. Rain bucketed down, running freely over his face from the edge of his hood. He cleared his eyes with one hand and stared into the braided chasm below. Thick mist sparkled between long fingers of shadow, but it was not just the dawn that flashed among the droplets.

All around him, up and down the length of the canyon, small blue lizards darted in fits and starts from crevices where they made their homes. Wherever the sunlight pooled, they gathered. Jewel bright on rain-dark rocks, they lifted cerulean wings as if in tribute to the sun; then, at some unspoken signal, they launched into the void.

Wings fluttered like fragments of shattered summer sky. Tails flashed in the pearlescent vapor. Blue streaks, agile as eels, chased through the spray after glimmering rainbows of flying silver fish – a sight to rival the famed sky-veils of Manziat.

More than anything, he wanted Andel to see it, but he was afraid to leave even for one second, knowing that the moment would not last and that their psychic bond was not deep enough for him to share such wealth and do it justice.

As if his thoughts had been a cue, the sunlight was eclipsed by storm clouds and the magical scene darkened. Lizards still flew, fish still jumped, but everything was different. He stood and bowed in homage to the wonders of El's creation, and, after a last look, began walking slowly along the edge of the ravine, careful to avoid unwary lizards.

He wondered how the creatures survived the long winter, but in their short window of time they could only have the briefest of overviews. Mating displays and breeding behaviors were rarely glimpsed, and there were few clear clues as to how any of the myriad life forms on this complex world reproduced.

He paused to pull a vine from his path and looked up as flashing blue wings arced above the ravine. It puzzled him that many populations showed no evidence of variation in age. Where were their young? But these mysteries would have to wait until the next thaw-cycle, or the next. The Overlord was far more interested in the location of mineral deposits, and saw ecological systems in terms of dangers and assets rather than life and beauty valuable in its own right.

With other assignments, ten years was the accepted rotation … ten years on, ten years off until the new planet was well understood. Only then would the Imperial Explorers give their final reports and the Guild release the new world for utilization – or not. However, this one was only habitable for three standard years. It would be another seven before it thawed again; so a three by seven rotation. This would put the Uri'madu out of sync with other teams.

Then there was the difficulty with external communication. Soon after the summer solstice, there would be an eight-day period at a specific location in the north during which they could make contact with the outer realm. Eight days then nothing more until the navigator returned to their original Djan'rū site. They had understood these limitations before they had accepted the assignment, and they would be well compensated of course, but this was the longest any of them had spent in complete isolation from the Realm, and as the communications window came nearer, he expected tensions to escalate.

He left the trail and headed west through dense vegetation. *It's probably the nacrite that causes the communications problem*, he thought. He had never heard of so much of the rare metal on one planet. When nacrite escaped into the atmosphere it continued to rise, and at a certain altitude began to fragment. His theory was that the whole planet was blanketed in minute nacrite particles that formed a natural shield against telepathic contact – but there was no easy way to prove it.

A zigzag pattern on the ground caught his attention and he stooped to collect a cluster of large oval nuts. The greenish shells were tough to break, but inside was a thick layer of bright yellow flesh which was not only safe for annangi to eat, but was also delicious. There seemed to be plenty of them, so he gathered a few more, then headed back to their southern base-camp.

When he returned the sun was shining, although the air held a crisp, polar bite. Tam was waiting for the nuts, ready to chop them open. Ubaid took some yellow nutmeat from the bench. "Where's Lind?" he asked. "She was supposed to meet me here so I could teach her more about the testing of potential provender. This is a tricky one, not obvious at first examination."

The healer frowned for a moment and Huldar sensed Lind's reply. Her voice seemed muffled, as if the call had woken her from sleep.

"I'll be in my tent checking the assignment listings," Huldar said.

"Suit yourself." The healer shrugged.

Enclosed by familiar leather panels, Huldar slumped onto his bed. It was ridiculous, the way he avoided her, but Lind's presence made him uncomfortable. He had told no one of their conversation by the sky-step, but it was hard to pretend it hadn't happened.

He took out a list and mused over the sites they needed to visit today. They would probably need extra containers as well as a selection of charm-sealed bags and boxes, and maybe some small jars, left in storage back on their more permanent campsite on the Eastern Continent. He would have to send someone to get them. Lind was the perfect choice.

"Breakfast!" Tam called. "Wait till you wrap your teeth around these little beauties!"

Huldar steeled himself to look and feel casual while eating breakfast with Lind and Andel both present at the same time, then gave out the assignments for the day.

––––––––

Lind strolled into the now-empty campsite on the Eastern Continent and shrugged her jacket off. At least the weather was warm there. She scanned for Duvät Gok's presence. He was supposed to be minding their things, keeping the local fauna and flora from colonizing, but it seemed she had the place all to herself.

The marquee door was open. Her hand trailed against the leather as she entered, its texture smooth and soft against her fingertips. Inside was dark and cool. Empty cushions and rugs lay around a cold hearth. A slight film of dust already covered everything. She kneeled on Huldar's customary cushion and imagined him as storyteller in full cry, and her tears began to flow. She had held him in her secret heart for such a long time. Why had she held back? Why had she said nothing until competition arrived?

Because archangels do not marry angels, she answered herself. And it was true, most of the time. But Casco was a mixed-marriage child, and El would not have blessed his parents if the relationship was wrong, would He? There could be no child without a marriage, and no child except that El had blessed the union, so therefore, mixed marriages could be blessed.

She thumped the cushion. "It's not fair!"

Andel was fragile and beautiful with dark hair and pale skin, and a naivety about her even Lind herself found fetching. She hadn't set out to win Huldar's heart, and probably didn't even know that she had.

"And she saved my life!" Lind sobbed aloud. "It's not fair."

The cool cushions buffered her collapse and she cried until there were no more tears to come. Afterward, she lay with her knees drawn into her arms and her mind a welcome blank. Slowly it came to her that they were only halfway through their assignment. Somehow, she would have to put this behind her, bury her feelings, and keep going. When they returned to Giahn, she would apply for transfer to another team and leave them to their happiness.

Her eyes closed. She felt herself drifting off to sleep but had no will to prevent it. The team would have to wait a little longer for their spare bags and jars.

She awoke to the sensation of being watched. Her mind reached out and found the Overlord standing not far away. She turned and sat up. His eyes followed her contours in a way she would have welcomed from Huldar.

"Aren't you married?" she snapped.

Duvät Gok nodded once, but his lips shrugged as if the admission meant nothing.

"Why are you looking at me like that?"

"You are beautiful."

He backed away a step, but his haze oozed attraction. He was still Duvät Gok, their despised Tiamäti Overlord, but his attention was like a warm fire on her jaded heart, and his yellow, archangel eyes wanted her, just as she wished Huldar's would. When he smiled, she smiled back, and when he tipped his head for her to follow, she did.

He held open his tent and she passed beneath his arm. Every sense felt alive in a way it hadn't for too many years. His eyes glittered down into hers. His finger passed across her lips, leaving a tingling trail. He was not beautiful, but he was powerful, and he wanted her. His hand felt clammy and soft in hers, but when their hazes touched she felt his excitement and, in that moment, nothing else mattered.

She fell onto the bed and he tumbled down on top of her. Beneath his shirt his chest was a little fleshy but still masculine and strong. He squeezed her breasts. She noticed the blue polish on his fingernails was chipped in several places. Moist breath panted against her neck as he pushed her legs apart and fumbled with the fastenings on his trousers. She wondered why he didn't use his mind.

Won't your wife know? she whispered.

I am Duvät Gok, he growled. *I take what I want!*

With one hand, she held her underwear aside. He gasped as he plunged himself inside her. Her ankles locked over his heaving back. *Slow down*, she said, but he grasped the frame of his bed and grunted with each thrust, absorbed completely in his own pleasure. As the tempo increased, he pressed his lips against hers and when she did not respond, he forced her kiss with his mind. Her mouth was filled with his tongue. His rutting vocalizations breathed into her lungs, owning them.

Trapped beneath his weight, she felt excited by his dominance. She ground her loins against him. He made a strange squeaking sound, and with a long groan, rolled off her, spent.

After a few moments, she sighed and wondered what to do. Then he started to snore. With a grimace she turned to look. There was a lumpy bag beneath his pillow. Herbs to help him sleep, perhaps? If so, he hardly needed them at the moment.

Her fingers crept forward. His breath was warm against the back of her hand. Her fingertips stroked the bag. The bulges were hard and round.

Duvät rolled over. She snatched her hand back. But then he snuggled deeper into the pillow and a little more of the bag was exposed. After a long moment she reached out again. The top was tied with a purple string. It had a silken gleam – probably charmed. "But right now, he probably wouldn't notice if the tent fell down," she murmured, and after a short hesitation, she touched it anyway.

The tie vibrated quietly between her fingers but she was no Shamkarun to be able to sift the notes free. She had an image of Huldar, his Shamkar glowing with a soft white light as he sang magic into a piece of driftwood then gave it to her, charmed to keep the zilla-flies away, but that was on another planet, at another time.

She gave the cord an angry tug and was startled when the knot came loose. Yes, it was charmed, but Duvät had been careless and not sung the seal. Carefully, she pulled it again and the loops fell away. The puckered top eased and she noticed something strange.

Is that colored light … coming from inside the bag? How could that be?

When she held her hand in front of the opening, a rainbow shape shone onto her palm. She probed inside and found a smooth surface, cool … like crystal. With barely a pause, she pushed back the lip to see more.

Rainbow light flared against her face. Everywhere it fell, on her arms, her chest, on the leather tent above, a rippling aurora transformed that object into a thing of transcendent beauty. Duvät Gok, Huldar's rejection, all was forgotten as she reached into the bag and withdrew a shining orb.

She eased her legs over the edge of the bed. The crystal nestled into the palm of her hand. It was clear like water yet alive with color. She could not stop looking at it. Whenever she moved, its colors would momentarily scatter then realign into a brilliant, cohesive aurora. She rolled it to and fro, lost in wonder. What was it, and why did their Overlord have a bag of the things lying under his pillow?

A cold shiver went up her spine. The hairs on the back of her neck pricked sharply and she turned to meet the Overlord's stare. Outrage filled his yellow gaze. She closed her hands over the light of the gem.

"Give it back," he snarled.

He snatched it from her and quickly returned it to the bag. Without releasing her gaze, he pulled the drawstring tight. His lips muttered the charm that should have held it safe from prying.

"I'm sorry," she said. "You were asleep. I didn't know. I won't tell anyone, if that's what you want."

His eyes burned uncertainly. The red stain on his haze intensified. Slowly, she stood up from the bedside and backed toward the exit.

"I don't know what they are and I don't want to know," she said. "I can screen. I won't tell." But with two strides he was beside her and gripped her arm with surprising force. She had never realized how tall the Overlord was, never thought of him as dangerous, until now. He threw her to the ground and stood astride her. She gasped with pain as his mind invaded hers.

YOU WILL TELL NO ONE! His voice reverberated, heavy with malice. She felt a snap as something altered inside her head. She tried to complain but the words would not form. It was as if her voice had frozen. Tears left cold trails. She lay motionless, face averted, barely breathing.

"Look at me!" he shouted.

Slowly, she turned her head. The penis that dangled beneath his shirt was becoming erect.

YOU ARE MINE! he yelled. *MINE!*

He kicked her legs apart and kneeled between them. She stared into his angry eyes, afraid now to look away.

He put his mouth close to her ear. "You will do my bidding, obey my every word because I am an archangel and you are pathetic, and if ever you breathe a word of this," he rasped, "or share even the faintest glimmer of a thought, I shall make you my slave!" His mind projected the image of a silvery neck-chain. His lips found hers in a lingering kiss. "Every thought you have, every whim – your entire self will be mine to know." His finger ran from the tip of her nose, across her lips and pushed them apart. "Have you seen it?" His finger stroked her tongue. *Have you seen what the chains can do?*

She shook her head. The finger almost made her gag. She did not move in such circles, but she had heard about the God-Emperor's household, about the slave-chains and silencers – the terror of every poverty-stricken angel.

Duvät removed his finger and made a wet line across her throat.

"If you do that," she whispered, "everyone will know about the ..." she tried to make herself say "crystals", but the word would not form. She tried "rainbows" but that would not come either. Even when she tried to image them her mind would not obey.

Duvät Gok smiled. With rough fingers he ripped her underwear aside and entered her again.

You are MINE!

His body thumped into hers. There was nothing but pain. When it was over, he stood up and shoved her with his foot.

"Get out."

She picked herself up and ran to her own tent.

Tears streamed down her cheeks. She cowered in the corner. What should she do? What had he done to her? Her mind felt as if it had been hit by a sledgehammer. It was already late and she had not returned with the containers she had been sent for. If she went outside, Duvät Gok would be there. What should she do? How could she hide this from the others?

The defiled clothing went into her brazier. As the smoke rose, she wrapped herself in a blanket and stared into the flames, wishing they could cleanse the Overlord's attentions from her body.

Lind?

She turned toward the call of Ubaid, still far south.

I'm fine, she lied. The healer knew of her episode with Huldar. She had told him much of what had happened while he treated the bites and the sprained ankle – but Naghari were deeply empathic. Ubaid was already concerned for her wellbeing. How could she keep them from finding out about Duvät's attack? But if she didn't, or he even thought she might not, he would kill her. Of that she was certain.

The others will return soon, Ubaid said. His tones were caring. *Don't be too much longer.*

A burst of energy galvanized her. She found fresh clothing and as she left her tent she carried herself as confidently as if nothing had happened, for so it must be. Thankfully, Duvät Gok was nowhere to be seen, but she could feel his presence like a slumbering canker. After gathering the containers from stores, she stepped through a series of portals and was back in the southern camp. She unloaded her cargo with brusque movements, ready to retreat to her own space as quickly as possible, but standing in her way was Ubaid. He looked at her with kind Naghari eyes, and suddenly it was too much.

Shh, he said, *shh* … and held her while she sobbed into his chest. She knew he would never pry – it was not the Naghari way. When she had calmed he stroked her head and looked into her eyes.

Better?

She longed to tell him that nothing could make it better.

There will be others, Ubaid said. *Huldar is a fine leader, an exceptional ecologist, but he is not the only person in the Realm.*

More tears came and she wiped them away. If she said nothing more, the others might believe that too.

Tam called out as Arko and Gento returned from the field. The smell of cooking made her queasy. She pushed her lips into a smile. *I'll be all right.*

Ubaid's expression was understanding. *You just need time.* He took her hand and a wave of healing travelled up her arm, warming her from the inside out. With a swift nod he released her. *You know that Alis and I are here for you.*

Sari and Nachiel were next to arrive through the portal. When Sari saw her, she came over. "Are you all right?"

Lind nodded. "Just a bit off color. What were you two laughing at?"

"Nachiel was doing one of his impersonations. Guess who!" Sari assumed a haughty expression. "Where are those reports? I am answerable to the God-Emperor himself!"

Lind overcame a sudden wave of panic and did her best to laugh along with her friends, but when Duvät Gok arrived for dinner, it was all she could do not to vomit. As she left the marquee, she felt him watching and straightened her spine. Whatever came next, she would never give him the satisfaction of seeing her fear again.

HEADING NORTH

"Tomorrow we go north," Huldar said. "The polar opposite. Days will be short. Time will be tight. Temperatures colder than here, but endurable. I have found a site for us on the shores of a narrow inlet. It's sheltered from the winds, but that's about as good as it gets. Take only what we need, and remember, up on the Northern Shelf, just like here, it turns from cold to frigid in an instant.

"We'll concentrate our efforts on the areas the Overlord has marked, but I'll not risk our lives unduly. If the weather is unfavorable, well, he'll just have to live with that."

"He still spends his days lounging in the eastern continent foothills, the lazy kalla," said Bush. "Then he expects to be fed! When's he going to start pulling his weight?"

Casco squinted at the fire. "Can't say I miss him, but what's he up to?"

"Well, he'll have to join us at some point if he wants to make contact with the Realm," Huldar continued. "The weather is our ultimate enemy. When it turns, I believe the change will be rapid. When we're done at the northern end of the planet, we'll return here to the south. From here, we'll let the weather chase us east – then finally back to the center to wrap up."

"What about our communications window?" said Nachiel. "When will the Hermes contact us?"

"Do they message you first," Gento asked, "or the Gok?"

Huldar nodded. "I spoke to the Hermes before we left. He assured me he'd speak to me first, but Duvät is our Overlord and we have to respect that."

"So long as he doesn't spend all our time whingeing to his wife!"

Huldar lifted his hand. "I raised similar points with the Hermes and he said that if such a problem became apparent, he would assign a second Ziquarudjan to us."

"Good!" said Casco.

"One more thing." Huldar hesitated. "We have been asked to say nothing of the nacrite finds as yet."

"Why not?"

"As you are no doubt aware, these deposits are extremely rare and valuable, but their mining potential has yet to be established. The Overlord has asked that we keep the knowledge to ourselves to avoid undue speculation."

"Until he can buy a stake, you mean!"

"Or sell the knowledge to the Faythans."

"Be that as it may," Huldar said, "he is our Overlord and he has asked this of us."

"Asked?"

"Ordered, then," Huldar admitted. "Despite the semantics, the effect is the same, so please …?"

With that, the meeting came to a close and, despite the complaints about Duvät Gok, Andel saw the mood of the group begin to ease. Bush and Topper laughed at something Arko said, Tam stirred the stew with renewed vigor, and even Ubaid seemed animated in his conversation with Alis.

"Who will you speak to first, Lady Andel?" Sari asked.

"My father." She imagined the familiar sound of his voice, thoughtful and always full of questions. He would be counting the days until their contact, she was sure. "And you?"

"And me?" Sari's smile was gentle. "My sister's youngest, little Samiel," she said, then laughed. "Not so little any more. Six hundred summers; he'll be of age before we get back, strapping young lad he is. My sister said they'd have another bit of a ceremony after I get home, just so's I don't feel left out." The older angel sighed. "And I can hardly wait to hold the grand-babies in my arms again." She hugged her arms across her chest and rocked as if there was already a little one in them.

"You miss them," Andel said. "And the name – Samiel?" Her eyebrows lifted. "I have a friend whose son is called Samiel! It's rare for two people to have the same name. Maybe they were kindred spirits in their last life."

Sari nodded. "Kindred spirits? Maybe." But Andel could see her mind was still with her family. She turned to Lind. "What about you?"

Lind blinked as if the question surprised her. "I … haven't thought. I don't know."

"No family?"

"No. Well, yes." Lind shrugged her shoulders. "I have an aunt, and a cousin or two, but I don't know where they are. Not exactly."

"No," echoed Sari. "Not exactly." She bumped shoulders with Lind. "But we're your family aren't we – the Uri'madu."

Lind nodded and smiled, but Andel noticed how gaunt her cheeks had become. Her eyes seemed to fill her face, and she was often quiet now where once she had been brash and outspoken. Something profound had happened, and whatever it was seemed to have occurred at about the same time that Huldar had gone to her rescue.

That night, Andel lay in her tent, unable to sleep. Casco's laugh came faintly from the marquee where some of the team were celebrating the next day's move with drinks by the fire – she had made her excuses early, feigning tiredness. Although they were few, and far beyond the realm, time alone was hard to come by.

She took the Kaskarudjan's book from beneath her pillow and let it fall open. There were words, but it was the illustrations on the page that drew her attention – an indigo sky dotted with silver stars in the shape of a circle. When she looked closer, she could see a pink discoloration on the indigo, remarkably similar to the night sky she had been staring up at only days earlier.

Around the border, lizard-like creatures walked on two legs among swords and chains and two ghostly intertwining snakes, which she thought must be the Kaskaru, the twin spirits that made the Kaskarudjan what she was.

She peered at the writing, but the characters seemed slightly different from the style she was familiar with. The only ones that made sense were the House runes of Maatu, Tiamät, Rukh, and Leth. Then she saw rune of Trianog too, drawn beside Maatu as if they were married. She wished she knew what it meant. Had the Kaskarudjan seen the stars of this planet? Imahtara of Trianog had been strongly gifted. Perhaps she had seen these stars in a vision? If so, it must have been important or memorable for her to have drawn this picture and included it in her book.

She wished there was some way she could find out, but Imahtara had died soon after Andel was born. Her Kaskaru had passed to the current Kaskarudjan, Kariiel Enna, who was wife to Shamkarun Daniel Naghar, the Naghari House Leader.

What would it be like, she wondered, to have synergetic spirits living in your body, at your beck and call. Did they have conversations? Did they have their own desires? She studied the drawing again, marveling at the fine detail. It probably wasn't these stars, and the mark in the sky was most likely just a smudge. Perhaps Huldar would know more … if she was brave enough to ask.

CONTACT

Life on the Northern Shelf was bleak, but since contact with the outer Realm was possible at last, the climate no longer mattered. After her session with the Hermes, Andel left the campsite and wandered, drawn as if by gravity to the icy seashore. She pushed aside the fur of her hood and peered along a grey shingle beach cut short by a shallow headland – the most barren place she had ever seen. Unenthusiastic waves surged beneath a carpet of ice. They sloshed against the stones then snatched at pebbles and spindly fragments of driftwood while hissing a sullen retreat. She crossed her arms for warmth. The only other sound was the lonely moan of the wind. There was no life – no fliers in the skies, no insects, no plants, no shellfish – just rock and shale, snow and ice. No predators and no prey except for the fearsome cold and the Uri'madu.

She almost regretted taking the opportunity to speak through the Hermes. Normally the isolation didn't worry her; she even enjoyed it. But at this moment she missed her family fiercely.

Her father had been utterly enthralled by her descriptions of the planet and the challenges they faced. He loved her renditions of Huldar's Lethian accent, her images of the sky-step portal, and had nothing but praise for her actions in saving her teammates from the volcano. But when she had tried to describe their current location, a great sadness had welled up inside her. She had no idea where it had come from or what it meant.

The pebbles behind her clacked as Huldar made his way across the shore. His approach felt warm, like the sun on her back. She turned slightly. "I like this place. It's free and wild, but it makes me sad."

"Sad?" said Huldar.

"I don't know why." As usual, her heart beat more strongly when he was close. She peered out to sea, hoping he wouldn't notice.

"I had a lovely conversation with my father," she continued. "He is on Ekeridu. The Lord of Maatu has built a new library," she explained, "and Father found some rare texts he thought they might be interested in. Shamkarun Manu Maatu asked to meet him personally and show him around the new structure. Quite an honor!"

"An honor indeed."

"Apparently, Shamkarun Manu designed the building himself, supervised the Zaīkhanun, and even joined in the actual work of shaping the stone."

"Remarkable – although Maatu can be like that, always interested in everything."

She waited for him to continue, but although the air sizzled between them he said no more.

"The First of Maatu is a navigator, did you know?" She glanced at the sky, wondering what it was like to sing your way through the stars.

Huldar nodded.

"He's supposed to be one of the best," she said. "And very handsome. Tall, like you … and quite mysterious."

"Ahh, but can he tell stories?"

Andel grinned. "Well, he *is* a navigator, and the whole of the known is open to him. He must have seen a thing or two! Maybe he'll come for us instead of Kandät Enna?"

"I don't think so," Huldar said quickly. "A great lord like that? Probably far too busy."

"Oh, what a shame," she teased. "I was looking forward to meeting him. The famous Shamkarun Anu, First of Maatu!"

Huldar snorted. For a while they stood in silence. Andel enjoyed having Huldar's company to herself but concern for Lind churned in the pit of her stomach. Eventually he looked at her, his sky-blue eyes enquiring.

"It's Lind," she admitted. "What happened to her? She looks terrible."

"I …" Huldar started, but he looked away and did not go on.

"Something happened when you went to rescue her, didn't it?" Andel prompted. "Was she more badly hurt than she told us? It would be like her to pretend – to make an injury seem less important than it was."

Hurt … he repeated. The wave of sorrow that washed over his veil was seasoned with a touch of embarrassment. "It was a little more complicated than that."

"Complicated?"

"She staged the rescue," he admitted. *Please don't tell anyone!*

I won't.

He rubbed his hands down his face. *She wanted me to rescue her, so she could tell me … but I don't. We are friends, but I don't think of her in that way.*

Andel's brow lowered as she imagined the scene: Huldar sympathetic but firm; Lind's humiliation. No wonder she was troubled.

She took it badly? she said, but it was more of a statement than a question.

He nodded. *I'm sorry for her – her disappointment, but it's not right to lie about such things.*

And ultimately impossible, she finished for him. They stood together, staring at the sluggish waters as sadness washed between them. There was an odd scene she'd witnessed back in camp between Lind and Duvät Gok. She'd meant to tell him about it but it didn't seem right to bring it up now.

As if from a great distance, words came to her mind. "… Love unanswered is merely the shadow of longing."

Longing? he asked. "Longing for what?"

"For truth? I'm not sure. The words just came to me." She didn't know what it meant, or even why she'd said it.

He looked away.

"The truth is, Tsemkarun Andel ..." she heard him say. This time, when he turned to her, he held her gaze. The blue of his eyes was a revelation every time. Andel's senses tingled. Her heart beat against her ribs, waiting for him to complete the sentence; to say – whatever it was he was going to say.

"Ahh, there you are!"

They turned to the crunch of footsteps and Arko's jaunty wave.

Huldar's sigh was slight. She sensed a leaden plunge in his mood before he firmed his veil to stoic perfection. He muttered words beneath his breath. It sounded like, "Not again!" but they were faint and she couldn't be sure.

"'Scuse me, Lady Andel," Arko said. "I need Huldar, just for a moment!"

"No problem." She smiled brightly. "I have samples to label, a report to finish. I'll see you both at the evening meal."

Huldar's answering nod was polite. She walked as if by reflex toward the campsite. Her senses strained, hoping for verification of what she thought she had felt, but all she could hear was the murmur of the waves and the cold sigh of the wind.

As she neared the campsite, Sari waved her over. "How was it? Did you talk to your parents? Were they pleased to hear from you? They must have been excited."

"Father more than Mother," Andel said. "He was so interested in what we are doing, he wanted to hear everything, sometimes twice."

"Twice sometimes? Yes." Sari's smile beamed from somewhere deep in her soul. "I spoke to my sister and all three of her children, Samiel, Ginnic and Rathar, all full of Samiel's sword ceremony. It's only four months until his six-hundredth; where does the time go? They're planning a big party afterward – and maybe a little something when I get back, like I told you, just so I don't feel left out. Isn't that lovely?"

"Wonderful!" She returned Sari's smile. "Your sister is thoughtful, just like you. Do Lethians get an actual sword for their coming-of-age? I have always thought of you as a peace-loving people."

"A peace-loving people? Well, most of the time," she answered. "Sometimes there is an actual sword, for archangels and the like, but we don't actually use a real sword, not our family. But the meaning's the same: you know, cutting away the old, childish life and accepting the responsibilities of adulthood. The sword of the mind ..." she nudged Andel with her elbow "... the sword of the body ..."

"Yes." Andel laughed. "There's that, too! I still remember my father's words ... 'Through stone, air, fire and water a pure path is forged to the divine.'"

"To the divine? That's so beautiful!" Sari said. "What do you think it means?"

"I'm not entirely sure," Andel replied. "But Father says that swords are passion and reason tied together, and it is up to the wielder to discover the balance."

"That is a fine saying, Lady Andel," Gento said. "Very wise."

"Gento! You were listening?" In the bustle about the marquee she had not sensed his arrival.

"Talk of swords draws the ear – it's a Rukh thing," he said. "And we have a saying also."

"A Rukhish saying? Please tell us," said Sari. She turned as Casco joined them. "Oh, Casco! Gento was just about to tell us something Rukhish."

Casco looked at him inquiringly.

Gento held out his hands as if a blade balanced across them. "To hold a sword is acceptance of death."

"Acceptance of death?" Sari frowned. "I like Lady Andel's saying better."

"Even so, these are words we Rukh hold close to our hearts." He paused. "But if it displeases you, perhaps you would like another?"

"They have dozens of them," said Casco dryly. "We could be here for a while."

"Just this one, then." Gento composed himself again. "The body is transient. Only honor and love fly on the wings of El." He bowed to Andel. "I fear this may be your influence, lady diviner. We have all become philosophers!"

"Enough of swords," Casco said. "Tam needs talemgal for tonight's meal, and some of the seaweed we collected down south."

Gento grinned. "Let's go then. Anything to make our plate more interesting!"

After they moved on, Andel took Sari aside.

"There is something I saw, Sari," she said. "It was strange."

"Something you saw? Tell me."

"When I had finished with the Hermes, I came out of the tent. Duvät Gok was first to speak."

"Yes," said Sari. "We waited for ages!"

"Well, when I came out I was surprised to see him still there. He was watching Lind."

"Watching Lind?"

"Yes. But it was the way he was watching her … it made her uncomfortable – and me too. When she looked at him, it was as if she was afraid. Then, she went to him. He squinted … you know that look … when he's concentrating? She moved closer, almost haze to haze. Like they were lovers. It was very odd. What do you think?"

"Odd? Yes, indeed. I've never known Lind to be afraid, or to let Duvät Gok that close to her. Perhaps there's a report she hasn't done? You know how he is about those reports."

"Maybe," Andel said. "It could have been something like that." She could ask Lind herself, but after Huldar had shared about the rescue she'd staged, it would be hard for her not to betray his confidence. She decided to wait and see if any more strange moments occurred.

"The wind's getting stronger," Sari said. "Perhaps we should go in where it's warm."

Andel followed her into the marquee. The others were sitting by the fire discussing their brief contact with civilization. At the rear of the tent, Lind stood by herself, staring at the flames. Andel picked up two honey-cakes and went to join her.

"I thought you might like one?"

"No, thanks," Lind said.

"Talk to anyone?" Andel ventured.

Lind sighed and shook her head. "I have a friend on Hesh, but she's moved and the Hermes couldn't find her. So many people coming and going all the time. Hesh is a busy place."

Andel smiled. "I went to Hesh once. The markets? I'd never seen so many people all together at once, from all ten Houses, all with something to buy or sell. It was amazing. Is that where you live, when you're not on assignment?"

"Sometimes." Lind shrugged. "But it's difficult. No point in owning a place when you're never there – or anything really. I have my clothes, my boots ... a few books, and that's it. That's my home."

"All by yourself on such a flamboyant world?" Andel looked at her slim shoulders. "Sounds lonely."

Lind looked at her with strange intensity. "You don't know what lonely is." She turned toward the clink of mugs. "Hey, Casco! Pour one for me!"

DUVÄT GOK

Warmth bathed Duvät Gok's face as he stepped
from the Northern Shelf back to the Eastern Foothills.
Almost immediately, sweat began to bead his brow. He
shrugged out of his cumbersome fur jacket and cloak as
he walked, and a few minutes after entering his tent,
the rest of his clothes lay strewn across the bed as well.
He opened the eastern quarter up to the breeze and the
view. When papers blew from his desk he didn't race to
pick them up. No one would come here. His privacy
was complete, especially since Huldar was busy with
relocating the Uri'madu – and the other dozen or so
meaningless tasks he'd cleverly set.

But several issues clouded his satisfaction, not least
the discovery that Andel of Trianog had a beacon
charm. He unfolded his grandfather's map on the desk
and moved his blunt fingertips to where the beacon
was marked. Sure enough, his memory and the
vibrations on the map matched.

How had she found it? He had searched the area several times. It was close to where Huldar had made camp. Had she visited him and found the marker, or was it just a very similar charm? He shook his head. The style of the song was quite old and no longer widely used. He touched the map again. Had it been a mistake after all to include a Trianogi in Huldar's team? Had someone told her where to find the charm, or had Huldar found it and given it to her for some reason – and if so, why hadn't he mentioned it and how much did they know? Had Lind somehow managed to overcome the block he'd implanted in her brain? He thought it unlikely.

Occasional swarms still beached on the inner shores, always in the same locality. He tried to be there to greet each and every one, but that level of watchfulness was difficult to maintain.

He lurched from his chair and paced to the open side of the tent. There were too many uncertainties. Cool air caressed his thighs with gentle fingers, a reminder that Lind would come to him that night.

With brusque movements he returned to his bedside and pulled on a robe, then sat down to think on another matter – the wholly unsatisfactory interchange with his superiors at the Imperial Explorers' Guild. He had expected to speak to the Faythans first and bargain some concessions from them with the information about the nacrite, but the Guild must have been waiting as the Hermes made contact.

"Good news, Duvät Gok," they had said. "Your planet has been claimed for House Tiamät." Perhaps they thought he would be proud.

"How delightful!" he'd replied. Now he was even more determined that no one should mention the nacrite. He might be able to use to use the knowledge of their find to his advantage before his presentation to the high and mighty of the Explorers' Guild.

His neck prickled. Paper rustled. A lump formed in the pit of his stomach. He'd forgotten to put away the map. Someone could be far-viewing it, or worse still, a Ziquarudjan could be here in spirit! He had no way of knowing, no screens set, nothing to protect him from their scrutiny. After months of freedom, he'd forgotten the need for such measures!

With artfully casual movements, he returned to the desk and restored the map to Qalān. At least the bags of eyes were there already and secure. He imagined the furor if they were revealed prematurely. They would be claimed by the God-Emperor and he would have nothing for the Faythans. It would be a disaster.

The Eyes of Bel Nishani are mine by right! I braved the sea-worms! They are the future, and, one day, this whole planet could be mine!

"But would I want to live here?" he murmured to himself. "No ... I'd recruit mercenaries to harvest the riches for me. Let them endure the cold and the isolation." He smiled as another delicious thought entered his head: "They'd think I was going to pay them, but would I?" *Communication from this planet is limited; everything done here is utterly private, completely beyond censure ...*

The sensation of being watched faded. Immediately, he retrieved some of his personal belongings from Qalān and began to search them for a charm-sung lump of clear quartz.

Ah ha! he said when he found it. *I knew I had it somewhere.*

The crystal vibrated in his hand as if eager to do its job. He composed his mind and with a short string of notes activated the charm to shield his tent from psychic view. A second set of notes set an alarm that fizzed briefly against his exposed skin. Now he would be alerted if anyone tried to spy on his private space. The ensemble's range covered his tent and a small perimeter quite nicely.

He dusted off his palms. "Now I can sleep in peace!"

It was nearly midnight when he was woken by the alarm and realized Lind was waiting outside.

"Where have you been? I expected you earlier," he growled.

She hesitated. "I … I was busy. The others were watching. I couldn't get away."

He sneered. "I can read you as if you're my slave already. The God-Emperor himself designed the slave collars and instigated their use. Does that make the pretty silver links the will of El? They sever spirit from soul … how you will writhe! Bow before you enter!"

She made a sullen bow. The hatred in her eyes was almost as exciting as his vision of her collared. He grabbed the base of her braid and pulled her close.

I am your emperor, he said. *You want to live, don't you?* He made her head nod up and down. "Yess …" *Perhaps I will kill my wife and marry you instead.*

"El would never bless such a union," she whispered.

He smiled a cruel smile and pulled her face close to his own. "What makes you think I would want the Blessing of El?"

Lind closed her eyes, ready to endure what she must.

Or perhaps I should just kill you.

"Kill me?"

"It would be so simple," said Duvät Gok, "and so easy to hide. No close relatives? Who would receive your sad little death-cry, Lind? Who would care? Huldar rejected you. He'd be happy to have you gone so he can –"

"No … please!" Lind cried. "I'll keep you happy … I'll do as you say!

She gasped as the Overlord pushed her away.

"Pay attention," he said. "When we're done here, I have a task for you. It concerns Andel of Trianog and a certain stone – but I don't want her to know that I'm interested. Understand?"

RETREAT

Following the summer solstice, the global winter's relentless advance began more quickly than anticipated. On the Northern Shelf, bitter gales scoured the tents of the Uri'madu with hail and sleet that quickly turned to snow. Temperatures could plummet within seconds. Each day their range grew more limited. No one went anywhere alone or unplanned.

On their final day, the Uri'madu awoke to a campsite encased in ice and their door-flaps frozen shut. After breakfast, leather drummed as they beat the ice from their tents before packing them for their return south.

The marquee was last to come down and Huldar paused to watch. The baring of the hearth was always a poignant moment for him, as if a trust had been violated.

Andel crouched nearby, sorting geological samples into containers and labeling them with care. When she sensed his attention, he tipped his head in the slightest of gestures toward the beach.

She smiled and with an equally tiny nod, agreed to his suggestion.

On the quiet of the shore, she watched the horizon with narrowed eyes. Behind them, skies were dark, but to the south the sun was still shining. In the background they heard faint laughter as the demolition of their campsite continued.

Andel turned from her scrutiny of the seas and crouched to study the shingle on the beach. As he hunkered down to see what she was doing, his long, fair plait fell forward and danced in a sudden gust.

With one hand, Andel held her cloak firmly closed. The other stirred the air above a group of ice-worn pebbles as she pushed them to and fro into piles on either side. Whether her mind followed the gestures or vice versa, he couldn't be sure.

At last, a single pebble remained exposed against the rock. Andel studied it for a moment, then lifted her finger to levitate it neatly into her upturned palm. The stone's finely pitted surface was marked with alternating stripes like the shadows of claws.

She nudged it around her palm with her index finger. "It's strange, isn't it?"

"Umm …" He peered at the object in her hand. "The stone?"

She looked up. "Rock responds well to both force of mind and power of voice, but some things listen better to one or the other, not both. It's as if all things," she waved her free hand around her, "all these rocks and clouds and waves, all have life and make choices – just like you and I."

Huldar was captivated by the intelligence in her sandy brown eyes, vertical pupils round-edged and dark with mystery. As the sky dimmed beneath a lazy cloud, the light of her Tsemkar fell softly on delicate cheeks. Her slight build and airy fragility made him long to shield her from the oncoming weather, yet when she was divining, power coursed through her bones and she walked as if imbued with the life of the planet itself.

For a long heartbeat she returned his gaze, then she bent again to the pebble nestling in her palm.

"Yet the same planetary energies flow through all things," she said. She breathed onto it to brighten the colors then slowly traced her middle finger over its surface.

With a small, secret smile, Andel closed her hand around the pebble. Her Tsemkar glowed again and the stony shingle clattered back into place. She looked at him and it was as if she met his soul with a glimpse of her own. When she stood to return to camp, Huldar followed, still mute, wishing he could think of something to say.

In his pocket, he toyed with the opalized shell she had given him. Night after night he had picked at the dull stone that encased it and eventually the intricate ghost of a long-dead sea creature had been revealed in lacy filaments of opal that shone with all the colors of fire. With great care, he'd fashioned a leather clasp styled after the House Rune of Leth, just as his father had taught him. But the giving of such a gift was fraught with meaning. Tingling senses told him that Andel of Trianog welcomed his attention, but it was vital their small party remained harmonious. With many months of exploration still ahead and Lind still so sad, perhaps it was not a good idea to give her the opal just yet. But his heart raced as he walked behind her and the leather thong of the necklace tangled in his fingers as if refusing to be released.

All done, boss! Casco called out. *Ready when you are.*

Andel turned. *Thanks for the break,* she said, *it was just what I needed.*

She left with a smile, but her veil was tight and he sensed a wisp of disappointment. He desperately wanted to tell her of his feelings, but the time never seemed right. He fingered the opal in his pocket.

Casco came and stood beside him, watching as Andel made her way back to her collection of samples.

Give it to her! he said. *Get the agony over with! What's the worst that could happen?*

The worst? Huldar imagined her small hand pressing the opal back into his own. Her expression pitying. Worse still would be the disruption within their group. Lind's battered pride, team members taking sides …

That's an extreme projection and you know it, Casco said. *And Lind isn't the type to hold grudges.*

Huldar was about to answer, but when tent leathers began to flap free he ran toward the marquee.

"Ronnin!" he yelled. "Quick! Catch it!"

Casco shook his head as he followed. *Later,* he said. *You and I are going to talk this through!*

READY TO LOVE

The Uri'madu returned to the Southern Archipelago as planned, then, when snow started falling in earnest, they hurried back to the Eastern Foothills. There, the extended summer was slower to fade, but inevitably the weather turned and the cold caught up with them again.

On the western side of the continent, the shoreline receded fast as the ocean was locked in ice. Huldar took a last look at a massive iceberg trapped in the freeze and turned to leave. The ground crunched beneath his feet. Around him, hoarfrost hung from withered vegetation as if pretending to the life it had stolen. His breath steamed as he entered the portal, but as he stepped through it, the cloud vanished. Warmer air relaxed the skin of his face, and instead of ice he walked on mud. The campsite was only one hundred paces away, but his boots squelched in the heavy going.

Easy to see where the portals are, he thought. *Just follow the slush!*

As he paused to survey the savannah below, his gaze followed the shallow ridgelines of the stony dunes. Although the endless plains had been a desolate desert when the team had returned, at least it had been dry and warm. The water retained in Bush and Topper's cisterns had seemed ample at the time and work had continued. But as the dry season stretched on, water had become scarce. Soaring daytime temperatures made the lifeless gravel shimmer, but with sundown the air chilled, and at night the ravenous cold sucked the heat from their bodies. Now the rains had turned to sleet and the Uri'madu were ready to return to the Central Continent.

Andel's tent was close to the path. Earlier, she had been writing notes about samples and findings, but now she stood with one hand shading her eyes as she gazed at the faded grassland, while the other rested on her sagging guy-ropes. She acknowledged his approach, but did not turn from the view.

"After the drought broke, I could feel the energy in the flowers," she said. "The fire of life, their joy of being – but now they are gone." She turned to him. "Do plants have more awareness than we believe? Does Asheru sing them home to bathe in the Breath when they die?"

"Maybe ..."

He looked at her poorly tensioned guy-ropes. Water pooled in the bowing leather panels. How was it she could feel their surroundings with almost the same acuity as his own and divine with such power, yet maintenance of simple tent charms seemed beyond her?

"Perhaps I could sing these tighter for you," he offered. "I know you have a lot to do before tomorrow's move."

"Thank you," she said. "That would be most kind, Shamkarun Huldar."

She smiled and he felt his heart skip a beat, then with a quick nod, she turned and strode toward the work she had started. He liked the way her hair glinted red in the afternoon light. While the sun was shining she preferred to work in the open air, and he saw rows of containers and chunks of rock spread out in neat lines.

He rested his hand on the rope where hers had been and watched her bustle over her samples. Her fine fingers traced invisible lines in the air as small pieces of rock flew from box to box. Levitating several at once was a complex task, and the fingers seemed to help her keep track. Then her directing hand paused and the rocks waited in mid-air as she rifled through a sheaf of papers. "Got you!" she murmured. Huldar smiled when he saw a highly detailed list, similar to an accountant's ledger.

"For a Trianogi," he said, "you have a Cantori-like obsession with order."

A Cantori! Andel poked her fingers at him.

He grasped his ribs and twisted his mouth in mock pain. *All right! I'm doing it now.* He pretended to limp as he turned to sing her guy-ropes tighter, but the notes he needed were slow to come.

We're moving back to the Central Continent tomorrow … He pictured tropical sunshine, cool drinks and brightly colored vegetation.

Yes, I know, she replied. The flights of her samples resumed.

And all our tents will be dismantled, he continued. His heart raced. It was hard to keep his mind veiled in a polite state of calm.

Andel kept working.

Perhaps I could take yours down for you instead of fixing it? he blundered on. *You could share mine ...*

Andel's samples froze mid-flight once more as she turned to look at him. Her face revealed little. He waited. Suddenly it seemed she had been silent for too long. His mind raced ... He had been absent for long stretches without contacting her. Why did he think she would be interested in him? They had hardly spoken in months! He had been too forward. He was a fool and Casco had been wrong – but then her veil began to glimmer. A shy smile came to her lips and he could think of nothing else.

"Well, take it down then," she said.

"At once, my lady!" He jumped to obey before she could change her mind.

That night as they gathered for the evening meal, nothing seemed out of the ordinary. Bush and Topper joked about the food and Arko jumped to Tam's defense. Ronnin and Nachiel played ashut in a quiet corner, Lind discussed herbal remedies with Ubaid and Alis, while Sari and Andel chatted by the fire about what changes they might find on the Central Continent. For Huldar, every moment dragged unbearably, yet part of him wanted it to.

It was not uncommon for sexual encounters to occur while on assignment, and as fully trained Naghari Healers both Ubaid and Alis were well versed in the twenty-seven rules of touch. But it was rare for him – very rare.

He watched as Lind joined Andel and Sari. For a moment, their eyes met. The glance seemed knowing but her true emotions were tightly held, yet when Sari said something that made the three giggle, the tone of Andel's voice drew him again. For Lind's sake, he tried not to stare, but Andel's presence burned against his soul. The life force within him seemed to have doubled and was only barely contained by his skin.

Said something to her, haven't you? Casco brushed his fingers in the air. *Your haze …*

Huldar closed his eyes and regained control of his psychic emissions. *Better?*

Casco nodded and returned to his conversation with Gento and Cobar. Across the room, Ubaid met his eyes with a wry wink. Huldar smiled and a wave of humor compressed his lungs. He was behaving like a young one at first awakening. Then a wisp of sadness spilled from beneath Lind's veil and his mood levelled.

Soon afterward, he left the marquee for the safety of his tent and surveyed the interior, wondering if it was neat enough. With soft voice he tweaked its screens into perfect order. He didn't want Andel to think he was a poor housekeeper. A simple, collapsible desk held some interesting seedpods, the gossamer wing of a slug, a piece of ice-worn bone and some bright blue lizard scales from the Southern Archipelago. These were illuminated by a light-crystal enclosed in a web of fine curving branches. It had been grown by a friend on Haaseen, the Rukhish homeworld.

As he straightened his bedroll he remembered that he had no spare pillow so he took the fur-lined blanket from the top and rolled it into a tube. First he doubled it over and put it beside the pillow he already had, then he unfolded it and took the pillow away but it still didn't look right and besides, if the night became much colder they might need the extra warmth on the bed. He shook it out again and laughed at himself. Fancy inviting the female of his dreams then asking her to bring her own bedding! He could sleep without a pillow.

He scanned the marquee. She was still there. Perhaps she wouldn't come …

With a sigh, he pulled a book from Qalān and read the same line several times before closing it again.

When at last she left the gathering and stepped out into the night, his finely tuned senses came to life. He waited by the central tent pole and tried not to appear nervous.

She scratched the leather of the door-flap. "It's me, Andel."

He froze inside, unable to think how to answer. Why couldn't he just laugh and say, "Of course it is!" as if she were Casco, or another friend? After a brief pause, she stepped in without waiting for a reply.

Their eyes met, and suddenly he was trying not to laugh.

Her cheeks colored. "I brought my own, just in case."

She followed his glance toward the empty space at the end of the bed and grinned. He watched her place her pillow beside his, then floundered, trying to think of something suave to say. It was as if his brain had ceased to function. Then she stood in front of him, and for a while they just looked at each other.

Her mind brushed his with tentative contact. *I haven't done this before*, she said, *not here.*

Neither have I, he replied. *Well, I have … well, no, what I mean is …* but his words turned to mush again, lost in the fire as their hazes touched.

She reached for his hands.

I thought you'd say no … he said.

Andel shook her head lightly. *You hoped I'd say yes, and I have.* She stepped close and slid his hands inside her shirt and held them against her breasts. Skin to skin, her touch was almost overwhelming. A flood of subliminal messages poured between them. Without thinking, he bent his head to kiss her. She was so small and sweet, he was afraid to overwhelm her, but then she reached behind his head and pulled him down, and he kissed her again, harder.

The Mark on her forehead glowed softly and a light pressure tickled against his abdomen as the laces of his trousers pulled themselves apart. She smiled and searched downward with fingers inquisitive and warm.

How often had he imagined this moment, alone with her at last? He wanted to please her more than he had wanted anything in his life, but all the moments he had fantasized – what he would say, what he would do – all those charmed moments fled as the real charm took hold.

Her trousers dropped to reveal lithe and shapely legs and he met her gaze again, still mute with wonder. She laughed and drew him toward the bed. Her eyes would not release him. Her breathing was as ragged as his. With a gentle shove, she pushed him onto the fur-lined blanket and held him down.

Time later for play ... she whispered, and all vestiges of awkwardness were vaporized as instinct took hold.

Much later, wrapped in the warmth of his blankets, Huldar gazed down at her sleeping face and touched her cheek, softly so as not to wake her. Her features were delicate, he decided, but not pretty. Her ears stuck out a little too far, and her nose definitely had character ... but she was herself, and she was beautiful. The workings of her mind were an utter fascination – thoughts wound and twisted as if every surface of every single thing needed to be examined and assessed in a web of connections most could never imagine.

Beyond the campsite, the silence of the frozen night was complete. Nothing moved beneath the crystal shroud of ice. He lay down and closed his arms around her, holding her safe at last.

You are my truth, she murmured.

And you, mine. He kissed her hair and let her warmth seep through him as the rhythms of her mind returned to a deep and trusting sleep.

RETURN TO THE CENTRE

The Uri'madu left behind a crisp dry frost on the Eastern Plains, and stepped back through the portal to the Central Continent campsite. There they found a green wilderness where their encampment had once been. Five pronged bushes with floppy red fruit that hung from each point gave the place a festival air. Bright orange slugs browsed between green nodules. Multi-legged crawlers cricked and clacked while waving fluorescent paddles in defense of their territories. Thick moss coated the tree trunks with waving webs of sporangia.

Casco scratched his head. "Are we sure this is where it was?"

"Has to be," said Huldar.

"Looks like we were never here," Gento said. "Can't even see the escarpment."

"Or the stones that mark the Djan'rū."

Huldar listened for a moment and was relieved to feel it still resonating faintly. "Don't worry, I can find it easy enough."

"Talk about not leaving a mark!" Casco noticed a faint trail and pushed between the waving strap-tree fronds to see where it went. "Whose tent would've been here?" he called.

"The Gok, remember?" Nachiel rolled his eyes. "Hiding from the weather. Stayed here longer than the rest of us when we moved across to the eastern continent."

"More than two years ago by Giahn standard," said Tam.

"I know! Seems like forever, and here we are, running from the weather again."

Huldar smiled with Andel as she studied their surroundings. "I like the way the strap-trees wave, and the bug-things with the paddles? Aren't they cute! I hope they don't bite."

"I hope they don't bite," Sari echoed. "And I'm not sure I like the look of that bubbly stuff on the rocks. Isn't that where we used to sit sometimes?"

"Let me look at it," Nachiel said. He leaned over the pearly nodules and reached out to touch one.

Gento seemed about to say something until Huldar gave a mischievous shake of his head.

With a small *pop* the nodule released its payload of dusty-smelling spores, setting off an explosive chain reaction.

Nachiel jumped back and fanned his hands about. "Ugh! Right in my face!"

"I'd steer clear of that stuff if I were you," Huldar said sagely.

"You should have known it'd do that!" Gento said. "In the ravines – you drew pictures of it for Breath's sake!"

Casco sighed. "Put everything back where it was, boss?"

"You're right." Huldar looked around again. "Day's wearing on. If we collect the critters first – I think there's a safe space for them over there." He pointed out a gully to the west. "Cobar and Gento, could you work with Casco to clear the vegetation? And you two, if you could check the cisterns please?"

"Right you are, boss!"

As Bush and Topper pushed their way through the thickets, Andel smiled. "At least the sun is shining. Critter patrol? Let's get to it then, Sari. Something else I'll be able to tell my father about when I get home."

"Breath of life, would you look at this one?" Sari said. A black-and-red-striped creature squirmed as she held it up by one of its many legs. Outraged clicks emanated from yellow medallions spaced evenly along its body. "All that noise!"

"Here, I'll hold the bag open," Andel said.

When Sari popped it inside, the creature began a strident distress call, triggering its brethren to screech in deafening sympathy. Andel closed the drawstring tight, but the sound continued.

By midday, the site was cleared and the tents had started to go up, and by nightfall, hearths were glowing, dinner was cooking, and the Uri'madu had settled back in. Huldar accepted a mug of Besh from Casco and sat with his long legs outstretched toward the fire. They looked up as the marquee door swooshed open.

"Here he is!" Casco muttered. "The invisible Overlord."

There was a sub-audible groan as Duvät Gok walked across the carpets. His polished boots made barely a sound.

"Thank you for your help today," Huldar said.

"My duties do not include menial tasks," the Overlord replied. He hovered at the bench while Tam took his plate.

"You call this food?" he said. "I can't wait till we get back to civilization! What's that?" He pointed to a red sauce Tam had made from the five-prong fruits. "No ... more of that. At least I know what it is ... no, and the green one too."

"There you are, my lord," Tam said politely.

Duvät turned to Huldar. "Are the portals re-established?"

"They are." Huldar nodded.

The Overlord picked at his meal as if it were made from week-old leftovers. He winced as beyond the campsite hundreds of segmented refugees sang on in strident protest.

"I trust you are aware of the importance of completing the assessment of the gold deposits?" he said loudly.

"Yes," replied Huldar.

"And the tin on the northern ranges?"

"Yes. And the darsite on the southern flanks."

"Quite so." The Overlord pursed his lips. "But you neglected to properly investigate the inner shores on our first visit to this continent, a situation which must now be rectified without delay. I await your reports!"

He looked with disgust at his half-finished plate of food. "I can't eat this! Breath be praised our confinement on this dreadful world is nearing its end." He clanked the plate back onto the kitchen bench and strode from the room.

"Neglected? Did you hear that?" Casco snorted.

"Nearing its end?" said Sari. "Anyone might think he wasn't enjoying himself!" She turned to their cook and offered her empty bowl. "The food's very tasty, Tam, and he should appreciate the trouble you've gone to. In fact, I'd like some more, if there's enough?"

"Plenty more," Tam said. His expression relaxed into its habitual smile as he doled out a second helping.

Later that evening Huldar stared into the flames and nursed another mug of ale. Andel's presence was a warmth against his soul. Without consciously thinking about it, he was always aware of her position in the room. Tomorrow he had to go west, but Andel would stay here to work on the gold deposits in the long valley below the campsite. The longing to hold her was a physical ache, but she had set up her tent in its usual place and had given no indication she would be visiting him that night. Had he disappointed her? Perhaps, as he had feared, his feelings were not returned. But then her voice slid into his mind and his anxieties melted like morning frost in the sun.

Why so sad?

I won't be seeing you – for months perhaps. He knew he sounded sulky, and perhaps he was.

She paused as if considering. *Then we'll have to be creative.*

Creative? he echoed.

She sent an enigmatic smile and returned to her conversation with Nachiel.

That night, he lay in his bed and pressed his nose against his pillow to inhale the faint, sweet remnants of her scent. After so many years, why did it suddenly bother him to sleep alone? Then he felt her presence tickling at his mind and his eyes opened wide. He lowered his defenses and she swirled like a breeze through his inner self.

This is different! he said. A tangy scent wafted with her, and a fleeting annoyance that he could not quite place it.

He sensed her delight.

Hmm. Just an idea I thought might work, she answered.

Is it ziquarra? he asked. *I can feel your hand on my chest as if you were here.*

There is Hermes in our family lineage, so maybe. A great-great-grandfather. Do you like it?

Oh yes! he assured her.

Then let's see what we can do …

At first, as her psychic touch explored his body he found it pleasant but ephemeral, but as she gained confidence, he began to groan with delight as places of pleasure inside and out were aroused to exquisite life.

I don't think that's in the twenty-seven rules of touch! he gasped.

I'd be surprised if it was, she replied, *and maybe a bit disappointed.*

The next morning at breakfast, Lind claimed she had 'things to do' and left the tent early. Andel grinned at him over a warm mug. There was a wicked twinkle in her eye and before he had time to look away his cheeks had creased in an answering smile. The joy of their encounter was still with him long after he'd stepped through the portal with Gento and Nachiel to continue their exploration of the western sector.

ANDEL AND LIND

Andel watched as Huldar stepped through the portal. She knew she would miss his physical presence, but her experiment had proved a great success and the thought of honing her skills with more such adventures sent tingles through her body. Her neck prickled and she turned to meet Lind's sad gaze. The angel's haze seemed quite fragile, and Andel's heart went out to her. It seemed strange to see the brash explorer so at odds. They had barely spoken since the 'rescue' and Sari was quite concerned by her increasing isolation.

"It's as if there's a great weight on her mind," Sari had confided. "But she won't let me see what it is. It's as if something has made her afraid."

But what could be so frightening to the normally resilient angel? Was it her pride? Did she fear that the Uri'madu would laugh if they knew the rescue was staged? Or if they knew Huldar had rejected her? Andel shook her head. The close-knit team might joke around, but none of them would be so unkind.

She smiled warmly and walked toward her, but when she reached out, Lind flinched away.

"Don't!" she breathed forcefully. "Please, don't touch me."

Andel stepped back. "I'm sorry," she stammered.

Lind held her hands up. "No, it's not you. Really, it's not!" She looked around. "It's not any of you."

"What then?" Andel could feel her desperate unhappiness, and Sari was right, there was also fear. "What is it, Lind? I'm worried about you. Sari is worried about you." She averted her gaze, embarrassed to ask, but the need to know was strong. "Is it …?"

"You and Huldar?" Lind shook her head. "I knew it would happen from the moment I met you. Remember? I was so jealous – couldn't find anything nice to say. But then you saved us from the mudslide … lahar … and it's not you. It's not your fault." She took a deep breath and her haze regained some of its usual structure. "Please don't worry," she said. "I can take care of myself."

Andel recalled the time during their communications window, the odd exchange she had noticed. "Is it something Duvät Gok has said? Or done?"

Lind startled. "No!" She glanced across her shoulder as if the Overlord might be listening. "Of course not! Why would you ask me that?"

Andel shrugged. "Just something I saw … it was nothing."

"No! Of course it was nothing!" Lind said. "Slimy kalla's a monster whoever he talks to."

"A monster?"

Lind hesitated for a moment. "Well, he's very unpleasant."

"Unpleasant is an understatement!" Andel smiled into Lind's eyes and hoped her projection of love and care would make a difference. "We have to make a move soon and start on our new projects, but would you have time to share a cup of tea with me?"

Lind sighed and started walking with her.

"Nothing like the taste of warm …" Andel stopped to think "… dar-leaf – that's your favorite?"

Lind nodded. "But not yours! Sari tells me all the time: 'It's *galano* for Lady Andel!' … And here she is."

Andel smiled as Sari joined them. "Sari! We were just going into the marquee for a last cup of tea before we disappear into the wilds. You too?"

"Into the wilds?" The older angel beamed. "Lovely."

As they sat down with their warm mugs, Lind remained withdrawn.

"I've been thinking of going to Hesh when we get back," Andel said. "But I'd love to see more of Lentath."

"Lentath?" Sari beamed. "You and Hu–" She gave a guilty glance at Lind then continued more quietly. "You could stay with me."

"Do you know any charm-singers, Lady Andel?" Lind looked at her expectantly.

"Charm-singers?" Andel hesitated. "I don't know. Only Huldar, really. Why do you ask?"

Sari chimed in, "My sister's husband, Dursin, he's a charm-singer, remember? You met him once."

"Oh yes," Lind said.

Andel's shoulders lifted. "Do you need someone to sing a charm for you? Maybe Huldar could help?"

"No, I don't need one sung," Lind said. She studied her tea for a moment before admitting, "Duvät Gok asked me."

"Duvät Gok needs a charm?" Andel tried to understand.

"No … He asked me about a charm, a beacon charm." Lind shrugged. "I don't know why."

Something tickled Andel's memory, then was gone. "I can't say I know anything about charm-singing, Lind," she said. "What a strange thing for him to ask you about."

"Hmm, it was, wasn't it?" Lind's hands clasped and unclasped, fingers tying themselves into knots. "He seems to think that one of us has one."

"Is there a law against that?" Sari said. "Who does he think he is? We can have whatever charms we want! It's in the rules. It's not for him to say!"

"I have a beacon stone," Andel said. "I just remembered. Huldar gave it to me."

"Can I see it?"

"I suppose so," Andel replied. "It's in Qalān … yes, here it is." The rounded pebble nestled neatly into her palm. "He said if I had it with me he could find me anywhere."

"Find you anywhere?" Sari nodded.

Lind turned her head as if suddenly quite interested in her tea. Andel blushed and put the charm-stone away.

Lind got to her feet. "I must get going."

"I'm sorry, Lind," Andel said. "Please, stay a little longer?"

"Thanks for the company." Lind smiled valiantly. "I know you're worried, but it's nothing, really. Just something I have to work out for myself."

Sari held her gaze. "You know where we are."

"I know," Lind said. She sauntered away with a touch of her usual confidence in her stride.

THE PREDATOR

Duvät closed his eyes and scanned the campsite. Three people remained. Tam was at the hearth, preparing another experimental dish with the local fruits, Arko was in the work tent assessing what was left of their supplies, and Lind was with Arko, asking him for extra supplies to take to the healers, wherever they were. It didn't matter to him so long as he could get to the beaching shore undetected. Even though there had been no fresh waves of sea-worms wiggling up the sands for some time now, the thought of a missed opportunity spurred him to keep checking.

He pulled a bag of eyes from his pocket and jiggled the contents again. To him, the rainbow light shone like coins – rich golden imperials. He now had fifteen bags of high-quality gems stowed in Qalān and two of the inferior. Who knew what wealth they would bring? He stroked an orb with one fleshy finger before lifting it to his palm.

Lind!

She startled when he called. He savored her pulse of dread and caressed the shining gem again. In only eighty-two more days – not that he was counting – the navigator would come and this ordeal would be over.

"What should I do with my little plaything?" he crooned to the crystal in his hand. "What should we do about Lind?"

The hilt of his knife felt cold against his fingers. *How would it feel to kill an annangi?* he asked himself. She was strong, but only an angel. He had seen second-hand vision of the collared ones kept by the God-Emperor: silent and respectful, obedient to the slightest whim. He imagined they could be killed quite simply. Just a thought, a push, and their souls could be severed from their pliant bodies. Or he could make them stand and wait for the knife to descend … he would push it in slowly, savoring every agonizing moment. Enslaved minds were completely open, unable to be shielded. He could absorb their suffering and revel in it, much as he had with the sea-worms. But how much more powerful would the anguish of a dying annangi be?

With the riches from the sale of his Eyes of Bel Nishani he would be able to purchase many slaves and many more to replace them. But Lind? If he let her live, she would spoil his plans.

There was a muffled scratch against his door. He returned the gem and pushed the bag into his pocket.

Enter! He tried to make his mind-voice sound as regal and portentous as the God-Emperor's might.

Lind sidled through the door-flap and bowed. He grasped her mind with his own. *Come closer, slave!*

"Stop it!" she gasped. With a surprising show of mental dexterity, she shrugged off his hold. He slapped her. A red welt appeared across her cheek, but now she was expecting him, it would take extra effort to regain control. Angrily, he lifted his hand to slap her again.

Wait! Please! she said. *I have news.*

He stayed his fist, suddenly curious. *What news?*

About the charm-stone. You asked me to find out for you.

"The charm-stone?" He'd almost forgotten about the mysterious beacon. "Well?" he demanded. "Out with it!"

"Andel has it, Lady Andel."

He lifted his arm again. "I know that!"

Lind cringed and covered her face with her hands. "She got it from Huldar …" Her voice trailed sadly away.

"Oh," he sneered, "is it upset about betraying its leader? Where did he get it?"

"I don't know, I don't!" she cried.

There were tears, stupid tears. Anger swept through him again, so deep it was hard to contain. What right had Huldar to thwart him? Snooping about in his paperwork, entering his private space uninvited, and now this! It was too much.

"Leave me!" he yelled.

Lind scuttled away like the insect he thought she was. *What now*, he wondered? How to counter this new threat to his plans? Why had Huldar said nothing? Why had he given the beacon to the diviner? What did she know? Questions, questions, questions – and how could he ask them? If he did, they would know. And if they knew, they would expect him to share, or betray him to the Guild, or both. His life would be over.

With a roar of frustration, he swept his arm across his desk. Papers scattered. A ceramic bust of the God-Emperor flew through the air and shattered against the tent-pole. He picked up his chair and threw it as far as he could. It landed with a thump against his bed.

What am I to do? he raged.

Huldar must know about the eyes, or he would have said something. He was saving the information so he could tell the guild as soon as they got back to the safety of Giahn. All the sideways looks, the veiled threats, the pitying glances … what a fool he'd been! And the diviner. What luck had she bought? Would she and Huldar stand together laughing as all his hope, as his very life was stripped away from him?

He rested his forehead against the tent-pole and tried to think. *How can I gain the advantage?*

Huldar did not know that he knew. *The element of surprise?* Duvät clasped the hilt of his knife. He could sneak up on the Lethian at night while he was sleeping … but the death-cry. Where would Huldar's death-cry go? Who would hear him? His parents were dead, but he had a brother. What if he sent his cry to Arian Leth himself? Everyone knew what a hothead the Leader of House Leth was. He would never sit by if he knew.

Think, Duvät, think!

He could take the diviner as a hostage. Lind could lure her. He would kill her … kill them both if Huldar revealed what he knew. If he could just keep the Lethian quiet until the Faythans were paid! Breath's Design! It wasn't fair!

A finger scratched against his door.

"Lord Duvät Gok," Tam said. "I heard noises. Is everything all right?"

"Of course!" he snapped. "One of those confounded bug things. I thought you people had removed them all."

"I'm sorry, Overlord. Would you like me to come and remove this one for you?"

Duvät looked at the upturned chair, the remains of the ceramic God-Emperor and the loose papers now littering his floor. "No need," he said. "This one's dead."

LIND

Lind ran from Duvät Gok's tent and stood trembling before the southern portal. She had to get away, but it took a few moments to steady her emotions to safely sing. As she stepped through, it flashed through her mind that she didn't know exactly where she had sent herself, but then she recognized a small clearing not far from the healers' campsite. A few paces from the portal, she slumped to the ground. She could not stop crying. Soon she heard running footsteps and Ubaid kneeled beside her. His mind probed gently. *What's wrong, child?*

Lind buried her head in her hands and sobbed. She tried to answer, but no words would come. What had she done? The Overlord's slap still stung her cheek. Her body would never be clean again, and neither would her soul.

"Lind?" The voice of Alis was soft with kindness and care, but the love the Naghari offered was too far from what she deserved. Some things could never be healed.

"I have to speak to Huldar," she whispered, her lips thick and numb from crying.

"Here, drink this," said Alis. "Karientos."

The astringent aroma brought a fresh wave of tears. Alis held the pale green liquid closer.

As she accepted, Lind tried to hide the tremor in her hand but her efforts only made it worse. She drank quickly.

"Why do you need to speak to Huldar?" Ubaid said softly. "He is in a relationship with Andel now. I think you should try to accept that."

"It's not that!" she cried. "I've done something – something he should know about."

"Can it wait?" Ubaid said. "Your voice holds too much emotion. You should not try to sing through any more portals until you have regained some calm."

"It's too dangerous," Alis agreed. "You should wait until you are feeling better. If the notes are wrong you could get lost, end up anywhere ... or worse."

"Or let one of us take you?" Ubaid added.

"No! It's personal."

The healers exchanged a glance. Ubaid's understanding expression was exasperating.

"But not in that way!" she cried, or was it? If only he had loved her! Fresh tears rolled down her cheeks. The calming effects of the karientos seeped through her mind, but her eyes still wept. She struggled to her feet. At any moment the Overlord might descend upon Huldar's camp, yelling and screaming, demanding answers because of what she had told him. She had to get there first.

"I have to tell him everything ..."

"Lind, wait!" Ubaid called, "Do you even know the way?"

Lind stepped into the portal despite Ubaid's warning. Her senses dulled momentarily as the planetary network engaged with her, asking where she wanted to go. Now was the time for the notes to be sung. There was no need to voice them loudly, just a whisper would do, but as she opened her lips she realized Ubaid had been correct and she was not sure. Her voice faltered. She tried to redirect her song to the campsite, but with a sudden wrench the barely tamed energy took her in its grip.

She felt pounding pressure against her eardrums, but there was no noise. Colors flashed past then faded into white. Just white. She waited, but nothing changed. No exit appeared. What if it never let her go? She had heard this could happen – how the unwary or unschooled could be caught in Qalān and never seen again. It was thought they died a lingering death of hunger and thirst, their soul trapped forever beyond the Breath.

"Let me go!" she screamed.

The sound made Qalān jump. It shook her like a predator shakes fresh prey. She had to calm down. She had to think. Would another song work if she sang it now?

With a hesitant voice she started to sing the notes for the encampment on the desert plains. The portal gave a violent lurch but there was no release. Heavy sobs bubbled from her chest. She stared in desperation at a thousand shades of white. She tried to beat her fists against it but there was nothing solid to impact upon. When she collapsed, there was no sensation of landing, no feeling of location. She hugged her knees and rocked back and forth. This was the first lesson any child ever learned about portals: never to use one unless you are certain that you know the song of your destination and can sing it fluently. This was why emotional control was so important. Why hadn't she listened?

Qalān was outside their everyday dimension. No one could hear her call and no one could ever find her. It was impossible, even if they tried. Empty bonds, the connections of her life, flapped free. She cried again in hopeless sobs while Qalān bucked and shook, uncaring.

.

HULDAR

Huldar paused in his work and focused inward, listening intently. Gento and Nachiel exchanged a glance and waited.

"What is it?" Nachiel asked.

"Message from Ubaid," Huldar replied. "Lind's on her way here."

"On her way here?" Nachiel scratched his head. "Why is she coming here?"

Gento rolled his eyes. "What, are you Sari now, repeating everything?

"Don't be nasty!" Nachiel said. "You love Sari. We all do."

"He didn't say," Huldar went on. "Only that she was upset about something."

"Hmm, well. She's been upset about something since … for months now. Nothing you can do about that. You won't let it come between you and Lady Andel, will you?"

Huldar frowned. "I don't see how that's –"

"You must be the luckiest person alive," Nachiel said. "Lady Andel? She's so pretty, and clever and, oh! Did I tell you –"

"For Breath's sake!" said Gento. "Don't you ever stop nattering on? A whole planet and I'm stuck here with you!"

Huldar paid their bickering little heed; tempers were often short at the tail end of an assignment. He was more concerned with Lind's imminent arrival and finding out what had upset her. In Ubaid's message he had seen her crying. The last time he had seen Lind cry like that was when Joumelät Enna had died.

With a soft sigh, he returned to his work. Whatever Lind had to say, he would deal with it when she arrived.

He stared at the six-winged creature lying supine in his hand, temporarily stunned by a well-placed song. It wasn't insectile, mammalian, or even reptilian. He moved it to and fro to get a closer look. Its body was covered in flattened hairs, almost like leaves, yet soft and pliant. How did it coordinate its flight? Did all six wings move independently? With careful fingertips he took hold of one wing and moved it up and down.

The creature stiffened and stabbed down with its mouth parts. Huldar gasped with pain. He dumped the strange beast in the open box at his feet and sucked the side of his palm. A quick inner scan showed no toxins, but he was angry with himself for letting his guard down.

Nachiel laughed and shared a glance with Gento. "Perhaps his mind's not on the job!"

He shook it off the bright red blood that beaded from the wound and accepted the wad of spider silk Gento fished from their first-aid kit. The creature in the box buzzed its wings as if to fly off, no doubt quite satisfied with the quality of its defenses, but Huldar released a minute blast of sound that stunned it again.

"Not so fast, my touchy little friend," he murmured, and picked it up once more.

The afternoon wore on and Lind had not arrived.

"Probably gone off somewhere by herself … she does that when she's upset," Nachiel said.

Huldar nodded. "Sometimes."

"She'll be here when she's ready, won't she Gento?"

The Rukh groaned. "How would I know? She'd probably get here quicker if she thought she'd get a word in around your flapping mouth!"

As if on cue, an icy breeze whiffled through the trees. "I think we should finish up for the day," Huldar said.

Nachiel made a face at Gento. "Oh no! Your turn to cook," he said waspishly. "If Lind knew that, she'd make certain she didn't turn up till tomorrow!"

"Enough!" Huldar snapped. "Let's go."

Gento glared down at Nachiel. "I'll make sure you get a double helping then."

"I said, enough!"

Gento grunted. Nachiel closed his mouth.

"Lind will get here when she does," Huldar said, "and if she's upset, I doubt your squabbling will help."

They returned to their tent and retired early to bed. Around them, the once luxuriant vegetation had started to feel the chill. The tap and rustle of brown-edged leaves was constant. Fruits and seeds loaded the branches of some plants, while others withdrew into the soil and rocks.

Andel brushed his mind with an affectionate caress, but she was exhausted and did not linger.

Images of Lind swam in his thoughts, but the familiar sense of her presence would not come.

If she needs a little privacy to work through her feelings, he thought, *I might only make things worse if I contact her.* He prided himself on his ability to hear and disentangle even the most complex of planetary songs, so how had he not known the depth of her attachment for him. How could it be that he had not heard her song? Yet Andel of Trianog wove music through his being in a way he could not ignore. It was less than a day since he'd seen her, but already his longing was an ache in his heart.

Next morning, the dim light of the newly risen sun shone weakly through translucent panels in the top of his tent. His breath made small clouds in front of his face. The familiar scent of little attar drifted from the campfire, but a quick scan told him Lind was still absent. Something was wrong.

He rolled out of bed and dressed quickly. Nachiel greeted him with a bowl of porridge and a mug of sweet tea.

Gento looked at him expectantly.

"You and Nachiel examine the fruits of these trees." He shared some images. "Notes and drawings. Tell me what's feeding from them." He washed down a mouthful of porridge with a swig of tea. "I'm going to visit Ubaid."

Nachiel shrugged. "She's probably still off sulking somewhere. You know how she is."

"No," Huldar said. "I can't sense her. She doesn't answer when I call. I don't know what to think."

Gento and Nachiel looked at each other. *Dead?*

Huldar didn't know how to answer. That he could not connect with her at all worried him very much. "I don't know," he said. "Maybe she's just too far away to hear me."

"She can't be dead," Nachiel said. "And it's mean of you to say so! She's too careful. And there are no predators here."

"Not that we've found," said Huldar.

Nachiel waved his bowl toward Gento. "Now you sound like him!"

"I don't know!" Huldar said. "She could be unconscious somewhere, or it could be that she's hiding for some reason, or … Alis and Ubaid. They were the last to see her."

"She has been very sad," Gento said slowly. "I hope the call of the Breath has not overwhelmed … but no. She loves us; we love her. She would never –"

"No! No!" Nachiel backed away. "She wouldn't do that. Whatever her problems were, the Uri'madu are her family! She would send her death-cry to us. She's just lost!"

"Peace, Nachiel," Huldar soothed. "I am worried, but I don't think she's dead. I'll tell you as soon as I find her."

He drank the last of his tea and headed for the healers' camp.

Ubaid and Alis ushered him into their tent.

"Yes, she was quite upset," Ubaid said. "I asked her to wait until she'd calmed down – gave her a mild sedative, but she wouldn't stay."

"Do you know why she was in such a state?" He paused. "I don't mean to pry, but it could help me understand, and maybe help me find her."

Ubaid's gaze was penetrating. "I don't think it was you," the healer said. "I can see that the thought worries you, but no, it was something more."

Huldar sighed, surprised at the level of relief Ubaid's words gave him. "Then what?"

Alis leaned forward. "We have come to believe that her lasting sadness has another cause, but she won't take us into her confidence."

"Could it be an illness?" Huldar suggested. "Something she ate? A poison?"

Ubaid frowned in thought. "It's possible, of course."

"You are healers." His tone was sharp. "Surely you would know?"

The Naghari glanced at each other. "It may have been something the Overlord said," Ubaid admitted. "I glimpsed his face on the surface of her mind, and she had a welt on her cheek."

"A hand-shaped welt," said Alis quietly.

"The Overlord?" Huldar looked in the direction of their base-camp, where he knew Duvät to be. Perhaps that was why she had been so determined to talk, but although the Overlord was detestable, he found it hard to believe he was capable of such violence.

"When we left camp, Lind stayed behind," Ubaid said.

"She was going to gather supplies then follow us," Alis added. "Maybe Tam or Arko will know something."

Outside, it had started to rain. Huldar pulled his hood over his head and trudged toward the portal. Back at base the sun strobed through racing clouds, and although the rain had not yet arrived, he could smell it in the air. Tam was inside the marquee as usual, reading by the cookfire. Arko was nearby, snoozing on a bed of plush cushions.

"Nice to see you hard at work!"

Arko woke with a start. "I have been!" he stammered. "The day-packs and kits are all checked, the supply packs and emergency supplies are all in order. I was just resting my eyes."

"Lind is missing," Huldar growled. "Do you remember when you saw her last?"

"She was having a cup of dar with Lady Andel and Sari," Tam answered.

"After that, she was in the supply tent," Arko said. "Gathered supplies for the healers and left."

Huldar nodded. "She made it to there but left soon after. They said she was upset."

"She was fine when she left the marquee," Tam said. "Better than she's been for a while. No offense, Lord Huldar."

"Arko?"

"She seemed a bit flustered. Stuffed the stores into Qalān – jars and such … maybe a little anxious, but I thought it was because she was in a hurry."

"Did she see the Overlord?" Huldar asked.

"The Overlord?" Tam and Arko shook their heads. "There were noises in his tent," Tam said. "I went to find out if he was all right."

"Thumping and such," Arko added.

Tam frowned. "He said there was a crawler and he'd killed it, poor thing. I didn't stay. The Gok disgusts me. Why he didn't just call us to catch it, I don't know. I offered, but it was too late."

"No sign of Lind?"

The two shook their heads. Tam shared his memory of the noises he had investigated, and it did sound as if Duvät Gok had been chasing something. There were no other voices or sounds of a struggle, but that was not conclusive evidence that Lind had not been there. It could have been that she was too frightened to make a sound, and her terror well screened. Something had caused her distress, and the only other person in camp at the time had been Duvät Gok.

The first drops of rain had begun to spatter the path as Huldar scratched on the Overlord's door. "A word, Duvät Gok, if you please."

"What is it?"

"Lind is missing," Huldar said. He waited, and eventually the door-flap parted. The Overlord scowled into the weather.

"Missing?" He blinked as if genuinely surprised.

Huldar's gaze narrowed. "The healers mentioned a welt on her cheek," he said. "Would you know anything about that?"

"A welt?" Duvät Gok shrugged. "An insect bite, perhaps?"

Huldar shook his head. "A blow. The mark was in the shape of a hand."

"What are you suggesting?" the Overlord snapped. "I know nothing about Lind or why she might be missing. I hope you find her soon. There's work to do, and less and less time in which to do it!"

Huldar looked at the Gok's meaty hands. The delicately painted fingernails were a travesty. The Overlord shrugged, but a ripple in his over-shiny veil seemed suspicious. It would be deeply satisfying to burrow beneath that smug exterior and find out what he knew, or had done, but such abilities were beyond Huldar's skill, and like it or not, Duvät Gok represented the Imperium. Without hard evidence, he could not force the issue.

As he turned to leave, he glimpsed the Gok's sly smile. "Whatever it takes, you slimy bastard," he murmured, "I'll find Lind and I'll know what you've done to her."

SEARCH PARTY

Andel looked around the valley floor at frost-reddened wetland shrubs. Thin, high cloud prevented the sun's warmth from reaching them. Even the chirp of the swamp-dwelling creatures seemed dispirited. With a steady breath, she prepared to immerse herself in the valley's bedrock once more, but paused when Huldar stepped through the nearby portal.

He did not return her smile. "Lind is missing."

Missing? She tilted her head in confusion.

"She was coming to see me but never turned up. I can't sense her presence. She's gone."

"How can she be gone?" Andel cast about with her mind and found no sign.

"What's happened? Where would she go?"

He reached for her hand. "Let me show you what I know … "

With the extra insight, Andel's alarm escalated. She remembered the odd exchange between Lind and the Overlord, months back when they had still been on the Northern Shelf.

"What will you do?" she asked.

"I'm not sure." He rubbed his forehead as if trying to clear his thoughts. "Even if the Overlord has hurt her, he didn't cause her to become lost, and I can't believe he'd kill her. He has no reason to, and her death-cry would go somewhere – to one of us, surely. Someone would know ... wouldn't they?"

"There's never such a thing as simple truth," she said sadly. "Our veils are often as opaque to ourselves as to those who would know us."

He grimaced. "What's that supposed to mean?" He took his hand from hers. "Don't sprout Trianogi mysticism at me! Lind is lost," he barked. "Alone. What if she's dead, and I did nothing." *What if what I do is not enough.*

It's not your fault, she soothed. *You are doing everything you can.*

Patronizing! he snarled.

Patronizing? I'm trying to help! And you ARE doing all you can. Why are you so angry?

Huldar's struggle to get his emotions in order buffeted her mind. It was reasonable for him to feel upset, but it seemed like there was more to it.

If Lind was distressed, he said at last, *if she'd been crying, her voice might have been unsteady. She could have sung herself to the wrong location.*

The wrong location?

Or be trapped in Qalān. Huldar hung his head. *There is no way of knowing.*

You can't tell?

If she is trapped? No. He looked at her again. There was fear in his eyes. "It might be best not to mention this to the others. They'll be worried enough."

"If you think so," Andel said.

At that, he seemed to come to a decision. He started back to the portal. "I'm going to call everyone to base and organize a search," he said.

"I'll be as quick as I can." *Cobar!* she called. *No more divining today. Lind is missing.*

While the Uri'madu assembled, Huldar laid the map on the table and checked to make sure all portals on the Central Continent were marked and their global linkages shown – but with the rest of the planet frozen by now, if she'd somehow wound up lost on the ice … it didn't bear thinking about. He drew a circle around the branch that led to the healers' camp, and divided its exits into seven sections. Only a few led to other continents. He hoped to find her before it was necessary to check them.

"There will be two people to each portal chain," he said. "Team up as you see fit. Stay on this continent. You will remain in contact with at least one other group at all times."

Casco looked around. "Where's the Gok?"

Huldar tapped the side of his head to signify that the Overlord had been in contact. "He doesn't want to be involved. Said we could waste no more than two days on the search … and he had no doubt we could find her without his help."

"Unbelievable!" Casco muttered.

Huldar closed his heart to the other words the Overlord had said … that after losing a team member under dubious circumstances on their last assignment, he'd better be sure not to lose another.

He whispered to Gento, *Go with the Lady Andel. Keep her safe.*

Andel was talking with Sari when the big Rukh joined their conversation. After a quick glance in Huldar's direction, which he tried his best not to notice, they headed off. Sari went with Cobar, and when everyone else had paired off, Casco remained at his side.

You and me, boss.

Two by two, searchers slipped through the portal on the westerly side of the encampment, each singing a subtle variation of the same string of notes.

Ready? Casco asked.

Huldar found his emotions ice-calm.

We will find her, Casco said.

"I hope so, Casco. But even if we find her dead, I'd rather know she was safe in the Breath than trapped in Qalān. Lingering for weeks, total isolation. Navigators are trained for it, but Lind …"

Casco rested his hand on Huldar's shoulder. "Try not to think about it."

They emerged in a sheltered gully in the foothills surrounding the inland sea and hiked to the ridge-top to view the terrain. Huldar was amazed to see the straits were now empty and the sea completely contained.

"I've not made portals to cover the exposed sea-bed," he said absently.

Casco raised his eyebrows. "So we won't be searching there just yet." *Could you show me again what she was wearing? Might get a visual on the colors if she's injured and too far gone to sense.*

Huldar shared the image of Lind in a red-ochre jacket with pale fur lining over a dark green shirt and pants the yellowish tones of kahmayre. But Casco's request worried him. Would the others remember? Perhaps he had not been accurate enough in his transfer of the image.

"It's me," Casco said. "I wasn't paying proper attention. Distracted by the Gok, or lack of him."

"I know, but we can't think about that now," Huldar said. "We have to concentrate on finding Lind." He held out his hand. *Join with me?*

With their strength combined, Huldar and Casco called out for Lind in unison, then closed their eyes and listened for a reply, however faint. But the ether held only the voices of other teams, all calling the same name, all receiving the same response.

Although unmarked, Casco was stronger in far-sight than many archangels, and Huldar left it up to him to pilot their search. They took their time, searching for a flash of ochre, or distinctive yellow-green. They looked beneath rock overhangs and followed creeks and ravines, rifled with their minds among the piles of vegetation that had already succumbed to the changing of the season, and hunted beneath the bright red canopies of fungi that grew like giant gills from dead-fall on the leeward sides of the mountains.

After many hours, Huldar groaned to his feet. The other search parties had already reported their first and second search results – like theirs, all negative.

If they don't find her, I'll take either you or Andel and search those areas again, he said.

Casco sighed. *I wish I had my father's stamina*, he admitted.

The archangel?

Yes. But luckily we have the Lady Andel's strength to draw on.

As if she had overheard, Andel's thought touched him for a moment then passed on. He wondered if she had seen him. With her at his side, they could possibly cover even more ground, but Casco had joined minds with him on many occasions and their bond was familiar and comfortable. Such a bond with Andel would be fraught with novelty and distraction. He fingered the opal necklace in his pocket and wondered why he still hadn't given it to her.

Casco nodded ahead and they set off for another portal in the chain.

That night as he lay exhausted in his bedroll, he felt Andel's presence tickle his mind.

How are you? she asked.

He tried to answer, but what could he say? First Joumelät Enna, and now Lind. *Worn out,* he said at last.

The sensation of her caress was as warm as any physical touch could be, so much so that he almost reached up to catch her hand and keep it with him. Then she was gone, and her absence left an extra knot of loss in his heart.

LOYALTY

After a difficult night's sleep, Andel struggled into layers of warm clothing before emerging bleary-eyed from the tent. After several days' search there was still no sign of Lind, and last night, yet again Huldar had rejected her company.

She sat on a rock while Gento fixed the fire. *He's very good with flame*, she thought absently, *and so is Cobar.*

I taught him everything he knows, Gento flicked back at her, and she apologized for thinking so loudly.

"We're both tired, Lady Andel," he said. "No apology necessary."

She gave him a rueful smile.

"How long have you known Huldar?"

"Five hundred years … four planets." Gento turned to look at her. "Be warned. We Rukh are loyal, sometimes to the point of idiocy."

She spluttered a protest, but he continued, "It's a sad fact. The gift and the curse of our House. Rukh strive for lives of simplicity lest they become a tangle of conflicting obligations and ideals … and so, whether angel or archangel, we are taught from an early age to choose our companions with care." He smiled and gave a knowing nod. "Huldar is well worthy of my loyalty."

Andel put her face in her hands. She knew that Gento's words were true and the gift of his allegiance was a huge honor, but it didn't answer the questions in her heart. Why did Huldar reject her? He had courted her, in his own way, for over two years and never lost interest. Their relationship had blossomed easily and naturally into something deeper than she could have anticipated. It seemed she had found a life partner, maybe even the mate of her soul, so why did he block her out? Why now, when crisis had struck and they needed all the support they could get ... and perhaps himself most of all.

"Did he love Lind?" Her voice sounded small in her own ears, almost child-like.

Gento shook his head. "In the same way he loves us all, but not in a romantic way."

She took the mug he offered and felt its warmth seep into her hands.

"You are the one he loves, Lady Andel. Have no doubts." He turned to pour tea for himself. "Grief is a road with no boundaries. Given time, his sadness will wash up against your shores, and you will find each other again."

She stared at him for a moment. Unshed tears burned behind her eyes. "I had no idea the Rukh had such beauty in their thoughts," she said at last. "I thought you a warrior people, interested in swords and battle."

"We are," Gento replied. "But to live on the edge of death tends to open one's awareness to the beauty of life, or so I have found."

Andel thought on this for a moment. Her soul brightened a little. "And what are we doing here, as Uri'madu, if not risking death every day in our explorations?"

Gento smiled and stirred the pot on the fire. "Life is beautiful, is it not?"

"Yes, it is," she agreed. "Come on, let's get breakfast done, then we have another whole day to search. Maybe today is the day we will find her."

He slopped some porridge into a bowl and handed it to her. "And here we have it, a lovely, filling bowl of little attar."

"And the beauty of life? How does little attar fit into that?"

"We must keep our strength."

As they shared a smile, Andel's anxiety receded. Perhaps everything would be all right after all.

DUVÄT GOK

Duvät stood in the empty marquee and considered his options. Even Tam and Arko had joined the search for Lind, so the campsite was deserted, and at last he felt a measure of freedom. The effort of suppressing all knowledge of his capture of the eyes as well as hiding his relationship with Lind had been, he admitted, very great. Under normal circumstances, it was only when he was far from camp that he could relax, and with the navigator almost on his way, he had thought those conditions would not come again.

He poured hot water onto some galano twigs and swirled the cup. It seemed that the Breath was still blowing his way. Wherever Lind was, this was the fourth day she hadn't answered their calls and as each moment passed it was less likely she would be found alive – if at all. There was still a slim chance she was unconscious somewhere, and of course if he knew where he would ensure that the searchers found only a body. But that was one stress he did not yet have to deal with.

Even better was the fact that neither Huldar nor Andel of Trianog seemed to connect him with the beacon stone, and as for the mark on Lind's face, without proof, Huldar would not dare accuse him of anything. There was only the word of the Naghari that there was a mark at all, and the vague idea that it may have been a handprint. *Could have been anything, really,* he thought to himself.

"Do you know anything about that?" Duvät sneered. His head wobbled as he repeated Huldar's words. The Lethian might suspect he had something to do with her disappearance, and if she'd waited a few more days before getting herself killed, their intrepid team-leader would most likely have been correct. But Lind had removed herself from the equation and taken her knowledge of the eyes with her, Huldar was completely distracted by his efforts to find her – driven by guilt he had carefully stoked – and no one was interested in their Overlord now, nor likely to be.

A flash of black and yellow caught his eye as an opportunistic clicker-bug made its way, one spidery leg after another, into the warmth of the marquee. Its fine whiskers stiffened as it sensed him. Six small eyes turned in his direction. With murder in mind, Duvät took a slow step toward it. The creature seemed mesmerized. Perhaps it could feel his power! Another step and he was almost close enough to catch it. Should he seize it with his mind, or rend it with his fingers? He could almost feel its pain and the sticky juices on his hands.

With a *whump*, the wind gusted against the tent and the spell was broken. He unleashed a numbing mind-bolt but the creature was gone. Sparks swirled from the hearth. Rain began to pelt the leathers and the temperature plummeted, but Duvät hardly cared. Such a short time to go until the navigator would come to take them home. He could feel his victory beckoning.

URI'MADU

After eight more days of fruitless searching, the Uri'madu gathered once more in the marquee. Tam had cooked a stew, but no one except the Overlord seemed interested in eating. Andel and Sari huddled close together and Nachiel wept quietly in Ronnin's arms.

The Overlord cleared his throat. "We have searched. Lind has gone. We mourn her absence, but time is short and assessments must be completed."

Huldar felt Duvät's words bounce off him. Surely the Gok was not serious? It now seemed certain that Lind had indeed become trapped in Qalān, and the horror of her fate sat dark in their minds. He felt his legs propel him upright.

Fear crossed the Overlord's face. He shuffled back a step. "I am the Overlord!" he said. "I am the Imperial representative, which means that I represent the God-Emperor himself. You will show me due respect!"

"Then has the God-Emperor no respect for us?" Huldar glared into the Overlord's shifty yellow eyes. "Lind is lost! We need time!"

"Another gone?" Duvät sneered.

Huldar forced his breathing to be regular.

"You might feel the need to wallow in your emotions," Duvät said, "but the first snows have fallen. I expect every assessment to be completed and the reports in my tray within the time allotted! The Navigator will not wait. There can be no extensions."

Huldar pinned him with his gaze.

"No exceptions!" Duvät grunted. As he departed, a well of utter silence was left in his wake.

With his other senses, Huldar followed the Overlord beyond the marquee. Despite the Gok's orders he would continue the search. They were family. It was expected.

He turned to the clink of ceramic and saw Tam and Arko muscling a full crate of Besh onto the bench.

"It was her favorite," Tam said.

Huldar took a bottle from the crate and held it up. "To Lind!"

"Aye! To Lind," the others responded.

He took a deep draught then wiped his mouth. "My friends, we must continue our work as the Overlord has said –"

"What?" said Casco.

He held up his hand. "Yes, there are assignments to complete. But the search will not stop until she is found, or until we are forced to leave. I will make sure of it!"

Before first light next morning, Huldar woke Casco.

"What is it?" Casco rubbed his eyes.

"Come with me?"

"What – now?"

"Please?" Huldar said.

Still grumbling, Casco left his blankets and followed through several steps to the northern delta, now not much more than a vast mushy swamp. What decaying vegetation remained was frozen solid, and there were no obvious signs of life. Gelid air sat crisp and clean, magnifying the constellations above. The great wheel, having shown herself through the summer, was now slowly slipping beneath the horizon. Huldar wondered if another great wave had dowsed the Southern Archipelago, or if the seesaw of nacrite was more gradual in its release. And where did the blubber-worms go? Did they spend years beneath the ice, or perhaps they spawned and died, a life cycle he suspected many of this planet's life forms experienced. But if that was so, what happened to the carrion?

A gentle glow on the eastern horizon set the alps in stark relief. To the west, a gradual increase of light revealed banks of ice floes heaving and falling in sluggish waves.

I know she's still alive. He turned to Casco. *I just know it. She is trapped and afraid and I can do nothing!*

Casco turned to view the dying landscape. *What will you do?*

Keep searching. Huldar replied. *Will you help?*

A pang of hurt stabbed from Casco's mind. *How can you even ask? You are the brother of my heart. Lind was Uri'madu, our family.*

I'm sorry. Huldar bowed his head. *I just ...*

Let it go! Casco cried. *Joumelät Enna died because she let her guard down. We all knew there were predators about. It was not your fault! And it was not your relationship with Andel that killed Lind, so please, stop punishing yourself and tell Andel how sorry you are for excluding her.*

She doesn't need to share my pain. I can't inflict that on her. She has sorrow enough of her own.

Rubbish!

"Look!" he said. From his mind's eye, he shared Andel's sad gaze.

"She's pining for *you*!" Casco shook his head. "How can you be so brilliant and so thick at the same time?"

"Ah," Huldar said. "So that's what you think of me?"

"Huh!" Casco grumbled. "We didn't have to come all the way to a frozen swamp for me to tell you what you already know."

For a while they stood in silence. Huldar sighed. Casco was probably right. He usually was.

"Look!" Casco pointed at a shooting star.

As the meteor blazed across the dawn Huldar knew it was time to return to camp. His team would expect him to tell them what to do. Some would be ready to return to their tasks, others maybe not. In the days before the navigator was due, there would still be time for many of their projects to be completed, although the weather was rapidly deteriorating. The Gok had been right about that at least.

As for himself, Huldar decided he would go west again, toward the falling star, and see what he could find. Maybe Lind would be there. Her early life had been marred by sorrow; she had been orphaned as a child and raised by her grandparents, now both long gone ... Would her death-cry have come to him?

"Are we done here?" Casco asked.

Huldar shivered. "Yes, we are." He clapped Casco's shoulder. "Let's go."

THE LOST ONE

In the never-ending silence, Lind rocked herself back and forth. After a while, she leaned forward and counted her toes again ... still ten. Her boots were gone – who knew where? Where did things go when they were lost in Qalān? The voices had started, but she knew they were lying. No one was looking for her. Soon she would die and her toes would drop off ...

Lind? LIND?

She looked up. Her boots were talking to her now? She must be mad.

"Lind, darling?" a soft voice said. "Oh my baby, my blessing, I've missed you so much!"

"Mother?" The word seemed obscenely loud and she cringed as Qalān reacted with a violent shaking.

"Why did you leave me?" her mother said. "I cried for you."

Lind shook her head. "No! Mother! I didn't leave you," she whispered. "I would never leave you. The healer was there and she took me away, and I cried. I cried! It was me, not you."

A pale round shape stabilized into a ghostly face with fair hair and blue, Lethian eyes - so like Huldar's. The generous lips parted in a smile.

"Come to me, darling, my sweet little one," the lips crooned. "Let me hold you. I can take you with me. We'll be together at last and I'll never leave you again." Her hand gestured lovingly. "Come ..."

Slowly, Lind unlocked her grip on her knees. Her mother beckoned again. Fragrant pink hereny flowers fell like rain. She climbed to her feet. Could she walk? She had to try.

Her mother frowned. "Where are your shoes?"

Lind looked down. Her toes were gone. Where were her toes? "I don't know, Mama," she said. "I lost them."

"You lost your shoes?"

The rain of flowers evaporated. Lind nodded, suddenly ashamed. Her shoes, her best pink shoes with the shiny blue buckles; how could she lose them?

"I paid good coin for those!" Her mother's face was red and angry.

Lind stepped back. She stifled a sob. Mama didn't like it when she cried.

"They were your favorite color!" her mother shrieked. Blonde hair swirled as she turned and walked away.

"No, Mama! No!"

As her mother faded into the mist, Lind tried to run, to follow, but she could feel no surface beneath her feet, no traction.

"I'll find them, Mama." She crawled about, frantically searching. "I'm sorry!" she screamed. "I'll find them!"

The whiteness bucked and jumbled, sensitive to her cries. Her mother was gone. Lind froze. The head-shaking movement would stop if she was still – still and quiet like a beybey hiding in the kahmayre.

The nausea passed. She realized she was hugging her knees again, as if she had never released them, as if she had imagined it all, her mother, her shoes ...

Arba and Uba, she wept to her knees, *you are all I have* ... but the knobbly bones didn't answer. They never did.

Cottony whiteness closed around her and for one lucid moment she knew she could no longer distinguish between wakefulness and sleep, and if she didn't keep counting her toes she might not know if she had died. Would the whiteness go on and on even after her soul had discarded her body? Maybe the Breath was a myth and there was no El, and no Asheru to welcome her like the legends said she would. But then she remembered Huldar's Mark, and her heart stopped racing.

Who gave him the Mark if not El? she asked her knees. She leaned forward. Her toes were there again.

One ... two ... three ... four ...

STRANGE CREATURES

Huldar rubbed his hands together for warmth. A well-used pot hung on a tripod above the campfire, but the water was slow to heat above flames with no natural fuel.

Cobar emerged from their tent. "Fire not your strong point?" The Rukh squatted by the tripod and concentrated for a moment. "Ahh, that old song," he chuckled. "This should fix it."

With a small *whump* the fire doubled in size, and Huldar smiled.

"What did you do?" he asked.

"Changed the song."

Cobar passed on an esoteric image of a fire-working charm: a Tsemkar/Shamkar hybrid. Huldar smiled his thanks, but he had little talent for mind-power and wouldn't be able to replicate it.

While the water bubbled, he reviewed his plans for the day.

When Casco joined them, he looked up. "Glad you could make it."

"Give him something to eat, Cobar," Casco said. "Might improve his mood."

Huldar returned his attention to the map. "If we go here, and then here," he said, sharing images of locations. "I want to cover this feature, 'the road', before it's covered in snow. It is a mystery, isn't it? Seems to have come up from the straights, as if it crosses them, and if Lind was lost or dazed, she may have followed it."

"She might have ..." Casco said.

"Exactly. So, ready?"

"As soon as I've eaten."

"Then eat fast."

As they reached the end of a branching chain of portals, Huldar hesitated before kneeling to negotiate a further step through Qalān. This would be his first engagement with the planetary network since Lind's disappearance. No one lost in Qalān had been ever been found, but maybe, just maybe, there could be a first time. Maybe she would be there by chance or he would hear her echo in the web of songs.

He could feel Casco's eyes on him, but when the new portal was completed, he couldn't meet his friend's gaze. He climbed slowly to his feet.

"Nothing," he said. "Not even a whisper."

Casco nodded. He tipped his head toward the new portal. "Let's go then."

Maybe next time, Huldar said.

As they stepped through to the edge of the road, Huldar and Casco were astonished to see a herd of large, six-legged beasts moving slowly and deliberately along it. They stood in shocked silence as the creatures bugled softly to each other through drooping, flexible noses. Each was at least as tall at the shoulder as Huldar himself, some even taller. Their long, silky coats were in all shades of brown from pale cream through russet to the deep peaty brown of an estuarine creek. A tiara of spherical eyes encircled each head like a crystal crown.

The largest member of the herd aimed its nose at them and started forward.

Huldar and Casco sidled from the path, but the creature followed, nose outstretched. The herd quickly engulfed the portal site, and Huldar cursed that they had not escaped while they still could. Had this been Lind's fate, to be eaten by one of these behemoths? Why had no one seen them before?

Deadfall from frostbitten trees made a thick natural barricade on either side of the path. They ran close to the edge, hoping for a break in the debris. The creatures kept up without effort, making no attempt to overtake. When Huldar slowed, the herd slowed also.

We should stop, he said. *Keep absolutely still. If they come at us, I'll try and defend us, but we may have to go bush. Pick a path. I'll follow.*

Casco looked behind them. *It's impenetrable!*

Then we'll crawl!

He froze as the lead creature advanced. Although it seemed placid and showed no signs of fear, he remained on his guard. At two paces from contact it stopped and moved its head up and down as if to see him better. Its hair rippled and swayed, then it launched itself up onto its two hind legs and opened its four arms wide.

Huldar looked up at a towering underbelly marked with intricate rust red patterns against darker brown skin.

By the Breath! Casco murmured, too astounded to do anything but stare.

From the corner of his eye, Huldar saw several more of the larger animals separate from the herd. As they neared him, they also reared up. Each had patterns to show, no two the same in color or design.

Are these elders? he asked Casco. If so, this was the first species he'd seen to have clear age differences and possibly even hierarchy!

The main herd shuffled restlessly and kept their distance. They were grouped according to the shade of their coats. One lifted its nose and bugled, a long, plaintive wail ending in the sound of a 't'. Within the herd other, smaller creatures faced each other and mimicked the behavior of the older ones.

The elders lowered themselves back to the ground. They seemed gentle and emanated only curiosity, so when the first one extended its nose toward Huldar's face he stood his ground, but silently rehearsed the most powerful stun-charm he knew … just in case.

The tip of the nose touched his skin. Behind him, he could hear Casco's tense breathing. Soft whiskers snuffled the Shamkar on his cheek. The creature inhaled as if his Soul Mark had its own distinct scent.

After several minutes, it seemed to lose interest, but when it moved on, another shuffled forward to take its place. Eventually all the elders had examined him in turn. Some also displayed for Casco and took time to examine his scent, while others merely gave him a cursory head-bob and wandered back to the mob.

Their curiosity satisfied, the herd moved on, wailing to each other with long, mournful cries. "Way-e-n-n-tuh!" Huldar repeated the sound softly to himself.

Soon, the hairy backs had blended into the landscape and the huge animals were almost invisible. Despite their great size, their soft feet left no signs of passage, no blade of grass bruised or twig snapped, but as they moved on Huldar was sure he sensed changes in the song of the planet – random elements melded into more cohesive patterns.

Like spirit creatures, he said at last. He knew they were vital to the planet – his finely honed gift of ecological empathy told him so – yet he knew nothing else about them, neither where they had come from nor where they were going. How could such beasts have remained undetected? Their behavior fascinated him. Their markings seemed to have great significance, and by the segregation of coat color, he could see evidence of clan structure within the group, but there was so little time left for study.

"Where does the trail go from here?" Casco asked.

"I think it passes right through where Andel and her team are working," Huldar replied. "At this rate, they'll cross her path in ten days or so."

He walked to the center of the clearing and looked southward. After a moment, a broad grin split his face and he turned to Casco. "Don't breathe a word of this. I want to see her face!"

Casco laughed. *Cruel!*

Huldar tipped his head toward the portal. "I can't think any more. We'll come back later."

"At least we can tell Cobar, can't we?"

Huldar nodded, and with a last look at the empty trail, the two meandered toward the faint aura of their gate. Their thoughts were full of their amazing encounter. Shared images and conjecture filled their heads, but when they reached the portal, Huldar stopped. There was something on the ground that hadn't been there before. He turned toward Casco, not quite believing, but when he looked again it was still there.

It's a boot.

They stared at the red leather, creased and worn – rune of Leth embossed on the outer ankle – dark blue clips, one broken.

"Been reminding her for months to fix that," Casco murmured.

Huldar caught a glimpse of more red leather caught on a fallen branch.

The other one? LIND! he cried. He gathered the boots to his chest and cast about with all the strength his mind could muster. *LIND!*

They waited in silence, hoping beyond hope for an answer, but eventually he turned to Casco. "Not a trace. How can this be?" he whispered. Tears stung his eyes. "Is it some sort of terrible joke?" But as his fingers played over the well-worn leather he noticed it was utterly dry and not even cold. Had the boots come from Qalān, from the portal he had just made? He looked into the leaden sky, chill dampness all around … there was no other explanation.

They scanned again, pushing their minds to the limit, but found no further sign. Huldar screamed in frustration. Reluctantly, they returned to Cobar, and Huldar summoned the Uri'madu to come home.

Back at base-camp, he placed Lind's boots on the kitchen bench and waited while the others arrived. When Duvät Gok came in, Huldar saw his eyes flash wide, then narrow suspiciously.

"What's this about?" Duvät demanded.

"I'll explain when the others get here," said Huldar.

The Overlord approached the table with caution. "Where did you get them?"

"Huldar will explain." Casco said.

While the rest of the team gathered in the marquee, Huldar sat quietly.

Sari pushed aside the door-flap and stared for a moment before running forward. She reached out to touch the broken clip. "They're hers!" she sobbed. "They're Lind's. Where is she?"

Casco took her in his arms and let her weep against his chest.

"Huldar? What's happened here?" Gento demanded.

Andel picked up a boot and held it gently in her hands. She closed her eyes as if sensing Lind's presence in the leather.

"Impossible! They are not hers." Duvät Gok yelled. He pointed at Huldar, his finger shaking with rage. "This is in poor taste, Huldar of Leth. Just when we are beginning to recover from tragedy, you see fit to reopen our wounds."

"No," Andel said. "They are hers." Tears started to roll down her cheeks. "If you touched them, you would feel her essence – and her trauma. The last time she was in contact with this leather she was crying and in pain."

She held the boot out. Duvät Gok flinched as if it were poisoned.

"Return to work, all of you!" he shouted, then without a backward glance he turned and hurried away.

Huldar stared after him. *The Gok knows more than he's saying. I know it!*

Casco shook his head. *And what if he does? You have no proof. Nothing. No shred of evidence.*

He hit her!

Unless you actually interrogate him, you can't be sure, Casco said. They locked eyes. *Have you ever done that? Delved into the mind of another against their will?*

Huldar looked away. *No. You know I can't. The very idea repulses me.*

Then let it go. Sometimes the truth needs time to reveal itself.

That night, Huldar could not sleep. The cold seeped into his bones despite his warm bedding, and the frigid silence unnerved him. Eventually he pulled on his clothes and went to the marquee.

Lind's boots stood on the bench as if waiting to be claimed. If they had something to say, he wished he could hear it, but then he recalled Andel's words about Lind's anguish and turned away. Suddenly, the deep stillness of the night seemed preferable to the boots' accusations. He left the tent and wandered toward the bluff.

On the plains below, snow glinted blue in the light of the moons – apart from an occasional flash of fiery red as the volcano vented. The eruption that had marked their arrival was slowly losing power. Burning rivers of lava had dulled, and discharge from the crater was now no more than an artist's red spatter – but the sight drew him like a magnet. What secrets could it share? Did it somehow know the truth?

The air moved slightly, so cold it seemed to have substance. He pulled his jacket tighter and hugged his arms around his chest. The mountain belched again. Thoughts of Lind's torment would not leave him, nor would images of the Overlord's sly smile. What did the Gok have to do with it? What was he failing to see?

He started as a dry branch cracked, then Andel took his arm.

What is it? she asked.

He stared woodenly at the volcano. *What is it? She's lost somewhere in terrible pain. You said it yourself!*

Andel stepped back, but her gentle touch on his arm remained. *If you truly believe there is something you can do, let your heart guide you,* she said. *Do what you think you must. Take the chance. Otherwise, we will leave here and you will be haunted, not knowing – blaming yourself.*

He gazed down at the top of her head. She wouldn't look at him and he regretted his angry tone.

You don't mind? he asked.

Mind? She looked at him at last. ... *That you won't give up on Lind? Your loyalty and doggedness inspire me. I sometimes like to think that you would show such determination on my behalf ... although lately, I am not so sure.*

"Andel" he whispered, *please! With Lind ... and what has happened in my past ...*

Yes? What has happened? What is so bad that you can't talk to me? That you must shun me?

He turned to the volcano again. *I'm afraid.*

Why? What frightens you?

The smolder of the volcano brightened momentarily. His desire to go to it was disturbing. Andel waited, her haze spiked with frustration, deceptively fragile – so many contradictions.

I feel as if it's calling me, he said.

Then go! Follow your heart.

He clasped her shoulders, willing her to understand. *You are my heart, Tsemkarun Andel of Trianog.* Her gaze searched his soul as he tried to explain. *But Lind is my duty. We are her family, her only family, and I am head of that family and I will not, cannot desert her.*

She slowly reached up and placed her palm on his cheek. *I would not ask you to, Shamkarun Huldar of Leth. I ask only that you let me in once more, when you are ready.*

That I can do. He took her hand and looked across the plain. *Will you come with me?*

To the volcano?

He nodded.

When she hesitated, Huldar steeled himself to go alone. It was too much to expect, and to revisit the site of her brush with the Breath ... But instead of pulling away, she stepped forward and lowered her veil, showing him her feelings with complete trust. Fire rushed through their contact, and his soul returned to a balance he hadn't known, until then, was missing.

THE VOLCANO

Andel followed Huldar across the valley to the mountains. Their passage was much faster than when they had first arrived and were forced to trek on their legs alone. The place where the lahar had hit was now a shallow valley marked by a paler deposit that wound its way through the surrounding hills.

"It's strange to be here again," she said. "I thought I was going to die …" she picked her way gingerly over drifts of solidified stones and mud "… and I was disappointed because I hadn't had a chance to be part of the team, or see anything of the new planet."

It was a brave thing you did, Huldar said. He looked back at her. "Casco still has moments, wondering how you managed to keep all those loose rocks from sliding."

"So do I," Andel admitted.

They paused again as the ground trembled. Huldar pointed as the cinder cone puffed sullen gouts of magma. "I think we've come far enough."

"What are we going to do?"

"I'm going to try and commune with the planet," he said.

Commune?

"It's an ability sacred to Leth. Not everyone can do it and not every planet listens, but I did it before, near the ravines, so maybe I can do it again. Maybe the planet itself can help us to find her."

"Then why here?" Andel asked. "Why not return to where you were successful before?"

"Because I think it's called me to this place."

Andel turned full circle, as if registering their position. There was little snow on the ground; the heat of the volcano prevented it. Barren rocks were swept clean of ash by the prevailing winds.

"What do you want me to do?" she asked.

"Watch over me. If a fresh eruption starts, wake me up!"

She nodded solemnly. "So, what you're about to do, it's akin to divining – I think?"

Where do your ideas come from? He tilted his head. "I've not thought about it. Could be."

"But how do you seek out an alien consciousness with your voice?" she went on. "And how do you know where you are or where you've been when there are no physical anchors to define boundaries and mark progress?"

"I don't know," he said. "I'll just have to feel my way."

She nodded as if he'd said something profound, and he hoped he had.

"It's amazing to me … what you can do," she said.

"It will be amazing if I can do it for a second time!"

He closed his eyes and began to listen, casting about until he found where the vibration seemed strongest. There was no life in this bleak place, and the lack of distraction helped him focus. He kneeled and placed his palms flat against the rock. The planet had spoken to him once, but could so vast a being comprehend his search for a single lost annangi?

He stilled his spirit. The sulfurous air was heavy with ash. Devastation surrounded them. *I'm not sure if this will work,* he started to say, but then a deep resonance welled up from the core of the planet. It pulsed through his feet and into his chest, inviting his participation. The Mark on his cheek warmed steadily until it burned, and when his whole body was filled with the song of the planet he released a sound of his own.

At first it was no more than a single pure note, but his voice swelled and developed layer upon layer in concert with the huge chord that played him ... yet for all his effort, he knew he was no more than a single tone in a vast symphony, spiraling downward into a musical storm.

Then noise organized into words, and meaning drifted through his heart.

Dissolve ... it said. *Become nothing so that I may see your shape.*

Huldar did his best to quiet the raging song he had set in motion, and the voice of the planet slowly infiltrated. Piece by piece his vibrational structures crumbled before the onslaught, and when he teetered on the threshold of true absorption, the voice flowed through his soul again.

Ahh, creator and destroyer, the two are one ... already the flames dance in your heart. The words of the planet became a buffeting tempest. *The circle must be broken ... Small feet leave a vast trail ... The child of theft bears El's great blessing ... I weep for my people, my lives – why must this be?*

Huldar struggled to comprehend. He forced himself to picture Lind.

The planet seemed to breathe again. *Ahh ... yes.* Overwhelming sadness seeped into Huldar's heart as the voice resumed. *The eye in the center, the sacrifice foretold. These are its beginnings.* More words floated by, capricious as butterfly wings – *You will dance to the whim of the Breath until you are Breath itself ...* Then, after a long pause, his image of Lind seemed to flesh out and grow larger. Two sad blue eyes filled his mind.

Held ransom for what has been taken, the planet whispered, *yet she is not at fault. She has given enough.*

I don't understand! Huldar cried. *How can I find her? How can I bring her back?*

Give yourself to love; only as one may you find another.

In the dark, the voice paused as if gathering strength. A pale face swam before him but it was smaller and rounder than Lind's. Warmth seemed to come to him and a flash of sandy-brown and his being was filled with a strange smile, as if the beauty he saw was the sadness he felt.

Two souls and time a moving sea between you. This is the only truth. Seek that which searches and love may come again ...

The words drifted into silence as the planet's vast soul receded.

"I don't understand!" Huldar cried. "Please! Wait! What does it mean?" He could feel himself pushed from the depths, a leaf adrift in a river of sound. Then the voice came again, clear now as if it was breathed against his ear – although there was an accent now, as if the speaker was not quite familiar with the language of annangi.

"I dared the flame," it whispered, "and yet I live." *Remember me – remember this …* A song of great complexity distilled into his mind.

"Love lost is love's gain," the planet whispered, then Huldar opened his eyes. The ground rumbled. Slowly the wheeling stars above came into focus. Warmth against his skin was Andel's hand in his, and the joy of her smile was burned into his memory.

Two are one …

He drew her to him and savored the long kiss they shared.

When they broke off, she stroked his cheek. "You should visit the planetary consciousness more often."

There was a deep boom as a plume of molten rock leaped skyward, red against the indigo night.

What did you learn?

She's alive! Huldar got to his feet and pulled Andel up beside him. "There were words … I don't understand them. Well I might, if I think about them, but she gave me an idea. A gift. We have to go."

She? Lind?

Come on! We have to go!

The sky was still dark when they arrived at the portal where Lind's boots had been found, but the eastern rim was lightening. While they had travelled he had been absorbed in calculations, his mind alight with a revolutionary song derived from the cycles of the planet herself, adapted from what she had given him. Given enough strength, it could hold open the gate in Qalān, hopefully for long enough to locate Lind and get her out. He shared his idea with Andel.

I'll need you to join with me, he said. *I don't know how long we'll have. If we call, she might hear us and I can sing us to that point.*

But I can divine ...

Huldar looked at her, not quite sure what she was saying.

If we both try and go to her in Qalān, we could both end up trapped, she explained.

But if ...

Wait! What I'm saying is that if you can hold the portal open, I can divine Qalān for Lind! She smiled encouragement. *Like you just did with the planet, only much smaller.*

Yes, but you are familiar with rock. This is not rock – nothing like it! What if you get lost? You'll be alone ...

She reached up and kissed his lips. *If our minds are shared, we can't be lost from each other.*

Except in Qalān! he retorted. But the planet's strange words would not leave him; *Two are one ... only as one may you find another.*

Andel seemed to think for a moment, then her lips moved and she opened her palm to reveal the beacon stone. *You said you could find me anywhere ...*

He looked at the striped orange pebble. When he opened his mind, the call of the charm was so loud he could almost see its emanations. Slowly he nodded. *Let's hope it's true.*

When the song had been rehearsed one last time and he was certain that the correct intonations were embedded in his mind, Andel took his hand and entered his thoughts. Qalān was before him as waves of color punctuated with brighter points of connection. The portal waited, calm and unsuspecting, then sound arrowed from his mouth into the opening and Andel's hand gripped hard as she stepped into the blank space it had become.

Face to face with the featureless whiteness of wild Qalān, Andel was suddenly afraid. Huldar's song bound them together, but she could no longer sense the outer world. His hand seemed insubstantial, a memory of meaning, and she knew that whatever grace he had gained, his strength could not hold the mighty forces at bay for long.

She thought of Lind as she knew her; capable and self-reliant, prickly and strong, non-descript fair hair, square, Lethian features. Her mind searched, but found emptiness. Their plan relied on her ability to divine, and unless she could turn her skill to finding a person, it would fail. Then it came to her. It was the essence of the ore that she divined for, not the color or the outer shell. For her efforts to work, she needed to search for Lind's inner self – the soul behind the veils. She remembered the words of the Kaskarudjan ... *The body is a dream we make real, a fancy for others to see, a shell around the mysteries we guard.*

What did she know? ... that Lind was lonely. She had sensed it many times, hidden beneath her brash behavior. This was the root of her desire for inclusion. She loved her life with the Uri'madu, yet she was afraid. Andel had felt that also, more often since Lind had called on Huldar to save her. Yet although her sense of worth had taken a blow, she had faced life as bravely as she could. Andel gathered these thoughts and delved for her again.

A hunched figure came into view. *It must be her!* Andel thought. *Who else could it be?* But the outline wavered as if wreathed in mist. Andel closed her eyes and let her mind reach out. Qalān appeared insubstantial, but there were edges, boundaries like syrup, and she oozed through them, seeking.

Lind?

The figure crouched tight, hugging her knees. Shoulder-bones and spine pushed against her clothing like the frame of a tent. Tangled hair brushed over bare feet.

Lind? Can you hear me? Andel said. From Huldar, she got the sense that he was tiring. She stretched her free hand forward.

Lind looked up, confused. *Mother?* she said. *You came back?*

No, it's me, Andel. Andel extended her hand as far as she could. *Lind, come to me! I can't reach.*

Lind shook her head and buried it against her knees.

Lind, please!

"Go away!"

As Lind verbalized, Qalān rocked around them. Huldar's grip loosened and Andel snatched tightly at his fingers.

It's all right, Uba and Arba, she heard Lind say. *I know she's not real. The Lady Andel? Why would she come? Mama has left us. The shoes are gone.* Then she started to count … *one, two, three, four …*

When she realized Lind was talking to her knees, Andel despaired, but she was almost there. She craned her hand forward. If she let Huldar go, just a little more she could touch … There!

At the point of contact, Lind screamed. Qalān convulsed. Andel clung to her arm, determined to keep the three of them linked, but in one violent lurch, Huldar's fingers were torn from her grasp.

Long after Qalān had settled, Andel peered into the whiteness where he had been. Tears fell and disappeared into nothingness.

Lind sat still and unresponsive, staring at the hand on her arm. Suddenly she lunged forward and wrapped herself around Andel like a spider traps prey, a grip so tight she could barely breathe. Skeletal fingers patted her back as if entranced by the sensation of touch.

Real – you're real, Lind whispered. With small movements she climbed into Andel's lap. Alternating waves of terror and relief bombarded Andel's mind, as if Lind was a baby without veils or boundaries.

"I love you, Mama," she whispered. "I'll find my shoes. I will, I promise."

The fog of Qalān closed in. Andel prized one hand free and held out the beacon stone, their only hope. Lind's skeletal bones dug in as she hugged her closer. Her whispering continued and Andel wondered whether the healers could save her even if they did escape. Slowly she calmed. Her head drooped, her body went limp and Andel held her close, listening to each shallow breath. How long it had been since she had slept? Time passed. She looked at the orange stone in her hand, willing it to work. Huldar would come for them.

But what if the weather gets too bad? she asked herself. *What if he freezes to death trying?*

She jumped as blast of sound chased the fog away.

ANDEL!

Lind woke, screaming. Qalān bucked and reeled.

I'm here! Andel cried. *Huldar! I'm here!*

Lind clung as if they were drowning.

Andel pushed the beacon stone forward as far as she could stretch, and after the longest moment, welcomed the pain as Huldar's grip crushed her fingers around the stone.

Qalān vanished.

Early morning sun washed her face.

All the sensations of a living planet flooded back in, and Huldar's love enclosed her with unanticipated intensity.

With stiff movements painful to watch, Lind slowly climbed to her feet and gazed mutely at her surroundings. Her eyes seemed to fill her face. Starvation had pared the flesh from her body. She waved her hands as if warding off flies then looked down at her toes and began to count them – one, two, three …

Huldar smiled. "Come," he said. "Let's get you back to the healers."

"Healers?" Lind whispered. *Healers? … healers?*

Andel fought back tears. "Yes," she said brightly. "Ubaid and Alis? They've been so worried about you."

Ubaid? Lind looked up. *Ubaid and Alis … my friends.*

"Yes, that's right."

"Sari?"

"Yes, Sari is waiting to see you too."

"Sari," Lind repeated. "Sari loves me." Then her face crumpled and she began to cry. She stared at her toes and started to count them again. Andel drew her into her arms. Huldar hugged them both.

"We all love you, Lind. All of us," Andel said. "There's no need to count any more. Come, let us take you home."

Lind walked, half sagging, between them. She seemed unable to fully comprehend her rescue. Although her face made the motions of a smile, it was as if she merely copied the expressions they showed her – until Huldar went to step them through the portal. At first she froze, then with surprising strength, she tore herself free and backed away, shaking her head.

"It's all right," Andel soothed. "Huldar's here. He'll sing us through safely." But Lind hid behind her and stared with big eyes at the portal's faint aura as if it were a dangerous wild beast.

Andel smiled reassuringly and drew her into her arms once more. "Then we'll stay here until you're ready, won't we, Huldar?"

"Of course we will." He came to her side.

Cloud covered the sun and the chill intensified. Andel draped a spare winter coat over Lind's bony shoulders, then wrapped a thick blanket over that as well.

Her bare feet were and blue with cold.

"Have these," Huldar said, and handed over a pair of soft, calf-high boots, fur-lined and warm. "Your own are back at camp, waiting for you," he said.

Lind looked at him blankly.

Andel took the boots and tried to put them on for her, but she stiffened uncooperatively. "Why don't you light a fire, Huldar," she prompted, "and make us some sweet tea? Something to eat, perhaps?"

Huldar opened a supply kit and took out some chunky brown biscuits. "Laced with kanth," he said, "for emergencies."

Andel gave up on the boots and pulled the blanket lower to cover Lind's feet, but Lind pushed it back until her toes were showing.

She took a biscuit and offered it to Lind, but she seemed uninterested.

While Huldar conjured a fire, Andel moved closer and patted the ground for Lind to join her.

Should we ask Ubaid and Alis to come? she suggested.

They may not be able to find us. His face brightened. *But Casco knows this place. He can bring them.*

Lind watched the fire grow. Slowly, she held her hand to the flame, closer and closer as if reluctant to believe. Andel gently pulled her arm away, worried she would burn herself.

"It's real?" she asked hesitantly. "Is this real?"

"Yes, it is." Andel forced a smile through tears, but it faded as Lind began counting her toes again, touching each one and numbering them one to ten.

"What are you doing?" she asked softly.

"I'm not dead?"

Andel took Lind's hand. "No, Lind. We are alive. We are really here. Huldar and I found you in Qalān. Huldar found us and brought us home – with this." She opened her hand and showed Lind the beacon stone.

Lind stared as if in shock, then began to cry. "The stone, the stone!" she sobbed. "He made me do it! I didn't mean it, Huldar, I didn't mean it! Don't hate me, please!"

"Shh, shh," said Andel. "You're safe now."

"No, no!" Lind cried. "He made me do it. He'll kill me!"

"The Overlord?" Andel asked her.

Huldar hunkered down beside them. "He hit you, didn't he?"

With a low cry, Lind buried her face in his chest. From her mind came images of Duvät Gok's vile behavior, scenes of the rape and petty brutality Lind had endured over many months. The information was streamed raw and unfiltered. As Andel and Huldar closed their arms around her again, their eyes met. Neither knew what to say, or how to respond.

"I'm so ashamed," Lind wailed. "So hopeless!"

"He won't hurt you again," Huldar said firmly. There was a savage note in his voice that made Andel look twice.

He'll kill me, Lind whispered. *I know secrets.*

Andel squeezed her hand reassuringly. "We know too now," she said. "We'll keep you safe." She looked up with relief as Casco brought the healers through the portal. He stopped in his tracks when he saw who was under the blanket.

Alis and Ubaid ran forward. With a little prompting, Lind relinquished her hold on Andel and Huldar turned to them.

Casco stood with Huldar by the fire. "How?" he asked quietly. "When I woke up, you two were gone, and now? I can barely look. When I ... I can hardly believe it. But she's so fragile. I can't imagine ... He looked at his friend with awe. "You've done what no one else can."

Huldar glanced at Andel and reached out his hand. "Long story," he said.

Despite his exhaustion, she saw a secret smile lurking just beneath his veil, and a certain sense of triumph. Her gaze was drawn to his cheek, where his Shamkar still glowed with residual energy.

"Your Mark's grown!" she said.

He put his hand to his face and explored his cheek, tracing lines of warmth.

"So it has," said Casco, brows raised in wonder. "Long story? Lucky you're good at those."

Andel saw fatigue descend on Huldar like a mantle. The song had come in a flash of brilliance, but it had taken all his strength to sing it. He'd not even known for sure it would work, although he'd believed with all his heart … then to sing it again after they'd been torn apart! It was a wonder he could even stand. His stubborn spirit had saved their lives. The Rukh were right: there could be no one more worthy.

"You asked me to tell no one, not even the healers, before we got here," Casco was saying. "Why the secrecy?"

Huldar's gaze narrowed. "It's best that the Gok doesn't know what's coming," he said. "But before I tackle the Overlord, if I don't eat soon I think I'm going to fall over."

THE SHAWL OF JUSTICE

Buoyed by a hot meal and plenty of adrenalin, Huldar strode toward the Overlord's tent. His veil was steely calm, but every stride betrayed the murder in his heart.

"Huldar!" Nachiel called, "Where have you been?"

"You'll find out soon enough," he muttered.

When he came to the Overlord's tent, he ripped the door open.

Duvät Gok!

"What is the meaning of this?" the Overlord cried, but with one look at Huldar, he backed away.

Huldar bore down on him. "I know what you did."

"What I did?" the Overlord spluttered. His eyes went to his desk. "What have I done?"

"Lind has been found. You raped her."

"Raped her?" Comprehension bloomed across the Overlord's face. "No, no, you misunderstand." He laughed nervously. "She likes it like that. She finds my strength –"

The crunch and judder as his fist struck the Overlord's face was deeply satisfying, and the Gok's shocked expression as he went down was an image Huldar knew he would remember for the rest of his days.

"Imperial representative?" He sneered, and spat on the ground. Duvät Gok squirmed backward. Huldar followed. "If this was what the God-Emperor represented then El would surely reject him. I will see to it that you are stripped of office," he said quietly, "and that you never work with the Explorers' Guild again!"

He reached down and hauled Duvät Gok to his feet, then gripped his suety arm and propelled him toward the marquee.

"What are you doing?" the Overlord stammered. "How dare you! Remove your hand from my person!"

Huldar unleashed a stun-song and smiled grimly as Duvät sagged in his grasp, but he knew the Gok would be wary if he tried the same thing again. As a gambler who mixed with rough company, no doubt Duvät had a few defensive tricks up his filthy sleeve.

———

Casco gave Huldar the time they'd agreed, then began shepherding the small group back to base-camp. Through every portal, Lind closed her eyes and clung to Andel's hand, but the healers' attentions seemed to make the process bearable. However, as they neared the marquee, she released Andel's hand and hugged herself tightly. The fear in her eyes grew desperate.

"I don't want to see him," she said. "Please don't make me!"

"No one will force you," said Ubaid, "But the others deserve to know what he did."

"I don't want them to know."

"It's best that you do this now," Alis counseled. "The pain will be great no matter what Ubaid and I do, but your overall healing may be hindered if you don't."

Casco stood close beside her. "We are your family," he said. "We'll be there. Sari, and Lady Andel too."

"You'll be stronger for bringing it all out," Alis said. "If you do it now, while you are brave, then we can all watch over you. Soon we'll return to Giahn and after that, you'll never have to see him again."

"I believe Shamkarun Huldar will make sure of it," said Ubaid.

Andel took Lind's hands and closed her mind to the terror that poured through. "He never gave up." She found Lind's gaze and held it. "He believed you were alive. He found a way where there has never been a way before."

"And you risked your life for me, again." Lind took a breath, and then another one. Andel could feel her reservations diminishing. Eventually she gave a hesitant nod. "I'll do it for you, Lady Andel, and for him, if you think it's right."

"I do think it's right," said Andel, "although very hard. Come. Let's go home. Everyone's waiting. They'll be so thrilled, so very relieved to see you."

As the small group entered the marquee, Sari's hand went to her mouth. "Lind!" she sobbed. "Oh Lind!"

Nachiel ran forward with her. "I can't believe it!" he cried. "When he said he had a surprise for us I thought it might be another case of Besh!"

Sari wrapped Lind in a delicate but determined hug, as if any sudden movement might shatter her. Ronnin soon joined them, then Cobar and Gento muscled in to engulf them all in a massive embrace. While the rest of the crew bobbed, impatient for their turn to welcome Lind back from the Breath, Duvät Gok stood stiff and diffident at the back of the room, watching with his one good eye. The other was swelling fast.

Andel glanced from it to Casco. *Huldar?*

I believe so, Casco replied.

"Good for him," murmured Ubaid.

Alis looked at the Overlord with open disdain. "He needn't expect us to tend it."

Huldar held Lind's shoulders and looked at her with concern. "Are you strong enough to do this?"

Lind stood straighter. "I ... think so. The Uri'madu – I am one of them."

Huldar blinked back tears and bowed. "It is an honor to have you back where you belong."

When Huldar had taken his place before the team, Tam handed him the storyteller's shawl. As the Uri'madu gathered close in anticipation, Lind and Andel positioned themselves at the front where Lind could see them clearly. She seemed pale but determined as Sari gave her a last brief hug.

If I don't do this now, Lind said to Andel, *I might never.* She turned and stared deliberately at Duvät Gok. He held his gaze straight ahead and would not meet her eye.

Look at him, she said. *Why did I ever think he had power over me?*

Andel noticed a hesitation in Lind's thoughts and wondered what it was she could not yet say, but after the extreme trauma she had experienced, it would be astonishing if she could face all that had happened with no qualms.

Huldar spread his hands. "Many of you are wondering how Lind has been found and returned to us." He fingered the aged fiber of the ceremonial shawl and waited for the rumble of comment to subside. "And why it is that the Overlord stands before you in disgrace. All must know what the Overlord has done; then, as team leader and ranking archangel, it is my right to pass judgment and be witnessed by all."

He placed the white shawl around his shoulders and bowed with his hands crossed over his forehead. "Bey Maat'aht ej El a'sien," he said solemnly. "Breath blows through me."

"Breath blow true," the Uri'madu intoned.

"I call Lind to tell you what she has experienced at Duvät Gok's hands," Huldar said. "I affirm that she has shared this information with me previously by way of direct imagery which cannot be manipulated or falsified. She may choose to share these experiences with any among you or not, in her own time and when she sees fit. Are we agreed?"

They bowed and recited, "Breath blow true."

Huldar bowed in turn and continued. "In accordance with protocol, if Duvät Gok has any evidence or anything to say which qualifies or excuses his actions, we will hear him after Lind has spoken. Then, in turn, we will listen to any among you who wish to present evidence or pertinent argument. Are we agreed?"

Again, they intoned the response.

Andel leaned closer to Sari and whispered, "The storyteller's shawl is the Shawl of Justice now."

"Justice, yes," Sari murmured. "It's on his shoulders … I wonder if this will be told as a story one day."

Huldar bowed to them again, and then to Lind. "Let us begin."

As Lind took the shawl, Sari gripped Andel's hand. Outwardly they smiled and nodded encouragement, but her skeletal appearance and psychic fragility moved them to the core.

"Where has she found the courage?" Andel asked softly. *And after such an ordeal, The terror of Qalān is beyond imagination!* "I know I couldn't."

Sari shook her head slightly, realizing Lind might find their whispering unnerving. *Courage? It is because she knows she must. She has faced danger before, many times.*

Sexual abuse, psychological torture – and he's the Imperial Representative, the ultimate authority of our group. Such fortitude is hard to imagine … except maybe among those of House Leth.

Lind fixed her gaze on Sari's and began. Haltingly, she admitted that her troubles began after she had "done something stupid" and been caught out. Duvät cringed as she described him pushing her to the ground and threatening her with slavery, but as the damning tales continued, Andel thought the Overlord seemed less concerned by the recital than he should. It was as if he was merely resigned to it, as if a game had been lost – not real life.

When Lind relinquished the shawl, Huldar offered it to him. The Overlord fondled it as if deep in thought, but did not put it on. Instead, he squared his shoulders and sketched a bow toward Lind. With his gaze focused on the opposite panels of the marquee roof he began in a clear and deliberate voice, "Lind, I am, of course, deeply sorry for any pain I have caused. For this, I can only blame the rigors of this most important job we do, and the stress – the huge responsibility I have to the Imperium." He paused, then added, "The isolation must have affected me more than I knew."

Huldar narrowed his gaze, sharing the skepticism felt by his team. When Duvät tried to return the shawl, he refused to accept it.

"Put it on, Duvät Gok," he said. "Tell us how you will make amends. An apology is mere words."

"I am sure you will pass atonement soon enough!" Duvät snapped. He examined the weave of the fabric in his hands at length, before resuming his veil of remorse. The Uri'madu shuffled restlessly. Red anger tinged their collective haze.

Andel watched Huldar, wondering what he would do, then just as he seemed about to lose patience, Duvät Gok tossed the shawl around his neck. He turned to Lind and cleared his throat.

"I will see that you are compensated financially. The coin will come from my own pocket." Then, as if sensing that this may not be quite adequate, he added, "And you will not be required to work for the remainder of our time on this planet."

Huldar waited.

With a shrug, Duvät took the shawl from his neck and stuffed it back into Huldar's hands.

Casco shook his head. *What's he trying to prove?*

We all know he's flawed, Andel replied, *but this? He violated Lind's trust, our trust!*

Huldar donned the shawl again and faced the gathering.

"Duvät Gok, hear the atonement I require. You will immediately resign as Overlord."

"Now?" At last, Duvät seemed genuinely engaged.

"Yes," Huldar said. "You are not fit for the position." After a slight pause he continued, "Your tent will be removed from the main encampment by more than fifty paces. You will surrender to this company all of the remaining coal in your possession. You may not eat with us, or come within ten paces of Lind unless she gives permission."

"Learn to cook, Gok," Tam sniggered.

"But I will be alone!" Duvät cried. "What if we are attacked? This is outrageous! How will I warm my tent?"

"There is more," Huldar said. "As soon as we arrive back in Giahn, you will accompany me to Guild headquarters. I will see to it that they are informed of your conduct, and removed officially from employment. At that time, I will collect one fifth of your overall contractual pay to be given to Lind as the financial compensation you promised."

"One fifth? How am I to live?"

Huldar bowed to signal the end of proceedings and closed his eyes as if listening intently to his soul. "I feel the Breath in my words," he announced.

"Breath blow true!" the company chanted. When Huldar removed the shawl from his shoulders the noise-level peaked as everyone started to talk at once.

"Casco, Cobar," Huldar called. "See to the removal of his tent."

Duvät startled, then hurried behind the Rukh. The company parted to let him through, but no one so much as acknowledged his presence.

"Look at him," Sari said, "scurrying behind them like the filthy kalla he is." She turned as Lind started for the door also. "Lind, you won't stay? Just for a wee while?"

"I ... I can't," Lind said. "I want to see my own tent. It's been so long ... I'm sorry."

Ubaid shepherded her to the door. "She has done enough," he said. "We'll see her safe, Sari, Lady Andel. Don't worry."

———

A few days after the judgment session, Andel and Sari sat with Lind while she picked at her morning meal in the glow of the fire. When Huldar entered the marquee, Andel gave him a small smile.

"Ladies of the Uri'madu, good morning!" He crouched beside Lind. "I have something for you." He handed her a woven leather thong with the orange stone suspended on it.

Lind took it warily. "Is that it? The beacon stone?"

Huldar's smile was encouraging. "I've changed the charm. It will alert me if Duvät Gok comes too close."

Lind closed her hands around it and listened. Although she had already put on a little weight, the gaze she turned to him was deeply haunted.

"Thank you." Tears glistened as she put the pendant around her neck and tucked it beneath her shirt. Sari reached out and lifted her hair free of the fastening.

"I'll be all right," Lind said. She wiped her face with the backs of her hands. "I'm feeling better already." She patted her chest. "Thank you for this."

"Have you seen him?" Huldar asked. "The charm will only react to his physical presence." He tapped his head. "Has he bothered you?"

"No. Only in the distance, standing by his tent. He looked lonely."

"Good!" said Sari. "Evil monster. So he should."

"But I don't want him excluded entirely," Lind said. "I don't mind if he comes to the marquee sometimes, so long as he keeps his distance."

"Are you sure?" asked Andel.

"I want him to see that I am loved and he isn't."

"He isn't!" Sari said. "So, I hope you won't mind if we don't actually speak to him?"

"That's exactly what I want," said Lind. "Let him live in a ghost world where nothing and nobody touches you or speaks and even if you think you see them they're not really real. Let him look in there and see. The silence is more terrifying than he could ever be."

For a moment, Huldar looked at her. Small creases worried his brow. "You are very brave, Lind," he said at last. He tipped his head toward Sari and Andel, "and I doubt you are in danger of too much silence ever again, now that you are back with these two. I am glad you are feeling better."

He signaled Andel. *Can we talk?*

Outside the marquee, dank mist crept between the tents, limiting visibility to a few strides. Dark tendrils of Andel's hair quickly coated with droplets and stuck to her face. Tenderly, he brushed them aside. A fleeting fear passed through him. What if he'd been unable to reclaim her from Qalān?

"I'm worried about Lind," he said. "Her eyes, her haze … I don't think she's slept yet."

Andel shared his frown. "She slept for a time while we were lost, but now, I think she's too afraid. There in Qalān …" She looked around at the flowing mist. "It was the most terrifying experience of my life."

He drew her closer and gazed earnestly into her eyes. "I would never have left you."

"I know." She glanced down as if studying the skirts of the tent. "But … I had no way of knowing if you could reach us again." Her gaze traveled toward the sound of a lonely clicker-bug, then back to him. "And then I heard your voice."

"I bet it never sounded so good!" He laughed into her eyes, but his happiness was muted by thoughts of Lind, and the terrors she had endured.

"I saw her counting her toes again," he said. How close he had come to losing them both.

Andel sighed. "She still won't wear her shoes." … *But the charm was a brilliant idea.*

I talked it over with Ubaid and Alis. They agreed that it was a good time to give it to her.

Andel nodded absently. *It was definitely the right thing to do … but I had become a little attached to it.*

His face creased with a smile. *I have something for you too.*

As he gazed into her eyes, he reached into his pocket and withdrew the fire-opal necklace. He placed in her palm and closed her fingers around it.

At first she frowned a little, but then her eyes widened as the charm he had sung into it came to life. *It purrs*, she said, and held it to her ear.

Delight curved the corners of his mouth, spreading like the warmth of strong liquor.

What is it? How does it work?

His thumb rubbed down, cool against her cheek. "The idea just came to me," he said. "Hold it between your palms," he nodded as she did so, *and whisper my name.*

She closed her hands around the gem and held it to her mouth. He smiled encouragement and she breathed his name, "Huldar." The vibration flowed through the opalized shell, honed by its spiraling structure, and sounded against his mind.

He reflected the sensation for her to share. *I will always come to you*, he said. Then with a last smile, he turned for the portal that would take him west again with Casco and Cobar to finish the assessment they had been working on before they found the boots. He paused as Duvät Gok's lonely abode momentarily emerged from its shroud of mist and cold. The Gok had not been seen since his public disgrace, but Huldar knew he was there, sulking in his tent.

And hopefully he'll stay there, Huldar thought to himself. He stepped through the portal onto crisp new snow, and reached into Qalān for a fresh lump of coal to throw onto Cobar's fire.

WANING DAYS

Andel gazed from the bluff, watching icy veils of snow beat against the mountains. Their ramparts reminded her of bony scutes, perhaps the backbone of a giant beast asleep within the terrain, and she wondered if the freeze had yet breached them to whiten the shores of the inner sea. For the past few days, even the volcano had been lulled into dormancy, and she missed its fiery glow.

After a nod to the majesty of the land, she walked back to the campsite and prepared to step through to her worksite. Beyond the volcano, in a wide valley sheltered from the encroaching snows, the Uri'madu hurried to complete their surveys before the whole planet became locked in ice.

When she crossed to the survey site, Sari was there to greet her with a warm, thick beverage that tasted of local berries.

"Here, this'll keep you warm," she said, and nodded at the tent. "Fire's going."

Andel cupped the warm ceramic in her hands and drank. She looked up as Casco emerged from the shelter and came to stand beside her. He eyed her steaming mug.

"I hate to say it, but we have a lot to get through today," he said.

"I know," Andel nodded. "I'll be quick. You on guard duty?"

"Me 'n' Cobar'll keep an eye on you while your head's in the ground."

Andel laughed. "If you put it like that!"

She looked up as a chill breeze rattled the branches, all that remained of a tropical forest now fallen prey to creeping winter's touch. The mysterious clearing, 'the road' as some were calling it, wandered between the forest remnants – a path of easier going for this, their last survey. She knew Huldar would be along later, to see how they were getting on, but for now he was buried in an avalanche of unfinished paperwork inherited from Duvät Gok.

She downed the last of the tea and signaled Casco, then, as her guardians took their places by her side, she stilled her soul and readied it to seep through rock and gravel. Hands still warm from the mug were left behind as she reached for a seam of copper, part of the rich bed that permeated the area between the ranges. It was not such a glamorous find as some they had made, but the work needed to be done and they were almost out of time. When the copper was found she began to walk, so intent on following her senses far beneath the ground that she was aware of nothing else. Time passed, but she barely noticed.

Then Huldar's voice came to her. *Andel. Look up …*

It was hard to put aside the thrill of his mind in hers, but this was not the time. She had to complete the survey.

His warning came again, touched with the faintest tickle of humor, *Andel, listen. I think you should look up …* but she continued raking her senses through soil and rock, maintaining a difficult balance. If she pulled out of this strata now, it would take hours to re-engage. Besides, if there was danger, Casco and Cobar were there to protect her, and all she could sense from them was the same amusement she felt behind Huldar's words.

LOOK OUT! he cried.

She reefed her mind from the ground and stumbled to a halt. She pushed aside loose strands of hair and blinked at the apparition before her. Colored shapes resolved into patterned skin: a tall creature still as a statue, dark against a backlit halo of waving corn-silk hair.

Shock pounded in her chest.

Stand still, Huldar said. *It means no harm.*

Four arms, each ending in a soft pad, stretched wide to display complex markings on the creature's under-arms and chest. Beneath its head, she could see a wide mouth held slightly open. Its long nose projected, straight and stiff like a baton.

Andel readied her mind to deliver an offensive blast. Why had Cobar and Casco done nothing?

Wait! Huldar said. *It's herbivorous. This is the only assertive behavior we've seen.*

Oh, thanks, she retorted.

You'll be fine, Casco said. She could hear him laughing.

From the corner of her eye, she saw a second creature moving slowly past. Long russet hair crinkled over its thick body. Its six legged stride seemed ungainly but resolute, each footfall cushioned and soft. As she watched, its swinging nose lifted in a long call: "W-a-i-e-n-n-n-t."

A sea of hair emerged from the clearing behind her. The gradual surge that enveloped the broad path was silent but for the occasional call and the silken rustle of hair.

She gasped as the giant beast before her lowered itself to the ground. Crystal balls regarded her. Hair rippled as if magnetized from beneath, then the nose extended toward the Tsemkar on her forehead. She tried to fend it off but the creature persisted.

Casco! Cobar! she called, but her guardians seemed unable to respond.

Just let it, Huldar said. *It's not going to hurt you.*

I don't want it to wipe its nose on my face! she said. "Get away!" She shooed with both hands, but her actions had no effect. When she stepped back, the creature followed with nose outstretched. Another nose started toward her.

Just stop, Huldar said. *It will be over soon and they'll lose interest. Did the same thing to me just before we found Lind's boots. Ask Casco! Unnerving but harmless.*

Casco? She called, but her erstwhile protector was leaning against Cobar's shoulder, convulsed with laughter.

She craned her neck until she saw Huldar's broad grin. He waved.

Villain! she cried. *You planned this. Why didn't you tell me?*

You looked so funny. He laughed. *I've never seen you so rattled.*

Ahh, that's right, said Casco. *You missed the charmed guy-rope episode.*

She stood still and endured as the creatures snuffled against her. They were soft and inquisitive – harmless, as Huldar had said, but she was still cross. However, the creatures themselves were fascinating. They were as bulky as the blubber-worms on the shores of the Southern Archipelago, but much more curious and strangely aware.

When each had displayed its underbelly and completed its inspection, the shaggy mounds wandered away, bugling to each other, "W-a-i-e-nn-nn … t!"

Huldar strolled over, still grinning widely.

"'W-ae-nn-nn … t'," Andel repeated softly, then she tried it again. "Sounds like 'went'," she said. "I wonder what it means?"

"I do-n-n … t' know," Huldar replied. She rolled her eyes.

"Wha-a-a … t's wrong?" Casco said, broad smirk barely hidden.

"Oh." Andel shook her head sadly. "I can see where this is heading."

READY FOR HOME

That night as they gathered for the evening meal, the tang of frying krale did little to disguise the pervasive, nutty smell. Tam was doing his best with meager supplies, but Andel was sure that once they got home she would never be able to face little attar again.

The mood inside the marquee was strangely disjointed. Andel waved as Sari looked up from an intense ashut game between Cobar, the reigning champion, and Nachiel, his most ardent contender. The match had attracted quite an audience. Firelight and crystal globes illuminated tired faces, some anxious and others excited by the prospect of their homeward journey and the end of their three-year separation from the Realm. Veils were thin and emotions were high, as if the cusp between worlds had eroded usual codes of behavior.

A sudden buzz of comments heralded a critical point in the game. Nachiel leaned back from the boards and clapped his hands. "Yes! Got you!"

"But that's the huntress!" Cobar rumbled.

"Well you cheated too with the blue fled!" Nachiel grinned.

Cobar glared. Two meaty hands clasped the sides of the table as he thrust himself to his feet. Spectators backed away.

Nachiel looked up, maddeningly unruffled. "Well, you did," he insisted.

Abruptly Cobar turned. The crowd parted as he stalked to the marquee door.

"Rematch?" Nachiel called after him but Cobar continued into the snow. Ashut pieces clattered back into their box.

Gento laughed and came with Sari and Lind to talk with Andel.

"How big were they?" Lind was asking.

"You should've seen her face!" Casco said as he joined them.

Huldar pushed through the door and went to the fire. "What happened to Cobar?"

"Lady Andel's face?" Sari leaned closer to Lind. "Well I was pretty surprised too, but Casco told me not to say anything."

Andel smiled up at Huldar. "It was a set-up," she said to Lind. "Here, I'll show you, if you'd like?"

"She'd like that, wouldn't you, Lind?" said Sari.

Lind nodded, and her eyes widened as Andel shared her memory of the giant creature with its four arms stretched wide.

"I wish I'd been there," she said wistfully. "Where did they go?"

"Should be easy to find: just follow that path, 'the road'," said Casco.

Andel turned on Huldar. "So that's how you knew!"

Huldar answered with a smug grin.

"Could we find them again, Huldar? I'd love to see them," Lind said.

"I suppose so," Huldar replied, "if Andel could far-search the path?"

"Tomorrow, after the weather has lifted," Andel promised, "I'll find out how far they've gone. But it means using portals, Lind. Do you think you'll be all right?"

Lind hesitated, just for a moment, then said, "I'll be fine. You'll be with me, won't you, and Sari?"

"Of course! And Huldar too. He has to go back there anyway. He thinks he might have found a potential Djan'rū site much bigger than ours. The navigators will love him!"

———

Lind gazed in wonder as the first shaggy bodies became visible through the snow.

"There they are!" she whispered. *So big and soft …*

Andel guided her forward. *Let them see you,* she said.

The slow-moving herd shambled to a halt. Snow slithered from silken fur as the elders came forward and reared up. When Lind lowered her hood her eyes were full of tears. She stayed still as the red-patterned elder lowered itself and began its snuffling investigation, but Andel could feel her amazement.

So many eyes, Lind whispered, *like drops of water. Like a crown! I feel as if it's reading me, as if I were a book or a scroll!*

Andel smiled. *Yes, it's magical, isn't it? They have absolute trust. I'm so glad you've seen them too.*

They are incredible, Huldar agreed. *I can hardly wait until I get the chance to study …* he paused as the creature began to sway. *What's it doing?*

The shaggy beast folded its forelegs and bowed its forehead to the ground. A deep drone came from its chest – its silken hair seemed to wave with effort. The three annangi looked at each other.

Amazing! Andel said.

Amazing! Sari agreed. *Is it bowing to you? They didn't do that before, did they?*

The vibration went on. They could feel it rise through their feet. Others of the herd gathered in a semicircle and lowered their heads. Hundreds of circular eyes glistened.

Should I be worried? Lind asked.

Huldar tilted his head, clearly puzzled. *I sense no aggression*, he said, *but perhaps we should back off, just a little?*

As they moved away the creature seemed not to notice, but when Lind was far enough from the droning one, another of the elders reared up before her.

"Are you all right?" Sari whispered.

"I don't mind," Lind whispered back. "They are so beautiful ... although I am a bit cold now."

With quiet movements, Huldar brushed the snow from her hair. *No wonder!*

Sari glanced at her feet. *Perhaps you could put some shoes on, just for now?*

Lind shook her head.

When the red one's drone finished, it gave her a last gentle snuffle and moved on.

"I have no idea what that was all about," said Huldar.

"Perhaps they have accepted us as part of the herd?"

Lind stared after them as they disappeared into the curtain of snow, listening as their plaintive calls faded into the distance. "I think we should name the planet after them," she said. "It's up to us, now, isn't it?"

Huldar nodded, and Lind continued, "We should call it 'Went', because that's what they sound like."

"Went?"

"Have you been to the planet Went?" Andel laughed delightedly. "It's certainly unique, like the planet itself."

"Yes, I like it," Huldar said. "Why don't we head back now and tell the others, before you get frostbite. And sorry to spoil the fun, but we still have plenty to do before we leave."

"The Djan'rū?" Andel asked.

"Yes, I have to make another assessment of the site, then see that the old one is correctly tuned so the navigator can find it more easily. I think we'll all be pleased if our departure goes more smoothly than our arrival."

The prospect of the return journey was something Andel had given little thought to until now.

"I was terrified!" she admitted. "Did I tell you I actually saw stars moving beyond the envelope?"

"No!" Huldar frowned. "I knew it was rough, but ..."

"I saw you," Lind laughed. "Looked about to faint!"

"And at least we are all of us going home." Andel made a solemn bow. "Bowed to by a Went? The others will be so jealous!"

Lind's expression grew pensive. Andel hugged her shoulders and steered her back toward the portal, but although she seemed thrilled by her contact with the Went and buoyed by the naming of the planet, darkness broke through their contact and every moment of physical touch was painful. As they neared the portal, Lind turned to her with sad eyes. "They have no toes," she said, then she started to count her own again, so softly Andel could barely hear.

LAST DAY

The morning was dark and bitingly cold. Huldar stomped the snow from his boots and entered the marquee, and warmth melted against his skin like a healer's touch. Andel's face shone dimly in the firelight. She looked up and smiled, then returned to her notes. They had both worked through the night, and now it was almost dawn he wanted to show her something.

Last page … she said.

"W-a-e-n-n … t some tea?" he offered.

She continued her work. "Look around, Huldar of Leth," she said. "The tide of humor has stolen your boat."

Boat?

Exactly!

Still mystified, he wandered toward the fire and the ever-present simmering kettle.

With warm cups clasped in their hands, Huldar led Andel the short distance to the Djan'rū. After many long hours incorporating the improvements Shamkarun Kandät Enna had shown him when they first landed, the charm was ready for his arrival. Its shimmering distortion spread in a large hemisphere, the vibration even and true. He liked to think the special bond he had with this planet had helped him – though without the regular input of a specialist, the work would gradually decay.

It's amazing, Andel said. "You've gained such skill with Qalān, you'll be apprenticed to the navigators next."

"Now that's an idea." Huldar laughed. "But seriously, I have no idea how they do what they do. Space is so much bigger."

Across the valley, the remains of vegetation poked like skeletons through the snow. The sun peeped over the dormant volcano like a child surveying the day's possibilities from the cover of warm blankets. Huldar pulled his fur-lined coat tighter, wishing a little volcanic warmth for himself.

As the dawn's first light brightened Andel's face, her sandy-brown eyes sparkled. She took a mouthful of rapidly cooling tea, tipped her head back and expelled a sputtering spume. Frozen droplets wreathed her in a bright cloud of ice.

His sudden bark of laughter was out before he could stop it.

You're an idiot! he said.

Made you laugh! she replied.

Her eyebrows lifted as his mind pulled her close, then her free hand felt its way around his neck and the sensuous tingle as their hazes began to blend inured him to the weather. The cold nose pressed against his cheek added fire to the heat of her lips, and as she drew him into a long kiss, her psychic touch feathered his body with a teasing caress.

Huldar's song shivered between them, building slowly with the whispered rhythm of his voice. Thin wind whined through cracked boulders. Above them, a squally mass of cloud loomed closer, its ragged edges illuminated as sunrise tiptoed across the land beneath. As if called by their song, an elemental gust battered stone with sleet, and he drew on its power, singing the wildness of storm into the music that bound them. As the raw note of harmony was reached, Andel's cup fell from her hand and shattered on the stones.

For a long time he held her, sharing the lingering heat; protecting her body with his as the elements rattled the rocks around them. Then as suddenly as it had arrived, the squall moved on.

They lifted their heads as the sun re-emerged on a landscape encased in translucent shards of ice.

He studied her face, unwilling to relinquish the moment. "I wish we had more time," he said. *Time with you here in this pristine place, away from the distractions of the Realm.*

Storyteller, she laughed. *You can't fool me! There's always one more mountain to look behind.* She reflected an image of himself back to him – a view of eyes as blue as a summer sky. He wondered if they really looked like that.

He pushed a damp, half-frozen strand of hair from her face. *You love this place too,* he said. *You wish we could stay …*

She looked outward to note the approach of another blast of sleet. *But the weather – and then there's Lind and the Overlord … it needs redress.*

Hmm … He tipped his head toward the camp, and with a last kiss, they turned their backs on the dawn.

He watched the top of Andel's head as she walked beside him, reminded of the strange, peaceful creatures, the Went, and a pang of regret crossed his heart. They were vital to the health of the planet, he was certain of it.

"I wonder how they cope with the big freeze," he said. "Do they hibernate? Their coats are thick, but they don't seem thick enough."

"Hibernation," Andel mused. "The sleep of death. Do they dream they are awake, or does darkness descend, making no choices? And how do we know when *we* have chosen? Maybe sentience merely glosses the driving of instinct with the veneer of free will."

She saw his mystification and smiled.

"Veneer or not," he countered, "I'm looking forward to coming back when the cycle warms again. And what about that road?" Huldar linked arms with her then jammed his hand back into his pocket. "All the way around the continent – a continuous clearing. Thousands and thousands of paces." He bumped her with his elbow. "I wonder how it would be to walk on six legs instead of two?"

Andel snorted. "I have heard there are creatures, the Simurgh, who can change shape at will," she said. "You should ask the first one you see!"

"The Simurgh?" He looked at her. "My family believed in their existence, but no one has ever seen one." His mind ranged ahead to the activity in the campsite. The tents wouldn't come down until the next day, but everything that could be packed beforehand should be. They could not keep the navigator waiting around in these conditions. He thought again of the Went. How intriguing they were!

"Someone must have made that path." He bumped her again. "I think it has something to do with your friends, the Went."

She shook her head. "Not enough of them, and you know how soft their foot-falls are."

"Maybe there're more of them somewhere else. Look at the way they stick to that trail. Maybe they've been following that exact path for so long that they've worn a hole in the biosphere, like a river."

"A river of hair? I wonder where the river w-a-e-n-t?" She snuggled closer. "Poetic, but I'm not singing along just yet."

Huldar looked across to the Gok's tent. Something about their ex-Overlord niggled at him, but it was probably nothing. It was easy to find fault in someone so despicable.

He returned to Andel. "I'm going for a last look at the inner shores, see whether ice is forming on the inner sea yet – and to say goodbye. Would you like to come?"

Don't you ever get tired? she sighed. "I think I'll get some packing done."

Huldar smiled as she rubbed her eyes. "If you had any sense you'd get some sleep."

"You're tired too!" she said. "You must be."

He opened his arms and pivoted around. "But this planet, 'Went', it's one of the most remarkable I've ever … She spoke to me, Andel. I want to fix one last image of her in my heart before we return to the tameness of Giahn." He continued walking. "I'll go to the central sea. It'll be the last thing to freeze over."

"Should I be jealous?"

He smiled and shook his head.

She paced beside him. "Why not take Casco?"

"Casco's busy, and I won't be gone long –"

Andel stopped. *Oh, no you don't!* "You'd be angry if you caught anyone else heading off alone." She crossed her arms. "I've changed my mind. And besides, you're right. It will be a long seven years before we come to Went. She's like a beautiful woman with veils and screens … the Kaskarudjan of planets."

He tipped his head toward the portal. "Let's go then."

But before they could take the step, Casco called out from beside the marquee, "Hey, Huldar! Join us for an ale or two before we get started? Warm your bones?"

Huldar grinned and gestured to the shimmer in Qalān. "Shall we?"

ON THE BEACH

Evidence of the big freeze hampered every step as Huldar and Andel made their way to the inner shores. Most things had died or retreated beneath their icy blanket to patiently await their time of rebirth. As he neared the final branch of portals, Huldar noticed one that was more stable than the others, as if from regular use. It led to a long beach on the eastern edge of the inland sea.

They stepped through it onto a sea of dunes and squinted against the prevailing winds. From this vantage, the long, graceful curve of sand contrasted with the rugged parapets of the ranges.

He touched Andel's arm and indicated a jumble of low mounds left high above the distant waterline.

As they made their way toward the shapes, Huldar began to recognize skulls and bones, as if a mass death had occurred. As he explored the tragic remains he thought of the strange life cycles of many species here, and the absence of age difference. Were these carcasses the remains of a natural event?

Andel crouched to examine one of the skulls. *Look at this ...* Her fingers followed deep incisions around the creature's single eye-socket. *Multiple teeth-marks?*

He hunkered down beside her. The skull in question sent chills down his spine. It appeared as if it had been stabbed.

Maybe the mystery predator of the southern seas has a nasty equatorial cousin? Andel suggested.

Maybe, Huldar ran his finger over the wounds, but they appeared too random for teeth-marks. Something terrible had happened here. He wished he could understand. The orange charm-stone came to mind, but what relationship could an unknown former visitor to this planet have to this slaughter?

Andel got to her feet.

Not the goodbye I had in mind, he said.

It highlights how little we know. She drew him up beside her and hugged his arm. *This has been the best three years of my life, and I wouldn't have missed it for anything.*

Even though you nearly died twice?

Definitely! She paused, then added, "And this is where we found each other."

Her shy smile imparted a lightness of being he had not felt before. He had heard of love and the effects it might have, but this was the first time it had happened to him. He wondered if he asked her to be dabaku, would she agree? The exchange of such a bond was a momentous thing, as permanent almost as marriage, although there was no chance of children between dabaku. If the bond was exchanged, their mental communication would be greatly enhanced, and in fact, when lovers took this step it was often a precursor to the most permanent bond of all.

She pulled him closer and kissed his lips. *It's getting colder. Let's get back.*

Getting warmer, I'd say, Huldar replied, but before he could return her kiss she had turned for home. As he bowed his head to follow, a swirling breeze uncovered something shiny beneath the sand.

He bent to pick it up and found a transparent globe that fitted neatly into his palm. As he looked more closely he was startled to see a rainbow of colors, although he had yet to hold it to the light.

What have you found? she asked.

I'm not sure. He held it to the sun. The rainbow neither brightened nor dimmed, although the light shone clearly through it. *A gem of some sort?*

Andel came to take a look. *Breath! It's so beautiful!*

He turned it over between his fingers. When he examined it at a deeper level, a sensation came to him, almost as if the bauble was alive, or contained a soul, yet when he tapped the surface it was definitely solid, like glass or crystal.

Mystified, he handed it to Andel. "Feel anything?"

"Like what?" As she stared, the rainbow reflected onto her face, shining in her eyes. He watched her Mark brighten then dim. She turned to him. *I don't feel anything special. Is it charmed in some way?*

He held out his hand for her to return the orb, and examined it again. It trembled, so faintly, as if it was troubled. He closed his eyes and extended his senses as if searching Qalān, but could feel nothing more until he held the stone close and looked into it – and saw something moving.

What is it? Andel asked.

A circle of crystals seemed to look out of the stone at him, and with a start he recognized it as one of the enigmatic creatures, the Went. It seemed sad, and somehow lost. Tears came to his eyes and he closed his hands over the crystal to shield himself from the pain.

Huldar, Andel took his hand. "What is it? Why are you crying?"

"I don't know. I saw something, a Went … it affected me this way."

"A Went?"

"A circle of eyes, looking at me."

"Could it have been the globe reflecting in on itself?"

He shook his head. It could have been that, perhaps, but he didn't think so. With great reverence, he replaced the globe on the sand where he had found it. The haunting sadness reminded him of Lind as he had first seen her after her rescue from Qalān. He looked up to see Andel's gaze on him, and words spilled out before he had time to consider. "Tsemkarun Andel of Trianog, would you be dabaku with me?"

He searched her eyes then looked away. Why had he spoken? As the silence stretched, fear gnawed at his insides. He forced himself to look again. He wanted her to see into his soul, to know how much she meant to him.

Then she smiled.

"Dabaku?" She said it as if the sound would make it real.

He nodded. "When we return to Giahn …"

She peered into his face with narrowed eyes, then with a flicker of her eyebrows she turned for the portal. "Let's get back. Big day tomorrow!"

He thought he heard traces of his accent in her voice.

"Come on!" she said, and he started behind her. The words were out there, waiting, working their influence on the world just as any sound would, but to him they loomed like giants.

She waited at the portal. It was uphill, and she smiled as he approached. *Dabaku?*

He nodded, certain she would hear his pounding heart.

Her eyebrows flickered. "We'll have to talk more of this, Shamkarun Huldar of Leth."

THE SEVEN BREATHS OF EL

By nightfall the most recent storm had passed, leaving drifts of snow huddled high against tent walls. Huldar paused outside the marquee and squinted at fat flakes floating down, thick and lazy like some Faythans he had known. He thought of Duvät Gok, thick and lazy indeed, but it seemed wrong to sully the purity of snow with Duvät's darkness.

Once inside, he sat close to the fire and wrapped his cloak tighter, watching the entrance.

Since inviting Andel to be dabaku, his emotions had swerved from exhilaration to despair and back again. Every time he saw or sensed her, his heart jumped, but he found it difficult to control which way.

He sensed it when she left her tent and headed for the marquee. When she drew the door-flap aside, her slight form filled his senses, blinding him to all else. She threaded between others of the team to settle beside him. Layers of warm clothing buffered physical contact, but the thrum between their hazes drew covert smiles.

She looked up as awnings bowed and creaked. Snow slithered from the roof with a crystalline crash and Duvät Gok ducked through the door.

"What's he doing in here?" Nachiel hissed.

"It's our last night," Huldar said. "If he keeps out of our way, he can share our warmth. Lind has agreed to this."

"It's my coal!" Duvät snapped.

"Was your coal," said Huldar. "Mind yourself or you'll be back outside."

Duvät glared at him for a moment, but the fire proved a stronger attraction.

A voice from the dark beyond it announced, "It's cold."

Huldar spoke as if to the flames. "If that's the best conversation starter you can come up with, Casco, our last night here will be a long one."

His eyes flicked toward the back of the tent as Duvät Gok cleared his throat. Clamped around a fine ceramic mug, the wretch's stubby fingertips glinted. Huldar shook his head. A spasm of anger became amusement. He still painted his fingernails the Imperial blue.

Orange tongues of flame reflected in Duvät's glare. He squared his shoulders and cleared his throat again. "Are the samples in order and reports completed? The navigator will be here at first light."

"Supposed to be," muttered Casco.

Andel nodded tiredly.

Duvät lifted his chin. "I am still accountable to House Tiamät."

"Yes, you are," Huldar said, "and the God-Emperor does not like disorder, as you are so fond of reminding us, so I'm thinking he won't be too pleased with you."

Tam slammed his mug down onto the bench. "Neither are we!"

"Peace!" Huldar's strong voice rolled over the impending melee. "Only a few hours left till we're on our way home. Let's not ruin it."

"What do you suggest, then?" Nachiel said. "It's too cold to get out from under these rugs, and my tea's freezing over while I look at it."

"Sing it warmer," Ronnin snapped. "Even you can do that."

Andel butted her elbow against his ribs. "Tell us one of your stories."

The ether calmed. A murmur of assent came back to them.

"A story?" Huldar's eyebrows lifted.

"Please?" Andel held his gaze with teasing eyes. *I'll make it worth your while ...*

Suggestions for personal favorites flew around the fire.

"Apen and Annan?" said Tam.

Huldar considered his collection of Apen and Annan stories. Apen and Annan were the father and mother of the annangi; however, though many stories of their exploits had been handed down through the ages, none seemed right for the moment.

"What about the Sajhar's nightmare?"

"Or the wings of Rukh?"

"No, we did that last time," said Nachiel.

Breath clouded from Huldar's nostrils. The tent bustled as people positioned themselves, ready for their entertainment.

"Tell us the Creation," Andel said. "The Seven Breaths. I haven't heard it for ages, and it seems right to tell it now, don't you think?"

Smiling in his mind, Huldar wondered if he could ever refuse her anything. "All right," he nodded, "the story of the Seven Breaths, then. The story of the Beginning as was told to me by my grandfather, sitting around a campfire much like this one."

"But warmer!"

"Not much!" he shot back. "Gets cold in the Lentath highlands. So, the shawl please, Tam," he beckoned, "if you will."

As the shawl was passed around the circle, Duvät Gok's expression was unreadable. When it reached Andel, she smoothed the wool as if she too was thinking of the last time they had seen it. Then she surprised Huldar with a cheeky smile.

"This is just a ploy to gain extra warmth, isn't it?" she said.

He winked, and with a laugh, she helped him arrange it over his shoulders. He lifted his hand for silence. Around him, friends and teammates stilled as he gathered the story to mind along with the charms he would use for its visual augmentation. In the pause that followed, he could feel the planet waiting, anxious in the creak of leather and subtle hiss of falling snow. Then his voice swept into the hush.

"The Seven Breaths, as told by House Leth, as told by all," he announced. "We honor El with this story of our Beginnings. Hear my words!"

His gaze travelled from face to face across the glowing flames. This was something he had no need to study; his ability for storytelling seemed to flow as easily as breathing, and the feel of an audience hanging on his words was a gift he deeply cherished. He steadied his mind and began:

"This is the story of Creation, from the time before time ever was." He moved his hand in a flattened arc. His voice stole through the quiet. "Imagine, if you will, when all was dark … no stars, no worlds. Nothing moved, lived or breathed, and in that timeless space, El became aware."

Above the fire, sparse clouds of stray sparks flew aloft. Between them, melting snowflakes glinted as they plunged through the smoke-hole toward warmth and death. Huldar felt the silence as the Uri'madu contemplated the idea of germinal emptiness. Did El exist before awareness came, or were cognizance and existence one and the same?

"Lying there, empty in the blackness, El perceived breath. El felt breath within and breath without, but the breath of time was, as yet, outside time, and all was stillness.

"When El drew Breath and spoke the First Word into the void, time began. Sound sped through the matrix, causing enormous eddies and great spiral clouds. Under the influence of vibration, matter was created and El saw beauty, but El was alone and could not share the wonder of creation."

The Mark on Huldar's cheek pulsed as he released a string of notes. The soft resonance captured snowflakes and whirled them in spirals with the sparks above the flames.

"El drew Breath again," he continued, "and the Second Word was spoken. Swirling matter coalesced into suns, and these clumped together to form galaxies like our own, spiraling and spinning, filling the void with color."

Huldar waved his arms, and above the fire, swirling galaxies of ice and embers formed and grew wilder.

"Within the galaxies," he said, "planets solidified like jewels around the suns. Meteors and comets formed. Wild motes sparkling in the vastness, they collided with planets and were eaten by stars. On the planets, volcanoes spewed gasses and molten rock, moons came and went, and all was chaos.

"But El was alone, and could not share the wonder and beauty of chaos."

The flurry of ice and fire slowed as Huldar's hands quieted, then the charm was released and the snow fell hissing into the flames.

"Once more, El drew breath and a Third Word was spoken. The Third Word found harmony with the two already in existence, and merged with their vibrations to create balance."

At Huldar's bidding, fresh snowflakes gathered to tempt ruin as they danced with sparks above the flames. Subtle changes to the charm's fluency caused the cloud to freeze into a three dimensional lattice, hemmed in by the watchful eyes of the Uri'madu.

"Patterns were born, and chaos was no more. Crystals formed, resonant to the Third Word. Suns and their planets vibrated in accord. Each added their own unique voice to the song of the universe, and flux and movement occurred all at one with the Great Design. But El was alone and could not share the wonder and beauty of harmony.

"Then El drew breath and spoke a Fourth Word. Uttered gently, it wove in and out of the harmony without disruption. This Word was the breath of life."

Above the fire, sparks and snowflakes snaked through the bright lattice in slow, serpentine strings. The strings began to move more quickly. Collisions sent sparks exploding into the darkness, then the colorful blooms were reabsorbed and sent weaving anew.

"Tiny creatures formed," Huldar cupped his hand and held it out, "so small they could barely be seen. Each had a beauty of its own. Feeding from the light, from the dark and from each other, they swept across planets, propelled by the movement of El's Breath.

"There was life, although it was unaware, but El was alone and could not share the wonder of its beauty."

While Huldar spoke, the strings had continued to grow and accelerate and the debris of collisions puffed bright clouds through the matrix. These formed more strings, which moved yet more swiftly, until suddenly the whole construction shuddered to a halt. The air hissed with the annangi's indrawn breaths. Several heartbeats passed with no sound but the brush of falling snow and the slow creak and pop of embers.

Then he wove a new charm, and the lattice reawakened. Moving strings became apparitions of things the Uri'madu had seen on their travels, and took the shapes of plants and creatures and all in between.

"El drew breath and spoke the Fifth Word, short and loud, shaking simple life forms into beings of greater complexity. Larger creatures grew and began multiplying."

Above the fire, images bloomed and were gone. Andel's enjoyment shone in Huldar's soul, warming his voice.

"There was life in the water, land and sky. Fish and seaweed, birds and trees, grasses, plants and animals. New harmonies flooded the song of the universe and there was life in abundance, but still El was alone and unable to share this new wonder of creation.

"Then, after long consideration, El drew breath again and the Sixth Word was spoken, calling forth sentience to share in El's joy."

The lattice dissolved and its denizens exploded outward, forming stars and constellations above their heads. A surge of light illuminated the rapt faces of the Uri'madu and Huldar's lips curved in a slow smile.

"Sentience was released to interact freely with creation, forming endless cycles of choice, growth and change. New harmonies added wild elements to the song of the universe. Some were discordant, but others were not, and good and evil were born of free will.

"Under the influence of sentience, a new awareness, Asheru, came into existence. Asheru felt the teeming, vibrant life born of the Breath of El and loved it, and loved El also, and El rejoiced to be no longer alone.

"Then El and Asheru drew breath together and uttered the Seventh Word as a shout of ecstasy, and Spirit was born to ensure the joy of creation will never be lost.

"Riding on the Breath of El and Asheru, all spirits return in their time and are breathed out again, refreshed and full of love, to continue their journey. Thus light and love will always prevail over the dark follies of wayward sentience."

Huldar made a slow bow to the flames. Sparks drifted freely again as the charm was released.

"We honor El, the Creator, and Asheru, the manifestation of love," Huldar said. "Hear my words!"

Andel drew the shawl from his shoulders and it returned through many hands to its keeper. Conversation slowly resumed. A mug of thick brown urmahji tea found its way into Huldar's grip. As he breathed in its steam, the woody fragrance reminded him of his childhood home by the highland lakes of Erithel.

He shared the thought with Andel. "My mother would search for urmahji root by the lakes in the summer," he said. "This is Lake Achaar."

Andel's smile became soft and reflective. "So beautiful … wild and rugged. Will you take me there?

In another part of the tent, Casco's voice lifted over the sounds of laughter and the clink of glasses. "The swamps of Karga'an!" he said. "Ah yes, I remember it well."

Gento snorted loudly. "If I recall, it was you who took us there – you who led us into the spark beetle nest."

"No, no, no!" Casco protested. "It was Arko!"

"Was you!" Arko cried.

"Well," Casco said. "Who could have known it would be so big?"

"Or smell so bad!" said Nachiel.

"Yeah," Gento rumbled. "Or that we'd end up covered in dung."

Andel rolled her eyes. "Ah, the glow-in-the-dark beetle dung. We both know how that tale ends. Let's go before they get too rowdy. We have important matters to discuss."

Important matters? His heart skipped a beat. "Yes, we do." He got to his feet. She stood up beside him. Her haze was a little pink, but her mind was tightly sealed. His heart raced. Had she come to a decision?

"Shh, not here," she said, then she blushed. "I have my pillow with me."

Lind watched as Huldar and Andel joined hands and slipped from the marquee.

Sari bumped her gently. "Are you all right?"

She hesitated. How could she explain? "Yes. I'm tired now though," she said. "I think I'll go to bed."

Sari looked around. "Just give me a minute and I'll join you."

"No, really. I'll be fine on my own."

Sari searched her face, her haze, and Lind knew she wanted to help, but there was nothing more to say. No words would make sense.

"Well … if you're sure now?" Sari said. "Your haze …"

"I am. I'm perfectly well." She tried to smile. "Just tired."

From the back of the tent, Duvät Gok watched with glittering eyes as Huldar and the diviner left the tent, then Lind. Stupid, he thought, the three of them. In the privacy of his exclusion, he allowed himself a moment to gloat over his victory. Huldar's threats – what would they matter once the untold riches of the Eyes of Bel Nishani were his? The loss of his position in the Imperial Explorers Guild would mean nothing: in fact, it was what he wanted. And as soon as they reached the first rest-stop, he would make contact with the Faythans to give them advance knowledge of the nacrite reserves, after he had negotiated a substantial reward for his efforts, of course. He closed his eyes to feel the Breath flowing through him, changing his fortunes for the better.

LIND

Lind realized she was whispering beneath her breath … "Three, four, five … Stop! Just stop!"

She clasped her hands to stop them from touching her toes as she counted. Tears leaked from her eyes.

Everyone was so kind, so caring, and she knew their love was genuine, but the cold lump inside her heart was a bottomless black well and there was nothing beyond it.

She smiled through tears as she recalled Huldar's story. The way he had woven charms with sparks and snowflakes was one of the most beautiful things she had seen. But he would never be hers. And all the while as the story was unfolding she had felt the Gok's eyes boring into her. She had agreed to let him enter the tent. It would show the Uri'madu, her family, that there was no need to worry. She was strong enough. She was coping well. All the work with the healers was not wasted.

One, two, three, four …

Sari turned in her sleep. Lind studied her face for a while: the kindest most beautiful face in the known. Sari was always telling her to put her boots on, and she meant well, but if her toes were covered, how would she know?

Sari would miss her the most.

As quietly as she could, she slipped from her bedroll. It was better to do it now, while she was stronger, while Huldar's story could still make her smile. In a few short hours, the navigator would come and the silence of the void would eat her again.

The snow felt crisp beneath her feet, but not as cold as she thought it would be. She pulled her jacket around her shoulders and kept walking. The glow from the marquee cast a faint orange shadow as she passed by. Tears froze on her face.

She found the rocks near the Djan'rū site and left the path to sit between two tall boulders.

High above, stars blazed in an indigo firmament. She shivered with cold. It was time. Every healer knew how to do this, to help another to rejoin the Breath with dignity. Ubaid and Alis had been so kind, but even they could not understand. No one could. The terror of sleep, the need for contact. She pretended for Sari's sake, but the pain would never stop. How could it? The past could not be undone. How could she face the Realm? The questions? They would look at her and know; they would feel it no matter how deeply it was veiled. She was broken. Worthless. It was better this way.

One last cold breath filled her lungs, then she centered her spirit and let it go …

Her body fell away like an outworn husk, like old boots whose comfort had worn thin. It had been a good body, but she did not know how to love it any more.

Suddenly, for the first time since Duvät Gok, her head felt light and clear. Then a sense of urgency overtook her. She should make her death-cry, but to whom, and what should she say? She had no direct family.

Time was slipping faster, her mind would not focus. Sari – she saw Sari swathed in warm blankets, still fast asleep. Then it came to her – what was really important here.

The eyes … she cried. *Duvät Gok has eyes* …

Sari sat bolt upright and screamed, but Lind had already turned toward the light and the divine Breath that rushed through her soul.

THE SONG OF WENT

The day had passed and the navigator had not come. As evening fell, the temperature plummeted. Andel and Huldar sat huddled in sadness with the rest of the team, waiting for his arrival. Gento conjured a fire and they clustered around it, but the heat barely escaped the flames. Pain weighed heavily on their hearts. Despite their efforts, somehow they had failed.

Andel's hand strayed to the pocket on her breast. *There is something I must do*, she whispered to Huldar.

He started to follow but she stopped him.

"I won't be long," she said.

He nodded and returned to his place. Her side was cold where she had leaned against him. He knew where she was going – just behind the rocks to the place where they had found Lind, her body still warm despite the snow all around it. They had sung for her until the corpse had dissolved and the elements that formed it had dissipated into the soil and the sky.

Andel kneeled in the snow and put her hands against the bare patch of ground, but all was at peace there now with nothing to mark Lind's passing but their memories. She took the stick from her pocket and admired its twisting pattern for one last time, then gently placed it over her grave. "I don't need it now, Aanjay," she whispered, *and if you can hear me, please, find Lind and love her as she deserves.*

She heard steps crunching through the snow. A warm hand clasped her shoulder, and she leaned back against Huldar's legs, but before she could say anything, a chord chimed through the ether and the navigator arrived at last.

———

In due course, the Uri'madu departed for Giahn and the small piece of patterned wood from Germane was buried beneath a ton of snow and ice; but on the planet the Uri'madu had left behind, the slow journey of the Went continued.

As the days froze together in the sun's declining light, survivors of the trail of trials reached the plains to settle into their homes at the foot of the mountains. While they regained their strength, the great beasts gathered in discussion and prepared for the long sleep. After the time of purification, the white waste would pass and they would awaken, ravenous. They must be prepared. The eldest were keen to pass their knowledge to younger generations. The songs of trail and trial must not be lost, and there were more observations to share.

Green-skinned Endowers showed their tribe the subtle changes in grass and leaf, and how to tell when the renewal was nigh. Pale ginger hair lifted, explaining how to find the last of the succor before it was lost to the waste and the time of purification began in earnest. The Eldest Stargazer raised indigo arms beneath russet hair and pointed out to its successors the signs in the sky of the white waste's approach. Grassmovers sang songs of the signs in the weather, brown hair moving with the language of blowing snow and forest crowns. The Eldest told of the time of storm and wind that heralded the renewal, and emphasized signs of the arrival of New Purpose. Singtellers raised blue skin and sang with pale coats to the Mothers and Enders of the storage of souls, and the end of life, and of the Great Circle; for the Mothers were the Keepers of the Circle, and the Enders were a mystery.

All sang of the Great Purpose, of the Circle. Everything, every aspect of life and their surroundings must be observed and recorded in the soul of the herd and sung to the Heart so that at the Time of Renewal, all would be regenerated as it must be. If all were sung in correct succession, the Circle would continue as it should.

As ice and snow grew thick over their tunnels and the time of purification was imminent, the Enders grew restless, anticipating the moment when they would shed their essence over the mother's gift and then they, too, would vanish into the Heart.

When it was done, with song and ceremony, the Mothers collected the Enders souls, then, with bellies distended by those in their care, they retired to the long sleep.

The remaining Went gathered and draped their heads to the ground so that the Heart of the World might know their song, carried in the drone of its accompaniment. With swaying backs turned to the outside, they shuffled sideways in a circling mass, each singing for as long as they could before ice filled their coats and rendered them voiceless. They sang of the Time of Renewal, when New Purpose would emerge from the sands to replenish and record the Circle so that it would never be lost.

Life comes from the sands
Life comes from the waters
Life comes from the sun.
Go to the sacred shores
Await the long reach of the Sky Circle
The sound of touch ends all sound
The sound of touch begins sound anew.
Where sand spirals in wind and water to join the circle of the sun
Purpose will be renewed.

When only the hardiest core of the herd remained, the eldest singteller, Fesneeth, gathered them in a last communion. Fesneeth, a veteran of four trails, used the wind in its coat to enhance the telling of another story while snow pattered in sad punctuation. The glistening eyes of the watching Went absorbed every nuance of the flow of Fesneeth's hair lifting and falling in a song of dark foretelling. New singtellers stood close to absorb even the faintest of whispers as a record for times to come.

The grizzled hair above Fesneeth's central eyes lifted and the ancient Went's coat began to move in stately patterns …

"Thus the song came to us from Shaartuhn Stargazer and Enzo Grassmover when they joined together in the place of foretelling to touch the darkened skies. They told of a time when the Circle would be broken. An empty time when the old purpose would fail and the Circle of Mothers would come to nothing. When the Heart cries out in loneliness and knows not what to do ...

The time of the broken Circle will come.
When the Circle of Winds will sniff in vain
And the Circle of Skies turns on emptiness
Weep for the purpose betrayed.
They will wait in the dark to mend what is take,
Blue of sky, gold of sun, white of dark in dark of night
Sing the rise of the purpose reborn.
We will trust the Circle to find its ends."

www.ingramcontent.com/pod-product-compliance
Lightning Source LLC
Chambersburg PA
CBHW030654120726
47905CB00001B/203